Harlequin

Desire

"Harlequin Desire…stories you can't put down."
—*New York Times* and *USA TODAY*
Bestselling Author Susan Mallery

Look for all six
Special 30th Anniversary Collectors' Editions
from some of our most popular authors.

TEMPTED BY HER INNOCENT KISS
by Maya Banks
with "Never Too Late" by Brenda Jackson

BEHIND BOARDROOM DOORS
by Jennifer Lewis
with "The Royal Cousin's Revenge"
by Catherine Mann

THE PATERNITY PROPOSITION
by Merline Lovelace
with "The Sheik's Virgin" by Susan Mallery

A TOUCH OF PERSUASION
by Janice Maynard
with "A Lover's Touch" by Brenda Jackson

A FORBIDDEN AFFAIR
by Yvonne Lindsay
with "For Love or Money" by Elizabeth Bevarly

CAUGHT IN THE SPOTLIGHT
by Jules Bennett
with "Billionaire's Baby" by Leanne Banks

* * *

Find Harlequin Desire on Facebook,
www.facebook.com/HarlequinDesire,
or on Twitter, @desireeditors!

MAR 2 2 2012

P9-ECT-192

Dear Reader,

I am, I confess, a lover of traditional story lines in romance. The boss/secretary story thrills me. Beauty and the beast. And sheiks. Okay, sure, the *real* Middle East can be a difficult place, but in romance, handsome princes are charming and honorable men who sweep away the women they love. The books are fun, sexy and there's often shopping.

The novella republished here in celebration of Desire's 30th anniversary, *The Sheik's Virgin,* was first published ten years ago. In that time I have grown as a writer, but in many ways I always come back to those traditional story lines. For decades, Desire has been home to romance that sweeps the reader away.

I hope you consider my story—and this anniversary Desire volume—a mini-vacation, complete with beautiful beaches and handsome strangers who take your breath away.

Happy anniversary, Desire.

Susan Mallery

MERLINE LOVELACE

THE PATERNITY PROPOSITION

Harlequin®

Desire

ISBN-13: 978-0-373-73158-9

THE PATERNITY PROPOSITION

Copyright © 2012 by Harlequin Books S.A.

The publisher acknowledges the copyright holders
of the individual works as follows:

THE PATERNITY PROPOSITION
Copyright © 2012 by Merline Lovelace

THE SHEIK'S VIRGIN
Copyright © 2002 by Susan Macias Redmond

Recycling programs
for this product may
not exist in your area.

www.Harlequin.com

Printed in U.S.A.

CONTENTS

THE PATERNITY PROPOSITION   9
Merline Lovelace

THE SHEIK'S VIRGIN   165
Susan Mallery

Books by Merline Lovelace

Harlequin Desire

The Paternity Proposition #2145

Silhouette Desire

*Devlin and the Deep Blue Sea #1726
†*The CEO's Christmas Proposition* #1905
†*The Duke's New Year's Resolution* #1913
†*The Executive's Valentine's Seduction* #1917

Harlequin Romantic Suspense

*Strangers When We Meet #1660
*Double Deception #1667

Silhouette Romantic Suspense

*Diamonds Can Be Deadly #1411
*Closer Encounters #1439
*Stranded with a Spy #1483
*Match Play #1500
*Undercover Wife #1531
*Seduced by the Operative #1589
*Risky Engagement #1613
*Danger in the Desert #1640

Harlequin Nocturne

Mind Games #37
***Time Raiders: The Protector* #75

*Code Name: Danger
†Holidays Abroad
**Time Raiders

Other titles by this author available in ebook format.

MERLINE LOVELACE

A career air force officer, Merline Lovelace served at bases all over the world, including tours in Taiwan, Vietnam and at the Pentagon. When she hung up her uniform for the last time, she decided to combine her love of adventure with a flair for story-telling, basing many of her tales on her experiences in the service.

Since then, she's produced more than eighty action-packed novels, many of which have made *USA TODAY* and Walden-books bestseller lists. Over eleven million copies of her works are in print in thirty countries. Be sure to check her website at www.merlinelovelace.com for contests, news and information on future releases.

Dear Reader,

With several sets of twins in our family, I've always been intrigued by their ability to communicate without words and the very unique personalities they develop despite their shared environments and experiences. So when a six-month-old drops unexpectedly into the lives of two rich, sophisticated and *very* handsome twins, I couldn't resist putting the Dalton brothers through all kinds of turmoil trying to figure out which of them had fathered the baby, and who the heck the child's mother is!

I hope you enjoy *The Paternity Proposition* as much as I did while writing it. And please check my websi at www.merlinelovelace.com or join me on my Facebook page for more information about this and my other books.

All my best,

Merline Lovelace

To my eighty-four nieces, nephews, grands and great-grands—it's been such fun watching you all grow. You've been the inspiration for *many* of my books!

THE PATERNITY PROPOSITION

Merline Lovelace

One

"Uh-oh."

The mechanic's muttered exclamation brought Julie Bartlett's head up. She was hot, sweaty, splattered with engine oil, and in no mood for another glitch. The PA-36 Pawnee they were working on was almost twice her age and had seen some hard years before being purchased third- or fourthhand by her new partners. No way she was going to take the plane up again until she and Agro-Air's chief mechanic had wrestled new rings onto the cylinder heads.

Agro-Air's chief and *only* mechanic. Tobacco-chawing Chuck Whitestone and Julie's other partner, Dusty Jones, had been in the agricultural aviation business for a combined eighty-two years. They'd scraped by during the lean times, when plummeting prices and widespread foreclosures forced so many Oklahoma farmers off their land. With U.S. crop production now on an upsurge, they should have turned the corner and be showing a tidy profit.

Should being the operative word. Dusty Jones could fly

circles around any pilot, young, old or anywhere in between. Julie could attest to that. He'd swooped in to dust her parents' wheat fields, taken their eager nine-year-old up for her very first flight and had her working the stick their second time in the air. Because of Dusty, Julie qualified for a pilot's license before she could legally drive a car. *And* paid her way through Oklahoma State University with a variety of flying jobs after her parents died. *And* got hired by a small regional airline right out of college.

Her plan at the time was to build up her cockpit hours and move into bigger passenger aircraft. Ballooning fuel prices had axed that noble goal. With commercial airlines shutting down routes and laying off personnel, she'd switched from hauling passengers to hauling freight. In the past four years, she'd flown in and out of so many remote locations in North, Central and South America that she couldn't remember a tenth of the places where she'd overnighted. She would probably *still* be hopping from country to country if Dusty hadn't tracked her down a couple of months ago and called to suggest she partner up with him and Chuck Whitestone.

He and Chuck were both on the down slope to seventy, he'd reminded her. They wanted to retire soon. If Julie stuck with Agro-Air for a few years, she could buy them out lock, stock and barrel. All they needed was a small infusion of cash to stay afloat until they rode the upsurge in crop production to a nice, fat retirement.

As it turned out, Dusty's definition of "small infusion" differed from Julie's by several decimal points. Still, she couldn't let him and Chuck go under. So she'd quit her job and sunk her entire savings into Agro-Air. But even someone with all her hours in the cockpit didn't just jump into aerial agriculture feet first. Zipping under power lines and skimming tree tops required a completely different set of flying skills. Also damned near the equivalent of a double PhD in biology and chemistry. Luckily, Julie had taken many of the necessary science courses at OSU. Still, Dusty had

insisted she do all the grunt work these past two months—
driving trucks, mixing pesticides, maintaining the plane.
She'd learned every aspect of the business from the ground
up, literally and figuratively.

During her hot, grimy apprenticeship, Julie had also discovered that one of her new partners hit the casinos almost as
often as he climbed into the cockpit. The cash she'd invested
in Agro-Air should have gone for new equipment. Instead,
Dusty had diverted it to pay his most pressing debts.

So here she was, trying to get this forty-five year old tail-
dragger back in the air. Consequently, she did *not* want to
hear Chuck had found another problem with the Pawnee's
engine. Mentally crossing all of her fingers and toes, she
popped her head up over the engine stand.

"Uh-oh what?"

The mechanic shifted his plug of Red Man from one cheek
to the other and spit out a black stream before nodding to
something over her left shoulder. "We got company."

Twisting, Julie peered at the heat waves shimmering above
the dirt road that led to Agro-Air's corrugated tin hangar/
operations center/business office. A plume of red Oklahoma
dust rose above the iridescent waves. Generating the plume,
she saw, was a low-slung Jaguar XFR.

"Crap!"

Her stomach did a swift free fall. She could think of only
one reason why a $70,000-plus sports car would bump down
a dirt road to a mowed-grass airstrip stuck smack in the
middle of the Oklahoma Panhandle. The same reason, apparently, had occurred to Chuck. Emitting another black stream,
the mechanic shook his head.

"Dusty's gone and done it again."

Jaw tight, Julie pulled a rag from the pocket of her coveralls and swiped at her grease-streaked face. The brutal July
heat had prompted her to stuff her unruly auburn mane under
an Oklahoma Redhawks baseball cap. As a result, she was
swimming in sweat and in no mood to threaten, cajole, bar-

gain with or otherwise attempt to fend off another of Agro-Air's creditors.

Except...

When the silvery Jag rolled to a stop some yards away, the man who emerged didn't look like the other collectors who'd harassed them about late payments. Julie slid her aviator-style sunglasses to the tip of her sweaty nose. With a pilot's quick grasp of the essentials, she catalogued sun-streaked tawny hair and linebacker shoulders encased in a crisp white shirt with the sleeves rolled up on muscular forearms. A silver belt buckle glinted in the July sun above a pair of pleated black slacks that only men with flat bellies and lean hips could carry off.

This guy did more than carry them off. He could have modeled them in any catalogue or on any website in the Western World, with some pouty, anorexic model draped all over him. Julie was thoroughly enjoying the view until he peeled off *his* sunglasses and hooked them in the open neck of his shirt.

"Omigod!"

She recognized those lean hips and wide shoulders now. She should! They'd pinned her to the sheets a year or so ago.

A different kind of heat slammed into her. Swift and furious and completely unexpected. She felt its scorch as images tumbled into her head. This man, lean and sleek with sweat, while she straddled his hips. His hands on her breasts, her hips. Hers exploring every inch of the gorgeous male stretched out beneath her.

And she could barely remember his name! Andy? Aaron?

Her inability to extract that bit of data from the searing memories acted like a bucket of cold water, dousing the heat and all but making Julie cringe. She didn't tumble into bed with complete strangers! Ever! Except for that one time, and never would again. She was too careful, too precise, and too fastidious for one-night stands.

Normally.

If he hadn't swooped into that small airport outside Nuevo Laredo in a spiffy, twin-engine Gulfstream…

If they hadn't bumped into each other in the operations shack…

If he hadn't offered to buy her a beer…

Oh, for Pete's sake! All the if's in the world wouldn't erase the idiocy of that wild night. Or her anxious hours after their insane marathon of sex. They'd used a condom. Several, in fact. But she'd been late the following month. Almost ten days.

She'd realized afterward that was probably due to her erratic hours and disrupted sleep cycles, but those were a tense ten days. Just remembering her dread when she'd walked into a drugstore to purchase a pregnancy kit made Julie shove her sunglasses back up her nose with a grimy finger. She wanted no trace of that nerve-racking experience to show when she greeted this ghost from her not-so-distant past.

Or didn't greet him. He flicked her no more than a quick, dismissive glance as he strode up to the engine stand and directed his remarks to Agro-Air's chief mechanic.

"I'm looking for Julie Bartlett. Is she around?"

Part Cherokee, part Afro-American and not particularly inclined to socialize at the best of times, Chuck looked the newcomer up and down.

"Might be," he drawled, shifting his plug to the other cheek again. "Who wants to know?"

"My name's Dalton. Alex Dalton."

Aha! Alex. The name clicked in Julie's head as Chuck gave the man another laconic once-over.

"You in the casino business?"

Obviously surprised by the question, Dalton shook his head. "No. Oil field equipment. Julie Bartlett," he repeated. "Is she here?"

Chuck left it to her to answer, which she did. First, however, she swiped her hands on the rag again and dragged in a long, steadying breath.

"Yes, I am."

She could accept the fact that he hadn't recognized her at first in baggy coveralls and baseball cap. She wasn't real happy with the second look he zinged her way, however. Was that surprise in those laser-blue eyes? Or disbelief that he'd hooked up with this grimy grease monkey? Whatever it was, it stung. Consequently Julie's next comment was more than a tad cool. "What can I do for you, Dalton?"

"I'd like to speak with you." He shot a glance at Chuck. "Privately."

She was tempted to tell him to say whatever he had to say right here. That brief look still rankled.

"All right. Let's go inside. The office is air-conditioned."

Even Dusty would admit "office" was a grandiose term for the plywood cubicle sectioned off inside the metal hangar. But it boasted an air-conditioner that sat on a precarious platform in the partition's only window and did valiant battle against the July heat.

The chilled air hit with a welcome slap as Julie motioned Dalton inside and shut the door behind him. He stood for a moment, looking around. She could imagine what the place must look like to an outsider. It had certainly made her gulp when she'd walked in two months ago. Weather reports, spraying schedules, fuel bills and chemical invoices littered every available horizontal surface, almost burying the computer Dusty had acquired sometime back in the Middle Ages. A crook-necked lamp tilted haphazardly on the Army surplus desk. A chair was wedged behind the desk, another in a corner next to a much-dinged and dented metal file cabinet.

Dusty's one-eyed, twenty-pound sloth of a cat lay sprawled across the seat of the corner chair. Belinda opened her good eye to a golden slit and twitched her whiskers, sniffing for the spicy tacos Dusty fed her two or three times a day. When she ascertained the arrivals had come empty-handed, she immediately lost interest and rolled onto her back to display a fat, freckled belly.

Julie started to nudge the animal off the chair when a glance at Dalton's crisp white shirt and black slacks stayed her hand. If he sat, he'd get up again wearing a layer of cat hair. He appeared to reach the same conclusion. After a glance at Belinda's freckled, two-acre belly, he opted to stand.

Julie still couldn't reconcile this cool, sophisticated executive type with the cocky pilot she'd hooked up with for a few, intense hours. 'Course, he hadn't been this cool or remote then. He'd been all over her, and she him. Cursing the flush that came so readily with her dark red hair, Julie shoved the lingering image of his hard thighs and muscled shoulders out of her head and leaned against the front of Dusty's desk.

"We're as private as we're going to get," she said with a nod to the cat. "What did you want to talk to me about?"

Instead of answering, he parried her question with one of his own. "Do you remember me?"

Like she could forget? Still, a girl had to save some face.

"Took me a moment after you got out of the car," she said with a shrug, "but I finally placed you. Nuevo Laredo, a year or so ago."

His gaze dropped from her face to her baggy coveralls. He did a better job of masking his thoughts this time but Julie could guess what he was thinking.

"Looks like you're having trouble placing *me,* though," she said drily. Tugging off her ball cap, she tossed it on the cluttered desk. Her sunglasses followed. "Does that help?"

Recognition registered the instant his gaze went from her tumble of auburn hair to her odd-colored eyes. One was green, the other a cross between hazel and brown.

He'd teased her about them, Julie remembered with a sudden kick, before dropping lazy kisses on both eyelids. After which he'd burned a slow, delicious line to her mouth, her chin and the hollow of her throat before contorting to torture the tips of her breasts with his teeth and tongue.

Just the memory of that erotic assault made the aforementioned tips get all tight and tingly. Then his mouth slid into a grin, and her traitorous nipples jumped to instant attention.

"Yeah," he admitted, "it does."

Whoa! There was the man she remembered. That slow, sexy smile crinkled the tanned skin at the corners of his eyes and transformed him from merely mouthwatering to Greek-god-gorgeous.

That's all it had taken, Julie remembered ruefully. That killer grin. Followed by dinner, a couple of beers, several shared war stories and two—no, three!—explosive orgasms.

Unfortunately, the cumulative effect of all of the above had made the other males Julie had since met seem too dull or flat or uninteresting to progress beyond the dinner stage. Not that she'd had much time for men, dull or otherwise, in recent months. Things could be looking up, though.

"You're a tough person to track down," he commented.

He'd been searching for her? Well, well. Things were *definitely* looking up.

Unless…

Had he driven out to this corner of the Oklahoma Panhandle in search of another good time? Another quick tumble? The possibility left a chalky taste in her mouth. Guess that's what she got for letting his handsome face and come-hither smile overcome her common sense.

Then again, he *did* drive all the way out here. That could indicate some level of interest beyond the obvious. If so, they would do things differently this time, Julie decided. Take it slower. Share more than a few beers and tall tales before they exchanged bodily fluids. Despite her firm resolve, the possibility sent a shiver of delicious anticipation down her spine.

"You were gone when I woke up," he commented, breaking into her thoughts.

"I had a five a.m. show time at the airport."

Also a major case of the guilts. She'd been dating someone else at that time. Not seriously, but regularly enough to add a nagging sense of disloyalty to her dismay at having done something so completely uncharacteristic. She and Todd had gone their separate ways soon afterward. Probably due to the fact that he—along with the two or three other men Julie had dated since—had suffered mightily in comparison to this one.

Okay. She could admit it. She'd thought about tracking Dalton down once or twice after their brief encounter. Might even have checked the logs at the Nuevo Laredo airport for his home base after she broke it off with Todd. But she'd taken a job hauling mine supplies in Chile immediately prior to buying into Agro-Air. That was a grueling, inter-Andes killer, and since returning to the States she'd had nothing but long days, exhausted nights, and too many Dusty Jones-style headaches to even consider a life outside fungicides and fertilizers. Thank God they were in that narrow window between spring harvest and prep for winter wheat planting. She finally had a few weeks to finish overhauling the Pawnee.

Reminded of the engine dripping oil outside, she decided to lay things on the line. "I'm flattered you drove all the way out to the Panhandle to find me, Dalton, but you need to know that I'm not the same person I was last time we crossed paths. A lot's happened in my life since then, and I don't have the time or the energy for a casual fling. Not that our last one wasn't fun," she tacked on when his brows straight-lined.

"I didn't come here hoping to pick up where we left off."

Ooooh-kay. Glad they cleared that one up.

"So why did you track me down?"

As soon as the words were out it belatedly occurred to her that he might want to talk business. Although they hadn't gotten around to sharing detailed family histories during their previous encounter, she'd deduced from the plane he was piloting and the very expensive watch he'd sported that he was related to the Daltons who owned a major manufacturing operation headquartered in Oklahoma. He'd just confirmed that a few moments ago with Chuck. As far as Julie knew, Dalton International wasn't into agricultural aviation but they could be considering it. The field looked to become extremely lucrative if recent crop trends continued.

Unless, of course, you'd bought into a company whose senior partner was addicted to the slots. Suppressing a grimace, Julie waited for Dalton to continue. He did, with no trace of a smile in either his voice or his eyes now.

"I came to find out if I got you pregnant that night in Nuevo Laredo."

"What?"

"You heard me." His expression was positively unfriendly now. "Did you get pregnant, give birth to a baby girl, and deposit her on my mother's doorstep two weeks ago?"

Her jaw dropped. She gaped at him, stunned into sputtering incoherence. "You're… You're kidding, right?"

"Wrong."

The flat reply snapped her jaw shut. This man had put her through a whiplash of emotions in the past ten minutes. Surprise had topped the list but fury was fast moving into first place. And here she'd thought… Sort of hoped…

Idiot!

They'd only been together one night. Never had time to get to know each other beyond that instant, sizzling attraction. But the fact that he would think, even for a moment, that she was the kind of woman who'd abandon her own child put fire in Julie's heart. Shoving away from the desk, she stalked to the office door and yanked it open.

"Take my word for it. If I did have a baby, I certainly wouldn't deposit her on your mother or anyone's else's doorstep. Now I suggest you climb back into your bright, shiny Jag and get the hell out of my sight."

He didn't budge.

"You took a job down in Chile eight months ago. Didn't come back until late May. The private investigator I hired hasn't been able to verify your whereabouts during that time."

No surprise there! Without resorting to her log, even Julie

would have a hard time remembering every remote strip she'd flown into during those hectic months. She didn't like that Dalton had put a bloodhound sniffing after her, though.

"Where I went and when I returned is none of your damned business. I don't know who you think you are, but...."

"I *think* I'm the baby's father," he shot back. "DNA tests show a seventy percent probability."

That sidetracked her for a moment. "I thought those tests were, like, ninety-nine point nine percent accurate."

"They are, in ninety-nine point nine percent of the cases," he replied stiffly. "There's a slight margin for error when the potential father has an identical twin."

"You're a twin?"

"Yes."

Good grief! There were two like him on the loose?

Or were they? On the loose, that is? Dalton hadn't worn a wedding ring when they'd met. Didn't wear one now, she noted with a swift glance at his left hand. Not that a naked ring finger proved anything.

"This is your problem," Julie told him, acid dripping from every syllable, "not mine. Now you need to be on your way. There's an engine outside that requires my attention."

She cracked the door wider and made a shooing motion. Once again, he didn't move.

"There's only one way to determine the baby's paternity beyond any doubt."

"And that is?"

"Match the father *and* the mother's DNA."

"I repeat. That's your problem. Besides," she added as a new thought pierced her simmering anger. "I can't be the only female you, uh, connected with last year. Have you searched your entire database?"

"As a matter of fact, I have. You're the last contact on my list."

Well, she'd asked. Now she knew. He'd gone through his entire black book before scraping the bottom of the barrel.

"Would you like to know what you can do with your list?"

Dalton's face flushed a dull red, and an anger that matched her own sparked in his eyes. "Hard as this may be to believe, I don't make a habit of hitting on every female I meet."

And Julie didn't usually let strange men hit on her. She was damned if she'd admit that, though. If Mr. Rich Guy Dalton wanted to think she was a tramp, let him!

Rigid with fury, she yanked the door all the way open. "Get out."

"All I'm requesting is a hair or saliva sample."

"Get out."

He moved then, but only to where she stood. Julie tipped her chin and held her own but she had to admit she didn't remember the sexy stud she'd hooked up with for one wild night being quite this tall. Or this intimidating. He stood so close she could make out the gold tips of his lashes, the faint white scar on one side of his chin, the utter determination in those deadly blue eyes.

Julie was no shrimp. At five-eight, she'd had to shoehorn into more than one cramped cockpit. She'd also learned to extricate herself from tricky situations while flying in and out of some less than desirable locales. Dalton topped her by a good four or five inches, however, and right now he looked as tough as any of the macho hotheads she'd encountered over the years.

"Look," he said, making an obvious effort to rein in his temper, "this isn't just about you or me. We need to know the baby's parentage for health reasons, if nothing else."

Well, hell! She hadn't considered that. Of course they would want to know if there was a history of serious diseases somewhere in the child's family tree. Julie almost caved then. Would have, if Dalton hadn't added a tight-jawed kicker.

"We'll pay you."

"Excuse me?"

"A thousand in cash for a DNA sample right here, right now."

She had to fight for breath. Not only did he think she would abandon her own baby, now he appeared to believe she had to be bribed to prove she was telling the truth. If Julie had a wrench in her hand right now, this jerk would be parting his hair on the other side for a long, long time to come.

"Get...out!"

His jaw worked. Those blue eyes iced into her. "This isn't over between us," he warned.

"What are you gonna do?" she sneered. "Get your PI to follow me around and snatch my coffee cup to steal a saliva sample?"

"That's one option. There are others."

He let his glance make a circuit of the messy office. Slowly. Deliberately. Then he brought that knife-edged gaze back to her.

"The offer's on the table for the next twenty-four hours. Think about it."

She ached to give *him* a few things to think about. A swift knee to the gonads came immediately to mind. She settled for slamming the door behind him so hard it bounced back and almost whapped her in the face.

Two

"A thousand dollars!"

Dusty Jones's creased, roadmap of a face lit up with delight. He'd returned less than a half hour after Alex Dalton's departure. A small, bow-legged old coot with wiry gray hair that sprang out in every direction beneath a beat-up straw Stetson, he strutted like a banty rooster whenever he wasn't in the cockpit. He wasn't strutting now. He was slapping his knee and whooping with glee.

"Whoooeee! A thousand for a hair or a lick of spit! That'll almost pay for the chemicals I ordered last week."

"You ordered a new load?"

Momentarily diverted from the subject of Alex Dalton's outrageous offer, Julie brought the front legs of her chair down with a thud. The violent movement provoked a hiss from Belinda. After scarfing up the tacos Dusty had faithfully delivered, the cat had draped herself across Julie's lap like a fat, furry blanket. She now proceeded to announce her displeasure at having her post-taco siesta disturbed by digging her claws into Julie's thigh. The needle-sharp talons pierced right through her coveralls and came close to drawing blood.

"Ow!" Julie returned the cat's one-eyed glare and detached her claws before appealing to the second man crammed into the tiny office. "Chuck, will you *puh-leez* remind our partner we still haven't paid for the last load of chemicals?"

The mechanic shifted his plug and dutifully complied. "We ain't paid for the last load, Dusty."

Julie ground her back teeth. If she didn't love these two geezers so much, she'd let them sink and get back to having a life! Hanging on to her temper with both white-knuckled fists, she glared at her partner.

"You promised!"

"I know, I know." Dusty rubbed a thorny palm across the back of his neck. "But we're coming up on winter wheat planting season. Can't make any money if we don't service our customers. So give this guy Dalton some spit, missy, and get us out of the hole."

"Didn't you hear me?" Julie asked, exasperated. "The man thinks I dumped a baby on his doorstep."

"Thought you said it was his mother's doorstep."

She flapped an impatient hand. "His, hers, what difference does it make?"

"Ha! You wouldn't ask that if you'd ever crossed paths with Delilah Dalton."

"And you have?"

"Yes'm, I have. Must have been thirty, forty years ago. Del and her husband were just starting out in the oil field resupply business then. He was what we used to call in them days a real rounder. Now Delilah..." He shook his head in mingled admiration and chagrin. "That woman was one fine female. Probably still is. But so uptight you could bounce a dime off her ass and get nine cents change."

"Which is all the more reason for me to refuse her son's

demand for a DNA sample," Julie huffed. "I don't want anything to do with him or his mother."

"But, missy! A thousand dollars?"

"No."

"Just for a little spit?"

"No."

He heaved a long-suffering sigh, as though *she* was the one who'd plugged last season's profits into the slots.

"Awright, already. I hear what you're sayin'. But…"

"No, Dusty."

He sighed again and retrieved his cat from Julie's lap. Belinda hung over his arm like a horse blanket as he delivered a last bit of advice. "If the Daltons are as hot to find the baby's mama as you say they are, I 'spect this isn't the last you'll hear from them. Or their lawyers."

"Lawyers?"

Julie swallowed a groan. That's all she needed. With a forty-five-year-old Pawnee leaking oil like a sieve and a partner who couldn't stay away from the casinos, she now had to worry about a horde of lawyers swooping in to gnaw at the flesh of Agro-Air.

"Look, I'll contact Dalton tomorrow, after I've cooled down a little, and confirm that I'm not the mother of his child. But I'm not taking money from the man, Dusty."

"I'm just sayin'," he intoned as he knuckled Belinda's head. "Better be prepared, missy. Dalton didn't look to be the kinda man to wait around for answers."

Alex's jaw remained locked for most of the two-hour drive back to Oklahoma City. Julie Marie Bartlett didn't have a clue who she was tangling with.

Who she *had* tangled with. Christ! He'd almost forgotten the dark copper hair that had first snagged his interest when he'd walked into that operations shack in Nuevo Laredo. And those odd-colored eyes. Not to mention the full lips, taut breasts and slender hips that went with them.

But the truth was, he hadn't remembered any of those enticing attributes until two weeks ago. That's when his mother had called and demanded his instant appearance at her Oklahoma City mansion. His, and his twin's. She'd met them at the door with a bundled infant in her arms. Alex could still feel the remnants of their collective shock when she'd announced someone had left a baby on her doorstep. Then she'd thrust out the note alleging the six-month old infant was Delilah Dalton's grandchild.

After they'd recovered enough to speak, both Alex and Blake had questioned the authenticity of the note. With good reason. In the past five years their mother had transitioned from wistful to vocal to downright obnoxious in her attempts to push one of them to the altar. Delilah didn't care which of her sons married which of the spouse candidates she'd thrown at them. She just wanted them settled and happy. And, oh by the way, producing grandchildren. Lots of grandchildren. As she'd tartly reminded them, she wasn't getting any younger. Nor were they. Her sons had chalked the baby up to another of their mother's Machiavellian plots until she announced she'd had a DNA test run.

Alex kept his eyes on the flat checkerboard of Oklahoma countryside outside his windshield but his mind replayed that surreal scene in his mother's living room. Either he or his brother had, in fact, fathered a child.

The shock of her announcement was still thundering in Alex's ears when he'd cradled the baby in his arms. Blue-eyed, pink-cheeked Molly had pretty much won his heart with her first gummy smile. Then she'd gurgled and blown him a bubble. Alex would have claimed her as his right then and there, but Blake had reminded him of the thirty-point swing in the DNA analysis and Delilah had stressed the need to nail down the mother.

As a result, Alex and his brother had spent the past two weeks contacting the women they'd connected with early last year. Their lists hadn't been anywhere near equal. As Dalton

International's Vice President of Operations, Alex got around a lot more than its Vice President for Financial Strategies.

Given the narrow window of opportunity, however, even Alex's list hadn't been all that long. It had included the lawyer he dated off and on for almost six months. The divorcee his mother had foisted on him when she'd realized he and the lawyer weren't serious. The mega-hot state senator's daughter Delilah had paired him with at the Oklahoma City Country Club's annual charity ball. And Julie Bartlett.

The first three had responded to his query with looks ranging from astonishment to amusement. The last...

It had to be Bartlett. She'd been out of the country for most of last year, moving from job to job and one remote airstrip to another. The PI Alex had hired to dig into her activities and physical condition during those missing months had hit a couple of blind alleys but should produce results soon.

Not that Alex needed further confirmation. Julie Bartlett wouldn't have refused to provide a DNA sample unless she *had* given birth and subsequently abandoned her baby.

His brother agreed with his assessment. To a point.

Alex cornered Blake in his office in the glass-and-steel tower housing the headquarters of Dalton International. The floor-to-ceiling windows showcased a bustling downtown Oklahoma City with its Bricktown Ballpark, busy restaurants, and newly diverted river spur ferrying tourists to the Land Rush sculpture park. Neither of the Dalton brothers had any interest in the colorful barges meandering the tree-lined river, however.

"The fact that she wouldn't voluntarily give a DNA sample is pretty telling," Blake agreed, "but not *prima facie* evidence that she's the mother."

"So where does that leave us?" Alex worked off his frustration by pacing the office. "Can we take her to court and force her to provide a sample?"

"Not without more justification. We would need hospital records, statements from witnesses that she was pregnant, some hard facts to support the petition for a court order."

Alex had expected the answer. Blake was precise and deliberate by nature, and the framed law degree hanging on the wall behind his desk had only exacerbated his tendency to examine any and all sides of an issue before jumping on it.

He'd been that way even as a kid. Alex would hurtle himself head first at every challenge, whether it was a new toy or a kite caught in a tree or a schoolyard bully. His twin would hold back and assess the situation, although Blake would always wade in whenever necessary—usually after Alex's nose had been bloodied or he'd shimmied up a tree and couldn't get down. The present situation, he thought grimly, had too many parallels for comfort.

"I should have just invited her to lunch," he said in disgust. "I could have picked up her fork or glass or napkin and strolled off with it."

"You could have," Blake agreed mildly. "None of which would have helped us in court. For a paternity suit, or in this case, a *ma*ternity suit, the sample has to be taken under controlled conditions."

"But at least we would know."

"Maybe. I've done some digging into DNA testing. There was a case in Virginia a few years ago. The principals battled it out in court for two years despite the fact that the DNA test showed an almost hundred percent probability the defendant was, in fact, the father."

"Yeah, we know about those probabilities."

"The judge finally ruled against the claimant when it came out that the DNA lab employed a total of five people processing more than a hundred thousand paternity tests a year, with one supervisor certifying the results every four minutes. The margin for error was too wide for absolute certainty."

Alex stopped his restless pacing and faced his brother. An outsider probably couldn't have told them apart. They were both six-two, blue-eyed, and built on exactly the same lines. But the differences were there and readily apparent to anyone who knew them well. Blake's hair was a darker gold and parted on the left. Alex sported a scar on his chin from a close encounter with a fence post as a kid.

They had that unique twin ability to almost read each other's thoughts, though, and Alex didn't particularly care for the vibe he was receiving at the moment.

"So you're saying Molly may not be ours?"

The possibility carved an unexpected hole in his heart. He'd had two weeks to get used to the idea of being a father. Or uncle. Either way, the idea that neither he nor Blake might have a claim on the baby left a hollow feeling inside him.

"I'm saying it might not hurt to run another test," Blake was saying. "Especially considering who arranged for the first."

"You're right." Alex huffed out an exasperated breath. "I wouldn't put it past our dear, sweet mother to have sent in baby hair from one of us instead of from Molly."

"Me, either." Laughter lightened Blake's somber expression. "How many prospective brides has she thrown at you in the past six months?"

"Eight. You?"

"Five."

Now they had a whole new set of issues to work. With his characteristic decisiveness, Alex wanted the matter of Molly's parentage settled. "Okay, here's what we'll do. First, we'll have another test run to confirm Molly is ours. Second, we convince Ms. Bartlett to submit a DNA sample. If it turns out she's not Molly's mother, we go back and…"

The buzz of the intercom cut him off. Irritated, Alex scowled when his brother reached for the phone.

"I told your secretary not to interrupt us."

"She's not a secretary," Blake corrected in his precise way. "She's my executive assistant."

As much as Alex loved his twin, there were times he

itched to stick a firecracker down his shirt collar and light the fuse. This was one of them.

"Just tell her... Oh, crap!"

He couldn't suppress a groan as the office door flew open and their mother sailed in. With her megawatt personality, waist-length raven hair showing only a trace of silver, and fingers flashing their usual ten or twelve carats worth of diamonds, Delilah Dalton tended to put a stone-cold finish to conversation whenever she made one of her flamboyant entrances.

The diamonds were absent today. She'd removed them two weeks ago to avoid scratching the tender skin of the infant now cradled to her chest. Instead, her tall, spare figure was encased in black leggings and a print tunic sprouting a profusion of leafy geraniums in eye-popping pink. The sling snuggling the baby against her chest was made of the same wild print.

"Well?" she demanded as she swept in. "How did it go with the Bartlett woman?"

Alex parried her imperious demand with one of his own. "Where did you get that outfit?"

"An on-line shop called Baby Glam and Mama, Too." Preening, she patted the baby's back. "It's got the most delicious inventory. I'm thinking of ordering matching leopard-skin tights and headbands for Molly and me."

Alex and Blake shared a quick glance. They knew their mother. Once she latched on to something, she didn't let go. If she'd decided Molly was really her granddaughter...

Aw, hell! Who were they kidding? Alex and Blake had latched on to that same possibility two weeks ago. Even if subsequent tests proved otherwise, the baby was now permanently etched on both their hearts.

That much was obvious when Blake rounded his desk and approached their mom. Smiling, he gazed down at the sleeping infant. His fatuous expression must have mirrored

Alex's because their mother could hardly conceal her glee as she glanced from one son to the other.

"Tell me," she demanded of Alex. "What did the Bartlett woman say?"

"Her name's Julie," he reminded her.

"Whatever." She flapped an impatient hand. "Did she admit to being Molly's mother?"

"No."

"Well, we'll soon discover the truth of that! When is she going in to supply a DNA sample?"

"She's not."

"What?"

Delilah's small shriek startled the baby. Molly's head popped up. She blinked and looked right, left, then right again. Driven by an instinct as nervous as it was protective, Alex reached for the child.

"Here, let me take her."

Delilah unhooked the sling and let him extract the baby. When she saw his smile as he cradled Molly in his arms, she had to bite back an exultant whoop.

She couldn't have scripted this scenario any better! She was ready. More than ready. All those long, hard years hopping around oil fields and even harder years expanding Dalton International to its present level of operations had taken their toll. Delilah wanted to kick back. Enjoy the wealth those grueling years had generated. Lavish all her loving energy on her tall, handsome, annoyingly independent sons. On the baby Alex now cradled in his arms.

"Tell me," she ordered again. "What did Bartlett say? Is she the mother or isn't she?"

"I don't know." Frowning, he brushed a knuckle over Molly's cheek. "I would have said no based on her initial reaction. But when I asked for a DNA sample, she got all huffy and hot-tempered."

"Ha! There you go! Refusing that simple request proves the woman's got something to hide. Did you tell her our primary goal is to ascertain Molly's parentage so we can do a medical history?"

"Yeah, I did."

His knuckle made another tender sweep over the baby's cheek. The sight would have filled Delilah with untrammeled glee if not for his grim expression.

"I also offered to pay for a sample," he related. "That seemed to set her back up."

"Then you didn't offer enough." The hard-headed businesswoman took precedence over Delilah's rampaging motherly/grandmotherly instincts. "Everyone's got a price. You just haven't found hers yet."

Alex knew she was right. He and Blake had stood shoulder-to-shoulder with their mother as she'd faced down competitors who made the mistake of thinking they could prey on their father's amiable good nature to cut into the Daltons' growing empire. Delilah had taught her sons to move in, take over, and leave no prisoners behind. As a result Dalton International had gobbled up their competition over the years, including any number of small, two-bit ventures like Agro-Air.

Their mother zoomed in on that like a crow diving on roadkill. "Did you check out this company she works for?"

"Of course," Blake answered. "We ran a complete financial analysis before Alex drove out to the Panhandle."

"And?"

"Agro-Air is operating on a shoestring. The old timer who founded it..."

"Careful!"

"The, er, *individual* who founded it is a throwback by the name of Josiah Jones."

"Josiah Jones!" Delilah looked as though the floor had just rolled under her feet. "Aka Dusty Jones?"

Alex settled the baby against his shoulder and shared a look with his twin. He couldn't remember the last time either of them had seen their mother's set back on her heels.

"I think..." Alex said slowly. "No, I'm sure Julie mentioned that was one of her partners."

"Oh, Lord!"

The two brothers locked gazes again. What the heck was this all about?

"You want to tell us how you know this Dusty character?" Alex asked.

The question seemed to shake her out of a trance. "We locked horns decades ago. Damned if I can remember why. But I *do* remember that bowlegged bastard could fly his rickety ole biplane like nobody's business."

"He's progressed from biplanes to single-wing PA-36's." A tight smile stretched Alex's lips as he recalled the oil dripping from the Pawnee's engine. "Still pretty rickety, though."

A familiar combative light leaped into their mother's eyes. "And that's who your one-night stand is partnered with?"

"Her name is Julie," he repeated tersely. "Julie Bartlett."

Almost purring with pleasure, Delilah eased the baby from his arms. Satisfaction radiated from her in waves as she tucked Molly back into the sling.

"Unless the Dusty I knew forty years ago has shed his skin and grown a new one, he's up to his elbows in one kind of trouble or another. Put that PI of yours on him. I'll bet my new chinchilla coat you'll find some leverage to hold over him and that tart you slept with."

"Julie," Alex ground out. "Her name is *Julie*."

"Like I care?" With a wave to her sons, she headed for the door. "This is your daughter we're talking about. Yours or Blake's. So don't screw around. Go for the jugular."

Alex took the elevator to one of the penthouse apartments on the top floor of the Dalton International building and put the rest of that afternoon and evening to productive use.

He knew he'd inherited his mother's killer instinct. More to the point, he itched to show a certain green-eyed, slender-hipped crop duster he was *not* someone she could eradicate from her life like she would a pesky aphid.

Okay! All right! It was more than an itch. During the long drive back to Oklahoma City, it had become almost a compulsion. He *could* chalk it up to his naturally competitive nature but he knew that was only part of the equation. As she had the first time they'd met, Julie Bartlett had spurred a gut-level response in him.

Once in his sprawling apartment with its panoramic view of the city, he splashed Crown Royal onto ice and settled at his desk. His first task was to turn his PI onto Dusty Jones as Delilah had suggested. It didn't take long for Jamison to come back with a report on the crop duster's personal ups and downs. Mostly downs in recent months, he related. Big downs.

While that was in the works, Alex spent several hours at the computer. He and Blake had already run the stats on Agro-Air's operations and revenue once. Wouldn't hurt to dig a little deeper. By the time he called it quits sometime after midnight and hit the sack, Alex suspected he'd gathered more information about the company than its principal owner wanted either of his partners to know.

Lacing his hands behind his head, he stared up at the moonlight streaming through the skylights. Now that he'd had time to sort through his roller-coaster day, he could admit the truth. It wasn't his mother's acerbic comments or his brother's legalese or the all-consuming question of Molly's parentage that had spurred all these additional queries. It was Julie Bartlett.

The prickly, uncooperative, grease-smeared redhead had gotten under his skin this afternoon, even more than the pilot who'd snagged his interest in down in Nuevo Laredo. His bone-deep competitive instincts wouldn't be satisfied until he knew whether she was or was not the mother of the child that might or might not be his. In the process, he might just finesse the woman into bed again.

Yeah, right! Like he needed that complication in his life right now.

On the other hand…

Images from their night together drifted into his mind, came into focus, sharpened. Alex was damned if he could remember the name of the restaurant they'd eaten at or the motel across from the airport they'd adjourned to. But now that he'd seen Julie Bartlett again, he couldn't get the vivid, 3-D image of her naked and flushed with desire out of his head. Grunting, he rolled over and punched his pillow.

Three

Alex's first call Wednesday morning was to his mother. Since she'd turned over most of the Dalton International's operations to her sons, Delilah had taken to sleeping more than the four or five hours a night she'd grabbed while she was raising her boys and building the corporation from the ground up almost single-handedly. Molly had rekindled old habits, however. Delilah was once again up with the sun and crashed as soon as she tucked the baby in for the night.

She sipped her first cup of coffee while she listened to Alex's plan. When he hung up, she sat for a long time in the kitchen of her sprawling mansion. She would never admit to either of her sons that she felt more comfortable in this cheerful kitchen with its watermelon striped wallpaper and collection of dented copper tea kettles than in any of the other seventeen rooms, all decorated by outrageously expensive interior designers.

She'd wanted more for her sons than the shack she'd grown up in. More than the tar-paper shanty their father had

called home before hiring out to Conoco-Philips Petroleum
when he turned thirteen. Neither she nor Big Jake had finished high school. Yet their sons had not only racked up several advanced degrees, they'd acquired a sophistication that
secretly thrilled Delilah almost as much as it frustrated her.
Alex and Blake should be married by now, damn it. Should
be giving her the grandbabies she craved. Babies like Molly.

"Ah, Jake," she murmured as she nested her coffee cup in
both hands and looked out onto a multi-terraced and elabo-
rately landscaped garden. "You ought to see the little one.
She has your eyes."

A familiar ache pierced Delilah's heart. She could only
pray that the shape of her eyes was *all* Molly had inherited
from her irresponsible, incorrigible, irresistible grandfather.
Then one of the monitors she'd had installed in every room of
the house recorded the sounds of the baby waking to a new
day and she catapulted out of her chair.

Alex's second call that morning was to Agro-Air. He
wanted to make sure the company's senior partner was present when he made the return drive to the Panhandle and presented his offer.

Dusty Jones was folded into the desk chair when Alex arrived at the hail-dented hangar that housed the company's
office. Julie Bartlett and the craggy-faced mechanic she'd
been working with yesterday were also in the office. The
two men eyed Alex with varying degrees of interest when he
walked into the hole in the wall that constituted Agro-Air's
office. Julie's expression was considerably less friendly than
her partner's.

She wasn't wearing coveralls today. What she *was* wearing almost stopped Alex in his tracks. It took some effort but
he managed to keep his gaze from skimming down the long,
fluid legs showcased by her cut-offs. He also allowed himself only a brief glance at the scoop-necked tank top, but the
image of the high, firm breasts showcased by the stretchy

tank stirred the beast within him. Ordering himself to get a grip, he focused instead on the dark red hair looped through the back of her ball cap and the destructive eyes leveled directly at him.

"I was going to call you," she stated almost before he was in the door.

"Were you?"

He did his best to disguise the sudden spike in his adrenaline. Was she going to admit the truth? That she'd given birth to his child? Or flatly deny it and provide the requested DNA sample as proof?

In that moment, Alex was damned if he could decide which option he preferred. This woman had eaten a big hole in his sleep last night. He wasn't sure how he felt about the possibility that a child might link them together for the rest of their lives, but the idea was inching its way into his psyche.

"You have something you want to tell me?" he asked, his eyes locked with hers.

"Yes, I…"

"Hold on there, missy!"

Alex's gaze shifted to the white-haired, weather-beaten man who popped to his feet and deposited his dirigible excuse of a cat atop the littered desk. So this was the Dusty Jones who'd locked horns with his mother sometime in the past. Alex sized him up, wondering what caused Delilah and this banty rooster to go toe to toe.

"Dalton here called us," Jones reminded his partner. "Let's hear what he has to say."

"I know what he has to say." The anger Alex had glimpsed yesterday flared in her unusual eyes again. She banked it with a visible effort. "He wants me to provide proof positive that I am or am not the kind of woman who would abandon her own child."

Dammit! Julie had promised herself she wouldn't get all hot under the collar again. Dalton had a legitimate need to

know the identity of his child's mother. Yet she could feel the
steam building as his blue eyes sliced into her.

"Are you?"

"Now just hold on a dang minute!" Swift as a snake,
Dusty drew their fire. "You said you had a revised proposal
you wanted to discuss with us, Dalton. What is it?"

"We're not interested in any revised proposal," Julie
snapped.

"We might be, missy. We might be. Let's just hear what
the man has to say."

The look she shot the old reprobate should have cut him
off at the knees. He ignored her.

"Why'd you want all of us here?" he asked Dalton. "Why
me 'n Chuck as well as Julie?"

"I realize I might have come across a little heavy-handed
yesterday," Dalton began.

"Ya think?" Julie drawled.

"But I've had time to reconsider," he continued coolly.
"Instead of a cash settlement, I'm thinking we might…"

"Cash is good," Dusty interrupted. "Cash works for me."

"…work out a business arrangement."

"What kind of arrangement?"

Dalton responded to Dusty's question but his eyes remained on Julie. "Dalton International hasn't moved into the
agricultural aviation sector. With the upsurge in the crop production, this may be the right time. We're prepared to make
a substantial investment in Agro-Air."

"How substantial?" Dusty asked eagerly.

"Enough to purchase another, newer plane. I checked and
found a used Lane AT-602 on the market, available immediately. It only requires one load to spray a 125-acre circle at
five gallons per acre. With this increased capacity and spread
ratio, you could double your business base."

He'd done his homework. Julie had to give him that. Despite herself, she felt a bump of excitement at the thought of
the 602's powerful engine.

"In the meantime," Dalton continued, "I'll have our engineers look at current applications systems. With Dalton International's resources and Agro-Air's expertise in the field, we should be able to come up with an even more efficient spread ratio."

"And what does DI get in return for this investment?" Dusty wanted to know.

"We take fifty percent of the profits until we've recouped the cost of the initial aircraft. We'll negotiate a percentage for the purchase of additional aircraft. As for the design and possible manufacture of a new application system, we'll bear the research and development costs but will pay for technical input and flight testing."

Dusty stroked his unshaven chin and peered at Dalton through eyes permanently reddened from dust and cigarette smoke. "That's it? DI takes a cut of the profits from the new plane and Agro-Air helps design and test possible new application systems?"

"No. There's a precondition to the deal."

"Ha!" Julie huffed. "I knew it."

"Did you?" Dalton's smile didn't quite reach his eyes. "Then you won't be surprised when I ask you to spend a week in Oklahoma City as my guest."

"Right." Forgetting that she'd already decided to call the man and assure him she was a non-mom, Julie made a moue of disgust. "I camp out in the city, you lift my DNA off a glass or a comb, and this generous offer from DI suddenly evaporates."

"The offer is solid. So is my promise that I won't take anything you don't want to give."

The way he said it sent a shiver down Julie's spine. Before she could block it, her traitorous mind recalled the mind-numbing pleasure this man had given *and* taken during their night together.

"I don't get it," she said, sternly repressing the memory of his mouth on hers. "How does my spending a week in Oklahoma City answer the question of whether or not I'm your daughter's mother?"

He hesitated and speared a glance at the other two men. Chuck maintained a stoic, unreadable expression. Dusty cocked his head and waited with as much interest as Julie to hear the answer.

"It doesn't," Dalton finally admitted. "What it does is give you a chance to spend some time with Molly and me, see how we fit together. Make sure this is what you want if, in fact, you are her mother. It will also give you an insight into Dalton International's operations," he added when her mouth opened on a hot protest.

Before she could voice it, Dusty leaped into action. "Wait outside," he ordered, shoving their visitor to the door. "My partners and I need to talk about this."

"No, we don't," Julie said indignantly as he slammed the door in Dalton's face. "I'm not trekking off to Oklahoma City for a week."

"You make it sound like the wilds of Africa. It's just down the road a piece, missy."

"Dusty. Listen up! I am *not* spending a week in Oklahoma City."

"Well, now, let's just chaw on that a bit."

Alex was leaning against his Jag when Julie exited the office some twenty minutes later. She stalked out of the hangar, her face stormy, those long legs of hers eating ground with stiff strides. He was careful to avoid any sign of triumph when she curtly announced they had a deal.

"But just so you know, I'm not happy about this, Dalton."

"I can see that."

"Nor do I intend to have you foot my bill. I'll make my own arrangements."

"If that's what you want," he said with a shrug. "But DI maintains a guest suite for out-of-town visitors. It's empty and available."

She hesitated, common sense warring with her obvious anger at being manipulated, then gave a grudging, "All right."

"Do you want me to wait here while you pack a few things or follow you to your place?"

"Just give me the address of the guest suite and a key, if you have one on you."

"I planned to drive you into the city."

"I'll drive myself. I've got some things I need to take care of first."

He'd won the battle. No need for additional skirmishes. With a tight feeling of anticipation he didn't stop to analyze, Alex extracted a business card and wrote the address on the back along with the keypad code for the door. "And this," he said as he added another set of numbers, "is my private line. Call me when you get in."

He handed her the card but held on to an edge when she reached for it. Her distinctive eyes flashed up to meet his.

"Thanks for doing this," he said quietly.

The wave of temper she'd ridden out of the hangar subsided enough for her to dredge up a reluctant smile. "You might not be thanking me when you end up with Dusty for a partner. He's the best pilot in twenty-six states but…well…"

"I can handle Dusty."

But could he handle her?

The thought added another edge to his anticipation as she made for a pickup parked to the side of the hangar with that hip-swinging stride of hers.

The next week, he told himself during the drive back to the city, should prove interesting.

Julie covered the same route later that afternoon. She still couldn't believe she'd let Dusty whine and weasel and guilt her into this ridiculous situation. She'd fully intended to tell Alex Dalton straight out to look elsewhere for his baby's

mother. Sign whatever release the man put in front of her.
Spit into the nearest empty cup.

Yet here she was, cruising east on I-40 toward the cluster
of skyscrapers that thrust up from the flat Oklahoma plains
like a bundle of steel celery stalks. The only reasons she'd
caved, finally, was because Dusty swore a solemn pledge to
stay away from the casinos if she agreed to Dalton's deal.
Plus, she would get a first-hand look at DI's operations, scope
out their engineering and test facilities. Added to that was
the fact that they were between growing seasons and Julie
hadn't had a vacation in longer than she could remember.

She would hit the shops, she decided as fallow, straight-
lined farm sections gave way to suburbs sprinkled with strip
malls and fast-food stops. Visit a couple of Oklahoma City's
world-class museums. Maybe catch the musical *Jersey Boys*
at the Civic Center. And, oh by the way, spend a few hours
with Alex Dalton and his family.

She'd looked them up on Google this afternoon. She'd
skimmed through all sorts of articles and financial publica-
tions chronicling Dalton International's steady rise from a
small family venture to a mega-corporation that manufac-
tured and supplied equipment to oil-rich countries around
the world. She'd also found a profusion of articles and photos
from various society pages. There was the two-page color
spread of Delilah Dalton's mansion, thrown open to the
public for a garden charity event last spring. And a profusion of photos showing one or both of the Dalton twins with
be-gowned and be-jeweled babes on their arms.

One Dalton in a tux had done serious damage to Julie's
respiratory system. Two had almost killed it. The picture also
made her realize how far outside the Dalton orbit she was.
She could relate to the cocky pilot who'd offered to buy her a
drink in a Mexican border town. Aside from flying, she and
Dalton really had nothing in common. Except, of course, one
night of steamy sex and a baby he thought she'd abandoned.

Scowling, Julie used MapQuest to guide her off I-40 and

through the city streets. She'd visited the state capitol many times, most recently when she signed over her savings to become a partner in Agro-Air. Yet the seemingly incessant downtown construction made MapQuest necessary to avoid detours and dead ends.

The thriving hum of traffic and tourists was a testament to a city that owed its origins to the 1889 Land Run, when the government opened lands in Indian Territory that weren't assigned to a particular tribe for settlement. More than ten thousand hopeful homesteaders had camped on the plain in anticipation of the Run. The sea of tents they erected prior to the cannon booming out had burst into an instant city.

By the time Oklahoma Indian Territory became a state in 1907, the boomtown had supplanted Guthrie as the territorial capitol. It continued to boom with the discovery of oil. In the 1940s, the massive gear-up for wartime production at the Douglas Aircraft Plant just outside town brought another surge in both population and revenues. That surge took a serious hit during the post-Vietnam drawdown in the defense industry and oil bust of the 1970s. Oklahoma City hung in there, however, its spirit indomitable—as the 1995 bombing proved to the entire nation.

The agony of that horrific incident had emphasized the best in the Oklahomans character. They were resilient, independent, fiercely proud of their roots. Julie felt every one of those emotions as she wheeled through the streets to the high-rise that housed the corporate headquarters of Dalton International.

A barrier and uniformed guard stopped her at the entrance to the underground parking. If he wondered what business the driver of a beat-up Ford pickup covered from hood to tailgate with red dust had with Dalton's chief operating officer, he was too well-trained to show it. Smiling, he passed her an electronic key card.

"Mr. Dalton advised you'd be arriving this afternoon, Ms. Bartlett. He's reserved a parking space for you next to the elevator. Just insert the card in the elevator slot and it will take you right up to the penthouse."

The penthouse? Well, well. This enforced vacation may not be so bad after all. Feeling almost resigned to a week of shopping and lazing around, Julie maneuvered into the designated parking space and plucked her carryall from the passenger seat. A glass-enclosed elevator whisked her from the dim, subterranean garage into dazzling sunlight, then climbed an outside shaft some thirty stories. The ride gave Julie a breath-stealing view of Oklahoma City's parks and winding river.

Once off the elevator, she followed the directions on a discreet bronze plaque to a set of double doors and keyed in the code. She stopped dead just inside the threshold.

"Ho-ly crap!"

Directly ahead of her was a solid wall of glass. The floor-to-ceiling windows offered a spectacular view from the oval ballpark to the bronze "Guardian" statue crowning the capitol's dome. She was still standing in stunned amazement, half in and half out of the suite, when she heard a door click shut further down the hall. A glimpse over her left shoulder kicked her pulse into sudden overdrive.

The guard downstairs must have notified Dalton of her arrival. He strolled toward her with an easy, confident stride.

"That was quick." She commented. "How'd you get here so fast?"

"I live here."

"Here?"

"Just down the hall. It's convenient for work and entertaining out-of-town guests."

"I'll bet!"

Her imagination took off, courtesy of all those articles depicting Alex Dalton and his brother with gorgeous females draped all over them. Julie would bet she wasn't the first "guest" to be housed so conveniently.

"If you think you'll just waltz through a set of connecting doors and pick up where we left off last year, you've got another think coming."

A smile creased his tanned cheeks, which only made her stiffen even more.

"Look, Dalton…"

"You've got the wrong Dalton."

"Excuse me?"

"I'm Blake, Alex's brother." He held out his hand. "And you, I take it, are Julie Bartlett."

"I, uh, yes."

The resemblance was astonishing. She was still trying to take it in when he took her hand in a strong, sure grip.

"Alex told me you'd agreed to his proposal." Keen blue eyes so like his twin's smiled down at her. "You're under no obligation to do this, you know."

"I got the impression from your brother that the Daltons were standing shoulder-to-shoulder on the issue of the baby's parentage."

"We are, but that doesn't mean we'll ride roughshod over you—or whoever Molly's mother turns out to be."

Julie almost believed him. Might have, if the elevator hadn't pinged at that moment and disgorged his twin. One Dalton packed a powerhouse punch. Two had her sucking air. Especially when Alex turned on an identical grin.

"I see you've met the runt of the litter."

"I have." She scrambled to recover. "He, er, mentioned that he lives on this floor."

"So do I."

A casual wave indicated another set of double doors to the right. Gulping, Julie realized she'd have a Dalton boxing her in on both sides.

"I made reservations for dinner at a restaurant here in town. Seven okay?"

It certainly was. She much preferred meeting his mother on neutral ground. Even the formidable female Dusty had described couldn't kick up too much of a ruckus in public.

"Seven's good."

"I'll pick you up here."

She nodded and let the door click shut behind her, wondering again why in *hell* she'd let herself get talked into this!

An hour later she was showered, blown dry, lip-glossed and encased in the only suit of body armor she'd brought with her.

She'd spent most of the past three or four years in jeans, cut-offs or coveralls. Hadn't had many occasions to "girl" up. As a consequence, she eyed her travel-proof, slinky black slacks and matching bead-trimmed tunic with some misgiving. The two pieces had proven fire-, smoke- and wrinkle-resistant. She'd crammed them into her carry-all dozens of times and could attest to their durability. Whether they were suitable for dinner with the Daltons was another matter.

The admiring gleam in Alex Dalton's eyes when she answered the door bell killed most of her doubts. At least she thought it was Alex. Yep, it was. The tiny scar on his chin ID'ed him.

Another memory suddenly surfaced. The man she'd locked lips and hips with all those months ago sported another distinguishing mark. A very kissable birthmark right...

Involuntarily, Julie's gaze dropped to a point about two inches below his belt. Just as swiftly, she whipped it up again. Hoping to heck her thoughts weren't blazing red in her face, she grabbed her purse.

"Blake enjoyed meeting you," Alex said as he stood aside for her to precede him out the door.

"I enjoyed meeting him, too." She glanced toward his brother's end of the corridor. "Is he driving to the restaurant with us?"

"We're walking, if that's okay. It's only a short jaunt. And Blake's not joining us for dinner."

"So it's just you, me and your mother?"

And possibly the baby. No, surely they wouldn't bring

an infant to a crowded downtown restaurant. As they approached the elevator, Julie geared up for her opening round with the no-holds-barred Delilah.

"Actually," Alex said, tossing a monkey wrench into her mental prep, "it's just you and me."

Four

"Just the two of us?"

Julie came to a dead stop and eyed the man at her side with instant suspicion. She had to admit he didn't *look* as though he was plotting something devious. Just the opposite, in fact. In crisply ironed khakis and a short-sleeved, open-necked shirt with a faint blue stripe, he looked good enough to eat. Whole. Without taking time to chew.

Still, there was the small matter of his thinking she was capable of abandoning her own child. And let's not forget blackmailing her into spending a week in the city.

"I thought one of the reasons behind this excursion was, how did you put it? So I could see how you and the baby fit together?"

"It is." Unruffled, he pressed the elevator button. "But before I throw you to the tiger otherwise known as my mother, I thought we should get to know each other a little better."

Better? Like they didn't already possess an inside and

very intimate track on each other? Her gaze made another involuntary drop to his belt buckle. Smothering a curse, she yanked it up again.

Damn! She'd darn well better control the images that kept jumping into her head at the most inopportune moments. If she didn't, this was going to be a looooong week.

They exited the DI building into blazing July heat only partially mitigated by the shadows of the downtown skyscrapers. Thankfully, the restaurant was only a block away. The elegant French bistro sat just off the lobby of a '30s-era hotel recently renovated to the tune of some fifty million dollars. According to one of the articles Julie had devoured, Dalton International had contributed a good portion of the renovation funds. Which no doubt explained why the bistro's chef/owner herself hurried around the stone counter separating the bricked-in kitchen from the main dining area.

"Alex!"

A petite bundle of sparkle and energy, she rattled off what Julie guessed was an effusive greeting in French. Laughing, Alex dropped a kiss on both cheeks and replied in kind before switching to English for the introductions.

"Cecile, this is Julie Bartlett. Julie, meet Cecile Duchamp. The lightest hand at crepes ever to come out of Maubec."

"Pah!" their hostess puffed. "As though she would know Maubec. It has not even a highway, only a two-lane farm road. But it is in Provence, yes, and all Provençal cooks prepare the crepes like you have never tasted before."

The smile she turned in Julie's direction didn't dim. If anything, it ratcheted up another notch. Yet the look that accompanied it was swift, assessing and distinctly female.

Uh-oh. Was Cecile one of the also-ran in the mother-of-my-child contest? Julie couldn't help wondering as the vivacious brunette escorted them to a circular booth tucked into a corner.

"I bring a bottle of red from your reserve, yes? And the crudités."

Alex looked to Julie. "Is red okay or would you prefer white? Or something other than wine?"

Like the Dos Equis they'd downed that night in Nuevo Laredo? Another memory shot to the surface, this one of Alex laughing at her grimace when she sucked on the lime wedge—right before he leaned across the table and kissed the pucker off her lips.

"Red's fine," she said hastily.

It was more than fine, she discovered when Cecile had decanted the wine. One sip evoked smooth velvet and giant sunflowers—fields and fields of them, bobbing on tall stalks with their faces turned up to the sun...probably because those particular flowers dominated almost every poster Julie had ever seen of the south of France.

"It's good," she told Alex. "Tastes a little like a Chilean syrah."

"You've got a discriminating palette. They come from the same grape variety."

His shoulders rested against the back of the booth but she wasn't fooled into thinking he was relaxed. Especially when he issued a seemingly casual request.

"Tell me about your time in Chile."

"This is what you meant by getting to know each other?" she said, bristling. "An immediate demand to know what I was up to last year?"

"Sorry. That came out wrong. Let me rephrase. What type of jobs did you fly down in Chile?"

"Mostly contact airlift for Caterpillar."

"One of our major competitors," he commented.

"I also flew for Komatsu, hauling equipment parts to Minera Escondida's gold and copper mines. As I'm sure your private investigator has informed you," she couldn't help tacking on.

Annoyance flickered across his tanned face. "I'm just making conversation here."

"Fine. Then why don't you tell me about yourself?"

"What do you want to know?"

She'd gleaned the basics from her Google searches. Age, education, professional associations. She'd catalogued far more intimate physical details during their night together. And she'd certainly had a taste of the ruthless determination that had taken Alex Dalton and his family to the top. Yet the man himself was pretty much an unknown quantity.

"What's it like to be a twin?"

He eased into a rueful grin. "All the cliches apply. Blake and I fought like hell from day one to maintain our individual identities. Fought each other, too. Sibling rivalry takes on a whole new dimension when you're half of a pair. We also rarely passed up a chance to pretend to be each other to confuse babysitters and teachers."

He took another taste of his wine. Julie watched his throat work and vaguely recalled burying her face in the hot crease between it and his shoulder.

"The bond is always there," he continued. "It's undefinable, intangible. Even when we're in different parts of the world. If Blake hurts, I feel it. If I get angry, his blood pressure spikes."

She traced a pattern on the table with her nail, trying to imagine that kind of closeness.

"How about you?" Alex asked, as if reading her mind. "What was it like to be an only child?"

"I loved it," she replied, with a familiar pang at the thought of the parents she'd lost more than a decade ago. "My folks spoiled me rotten."

"That must be how you talked them into letting you apply for a pilot's license at, what? Fourteen? Fifteen?"

He held up his palms before she could get all huffy about him prying into her past again. "I was curious about you after Nuevo Laredo. Did some checking."

"Which you didn't bother to follow up on until someone deposited a baby on your mother's doorstep."

Where did that come from? Julie sincerely hoped it didn't

sound as snarky to him as it did to her. Evidently not, since he lifted his shoulders in a self-deprecating shrug.

"Actually, I did try to follow up. By the time I got around to it, though, you were already down in South America."

"Oh."

That put a different spin on things. So different she found herself relaxing for the first time since Alex Dalton had walked out of her past and turned her life upside down.

They stuck to non-controversial subjects through an appetizer platter of crisp vegetables with a creamy Dijon mustard dipping sauce and a dinner of herb-crusted Dover sole that flaked off the fork. Cecile herself flambeed dessert at their table in a long-handled copper pan. Julie had to admit the woman hadn't boasted. The crepes Suzette were the lightest, most succulent she'd ever put in her mouth.

Not that she'd downed all that many. Having spent most of her cockpit time flying in and out of the Americas, she was a fervent and self-avowed connoisseur of tamales and empanadas. The spicier the better. She could get hooked on these paper-thin pancakes swimming in caramelized Grand Marnier sauce, though. Especially when Alex offered her the last of his after she'd finished her own with a near moan of ecstasy. His eyes dancing, he nudged his plate across the table.

"I warned you."

"Yes, you did." She stabbed the morsel and used it to sop up the remaining sauce. "Wonder if she does carry-out? I'd love to take some of these back to Dusty and Chuck. On second thought," she said after letting the heavenly morsel slide her throat. "I'd better not. Dusty would feed half of his to Belinda, and she certainly doesn't need the calories."

"Belinda being the mottled fur rug?"

"That's her."

"Unusual name for a cat."

He stretched a casual arm along the back of the circular

booth. It didn't come within six inches of Julie but she could swear she felt a slow flush crawling up the back of her neck.

"Belinda's an unusual cat. Dusty swears she can sniff out stinkbugs or wireworms a half mile away. I didn't believe him until I saw her in action. She made a believer out of me. A good number of our clients, too."

"Maybe I should make sure he includes Belinda in the inventory of Agro-Air's physical assets when we close our deal."

The reminder of their deal should have put a damper on Julie's after-dessert glow—and it probably would have if she wasn't so darned conscious of the tanned forearm stretched across the back of the booth. She could make out the hard muscles, the sprinkling of sun-bleached hair, the glint of his mucho expensivo platinum chronometer.

"Maybe you should," she said, deliberately angling away.

"Would you like coffee? Or cappuccino? Cecile makes it with honest-to-goodness whipped cream."

"I'll pass, but you go ahead if you want one."

"I'm good."

He eased out of the booth with a casual grace and came around to Julie's side to offer his hand. She hesitated for the barest instant as the glow faded and sudden, insidious doubts raced through her mind. Alex and Cecile were so friendly. Had he arranged for the chef to save the glass Julie had drunk from? One of the forks? Slip it into a plastic bag for shipment to a lab?

He'd promised he wouldn't take anything she wasn't ready to give. Could she trust him to keep his word? Instinct said yes. Logic argued no, that he had too much at stake.

Well, hell! This absurd situation was making her crazy!

Then she looked up into his eyes and went with her gut. Her hand slid into his. The strong, tactile fingers that had made her body sing closed around hers. All too aware of the sensations they once again generated, she eased out of the booth and withdrew her hand to reach for her purse. She led the way to the front of the restaurant and was mentally computing her half of the check when he waved to the owner.

"*Au revoir,* Cecile."

She saluted with a spatula from the open kitchen. "*Au revoir.*"

"We didn't get a check," Julie protested as Alex shouldered open the door to the street.

"Cecile keeps my credit card on file."

"She doesn't have mine." Julie halted just outside the door. The still muggy summer night flowed around them as she tackled the issue head on. "I thought I made myself clear. I want to pay my own way this week."

"It was just dinner, Julie."

"Funny, it feels more like a bribe to me. Some folks might even say this whole week smacks of blackmail."

He shrugged, completely indifferent to the accusation. "I consider it a precondition to a legitimate business proposition."

"So you're going to charge all my expenses to the company's ledger?"

"No, of course not. But…"

"No buts, Dalton. I've been pretty much on my own since I was seventeen. I pay, or I don't play."

Alex started to object when he remembered that the copper-haired pilot he'd hooked up with had roused before dawn and dropped a kiss on her half-asleep bed partner, murmuring that she had an early take-off. When he'd rolled out of bed and departed several hours later, the motel bill was already taken care of.

"Okay," he conceded. "I'll keep a record of all expenses incurred. We can settle up at the end of your stay."

Or not. He had no intention of presenting her with a bill. He'd dug through Agro-Air's balance sheets. He doubted she or either of her partners could handle a solid week of special reserve reds or dinners at places like Cecile's. Besides, by the end of her stay he would know for certain whether Julie was Molly's birth mother. If so, the expenses she racked up this week would drop below the noise level amid the much heavier negotiations to follow.

The idea that Julie Barlett would give up her child was looking less likely by the moment, however. The woman was fiercely independent. When you factor stubborn as hell into the equation, Alex couldn't see her walking away from anything, much less her own baby.

If not for those as-yet-unexplained gaps during her months in South America and her flat-out refusal to provide a DNA sample, he might have called a halt to this enforced visitation right then and there. Then he caught the sway of her hips as she pushed through the entrance to the Dalton building.

He'd give it another day or two, Alex decided, his eyes on her trim rear and slender hips. See if his PI could fill in the gaps. Peel another layer or two off Julie's prickly exterior.

When the elevator glided to a stop, that's all he intended to do. Just dig a little deeper. Get to know the woman inside the nicely packaged female. Was it his fault her use of the phrase "when I play" kept looping though his mind, repeating over and over like a damaged CD?

"Play" didn't begin to describe their interaction a year ago. There'd been some giggles on her part. He remembered that. Some laughter on his. Then everything had heated up. Time and the press of business had diluted the X-rated edges, but enough remained for Alex to use the pretext of outlining tomorrow's schedule to invite himself in for a nightcap.

"We've got a schedule?" Julie echoed, tossing her purse and key card on the glass-topped coffee table that ate up most of the sitting room.

"My mother quit the business five years ago but she has a hard time letting go of the reins." He felt the usual rush of affection too often strained to the limit. "She's got us down for brunch, ten o'clock. After that, I thought I would give you a tour of our local operations."

While Julie mulled that over, he crossed to the mahogany wall unit containing an entertainment center on one side and a fully stocked wet bar on the other.

"What's your pleasure?" Doors opened to display shelves lined with expensive brands. "We have all the regular labels, liqueurs, wine. Oh, and the speciality of the house."

"Which is?"

"A blend my father had bottled for him in Scotland. He named it Jake's Folly."

"Okay, I'll bite. Why folly?"

"He would never tell us. Neither will our mother, but she refuses to touch the stuff."

When Julie moved in for a closer look at the black label with a gold-embossed oil rig gushing crude, Alex breathed in her scent. Soap and shampoo and brandy from the crepes Suzette. Did she have any idea of how seductive it was? Or how the shimmering beads decorating the neckline of her blouse enhanced the color of her unusual eyes? One was the deep, dark green of a forest glen just before dusk. The other was that same glen, but with a touch of autumn in its gold and brown flecks. With their fringe of thick black lashes, they drew Alex in—and raised a new round of questions in his mind.

Molly's eyes were a grayish blue, but that could change. Most babies' eye color wasn't set until they were nine or ten months old, or so Delilah had informed her sons. Would Molly's eyes deepen to dark cobalt like his? Or shade toward green like Julie's?

For a moment Alex regretted his promise not to take a DNA sample without her permission. The sample may not hold up in court if it came to a custody suit but at least he would know.

He killed the thought almost as soon as it surfaced. He'd given his word. He'd stand by it. But he *hadn't* promised to back away completely.

"Your hair's longer than I remembered from Nuevo

Laredo," he commented, letting his gaze roam the shining cap.

She looked a little wary at the mention of their night together but shrugged. "I didn't have much time to fuss with it during the past year, so I let it grow long enough to pull back out of the way."

Casually, he curled a coppery strand around his finger and feathered the ends with his thumb. "I like it."

That wasn't all he liked. Using the dark red strand as a tether, Alex moved closer. "I remember a few other details from that night."

"So do I." Warning signs went up in her face. "Enough to let you know right up front there isn't going to be a repeat performance."

She didn't pull back, however, or tug her hair free. Alex noted both with a quick leap of satisfaction.

"No repeat performance, huh?" He pretended to ponder that. "I'm pretty sure I used most of my good moves that night. Given enough time and the proper incentive, though, I might be able to come up with something original."

Julie couldn't help herself. He looked so solemn, as though he was giving the matter some really heavy consideration. She let a grin slip past her common sense.

"Speaking from personal experience, I can verify that your moves were *very* good. And I suspect you wouldn't need much in the way of incentive to come up with some new ones."

"You're right. In fact, all it might take is this."

He tugged gently on her hair, urging her closer while giving her plenty of advance notice of his intentions.

Julie had more than enough time to deliver a swift kick to her conscience. She could put up a front with Dalton, but she couldn't lie to herself. She'd driven into the city with a very mixed bag of motives. It wasn't just about the business deal this man had offered. Or Dusty's sworn promise to refrain from feeding the slots if she complied with Dalton's outrageous precondition. Or even the innate sense of fairness that acknowledged this man had a legitimate need to know his child's heritage. The sad truth was that Alex Dalton irritated and aroused her in equal measures.

All right, all right! If she added up the minutes they'd spent in each other's company, honesty would force her to admit he aroused her a whole bunch more than he'd irritated her. That still didn't excuse her idiocy in tipping her head back for his kiss.

And idiocy it was. The shock that jolted through her gave ample proof of that. Not to mention the shiver that raced down her spine when he curved his free arm around her waist.

"The hair's different," he murmured, drawing her against him, "but you taste every bit as good as I remember."

His mouth brushed hers again. Lightly. Deliberately.

"Forget good," he said a moment later, his voice husky. "You taste great."

He punctuated that with another kiss.

He held her splayed against his long, hard frame. Every pressure point in her body was alive and kicking. Her breasts. Her hips. Her belly, where it pressed against the stiffening bulge just below his belt buckle.

Oh, God! It was just like last time. They'd barely slammed the door of that sleazy motel room before they started ripping at each other's clothes. She had the same urge now, could barely keep her hands from sliding up his ribs and down his muscled flanks.

And look what that raw hunger had produced, the last sane corner of her mind shouted. Two people caught up in a tangle of if's and maybe's. The thought acted like a fire hose on her raging hormones. It was time to end this charade, she decided grimly. Past time. Not even the shimmering vision of a brand spanking new Lane 602 could make her continue it.

"Alex, listen to me. I wasn't pregnant when I left for South

America. I didn't give birth in a Chilean hospital or some remote mountaintop clinic. I'm not the mother of your child."

She pushed away and put some breathing room between them while her fingers fumbled in her hair. She found a random couple of strands, yanked. Her breath still ragged, she looped them around the top button of his shirt.

"Here. Take these. Run whatever tests you want to."

Five

The abrupt command knifed through Alex's intense absorption with her scent and her feel. Mentally grinding his teeth, he forced himself to shift from lust to think mode.

Why the hell had she plucked those strands now? She could have waited the entire week to ensure he honored the deal he'd struck with her and her partners. Could have continued to feed his increasing doubts, let him struggle with the question of why a woman with her strong will and fierce work ethic would abandon a child. Instead, she'd laid her cards on the table. Or more precisely, wrapped them around his shirt button.

Slowly, the ice-minded executive preempted the hot-blooded male. Alex wanted this woman with an ache that wouldn't quit but he needed to understand her motives.

"Okay," he said slowly.

"Okay?" She blinked up at him. "Okay what?"

"Okay, I'll do whatever needs to be done."

She looked surprised and more than a little deflated by

his controlled response. "I thought you'd be pleased. Isn't that what you wanted? Proof positive of your baby's parentage? Or in this instance, proof that I *didn't* provide half of her DNA mix?"

Yeah, that's what he wanted. Most definitely. The uncertainty had been hanging over him and his brother for weeks now. Blake handled it with his usual deliberate approach to any and all problems. Alex was more impatient.

Yet instead of providing a definitive answer, Julie had just reopened the debate. If she wasn't Molly's mother, who was? The unresolved issue frustrated Alex almost as much as the hunger this woman stirred. It was still there, gnawing at him, as he fumbled for a solution that would keep her within reach.

"I'll send the sample in tomorrow. It'll take some time to get results, though."

"How much time?"

He decided not to mention the mountainous backlog of tests handled by various labs around the country. Or the court case Blake had cited, nullifying seemingly irrefutable results certified by overworked and overstressed lab supervisors.

"At least as long as you'd planned to stay in Oklahoma City," he said instead.

She took that with a philosophical shrug. "I guess the time frame doesn't really matter. You know the truth now. You can call off your private investigator. Or sic him on another candidate."

"There aren't any others."

"Oh, that's right," she recalled with a crooked smile. "I was the last one on your list."

Funny how that had worked. She might have been last on his list of possible mothers but since they'd renewed their admittedly brief acquaintance, she'd jumped to the top of another. One that had him sliding a hand through the warm silk of her hair.

"Now where were we? Oh, right." He dipped his head. "Just about...here."

He captured her mouth in an assault so swift and sensual that Julie never got a chance to vent her admittedly feeble objections. His lips moved over hers, demanding a response. She resisted for all of three or four seconds.

Sliding her arms around his neck, she angled her head. Alex took that as a green light to hook her waist and tug her against him again. One hand stayed buried in her hair. The other molded her hip, then slipped under her tunic hem. Her rioting senses registered its warmth, its strength, its tantalizingly slow glide to the small of her back.

She found herself riding a tidal wave of relief that she'd ended the DNA farce. Jumbled in with that were memories of their gloriously erotic previous encounter. But those were fast getting edged out by newer, even wilder sensations. She could feel his imprint on every inch of her body. Feel the heat of his hands, his mouth, his thighs. Hunger raged through her like an out-of-control bush fire.

An *almost* out-of-control bush fire.

Just enough sanity remained for Julie to tear her mouth from his. Panting, she willed air back into her lungs. It was a few moments, though, before she could trust her voice. Even then it came out low and husky and more tentative than she intended.

"This, uh, isn't a good idea."

The fire in his blue eyes scorched her. Julie couldn't decide whether she was more relieved or disappointed when he slowly, inexorably, tamped it down to a slow burning ember.

"Probably not," he agreed after a pause that had stretched her nerves to their max.

Ignoring her body's instant wail of protest, she put some space between them once again. "I'll leave tomorrow. No sense complicating an already messy situation."

"You can't leave."

Her brow creased. "Why not?"

Alex could think of a dozen reasons, not least of which was his now rock-hard resolve to finish what they'd started here.

"You haven't met Molly. Or my mother," he added to forestall the protest he saw forming in her eyes.

"What's the point?"

"The point," he said with more composure than he was feeling with his insides still tied in knots, "is that Delilah Dalton is a major shareholder in the corporation Agro-Air will become part of. You need to know who you're dealing with."

An arrested expression entered her unusual eyes. "You intend to honor the business end of our deal? Even though I've given you proof I'm not Molly's mother?"

Alex stiffened. "Did you think I wouldn't?"

"I don't know what to think." Scowling, she shoved a hand through her hair. "You... The baby... This whole crazy situation has got me caught in a vicious crosswind."

The admission eased his irritation over her assumption he would renege on their agreement. It also gave him the fierce satisfaction of knowing she was thrown for as much of a loop as he was by the way their past had unexpectedly collided with the present.

Deciding he'd better call it a night before he gave in to the urge to pull her back into his arms, Alex beat a reluctant retreat.

"Thanks for coming to Oklahoma City, Julie." He flicked the curling auburn strands wrapped around his shirt button. "And for these, although the fact that you volunteered them pretty much makes them unnecessary."

"Yeah, well..."

Uncertainty still clouded her eyes and pursed her lips. Before he could stop himself, Alex dropped a quick kiss on that pouty mouth.

"I'll see you in the morning. Mother's expecting us for brunch. Ten o'clock. We'll need to leave here about nine-thirty."

Julie was more used to getting up at dawn than lazing around until mid-morning. As a consequence, she woke the next morning at her usual time and futzed around the lavish apartment, making coffee and munching on one of the bagels included in the guest basket on the marble kitchen counter.

With another couple of hours to kill, she tugged on a tank top and a pair of khaki shorts and power-walked the still deserted city blocks. The morning rush was just starting to fill the streets when she took the elevator back up to the penthouse suite. A hot, stinging shower sluiced away the sweat. A frothy shampoo with the exotic mango scent provided by Dalton International for its guests left her hair soft and glossy.

Wrapped in a fluffy bath sheet, she slid open the louvered closet doors and surveyed her meager wardrobe. She'd found herself in some tense situations over the years. The terrifying time she'd flown through a storm into the remote Andean village and almost got swept down the mountain in an ensuing mudslide certainly topped the list. Going head to head with Delilah Dalton was fast taking on the same ominous overtones. So what the heck should she wear to beard a tigress in her den?

Not that Julie had all that many choices. It was either jeans or her trusty black slacks. She went with the slacks, pairing them this time with a sleeveless blouse in rusty rose and a black leather belt accented with hammered Peruvian silver. Dangly silver earrings added a finishing touch and gave her the armor she needed to confront the redoubtable Delilah Dalton. She hoped.

When she answered the bell, Alex approved of her choice. Although… She couldn't help noting that the admiring gleam in his eyes lacked last night's intensity. So did his friendly greeting.

"Good morning."

"Morning," she replied, trying not to feel as though he'd doused her with a bucket of dirty dishwater.

Okay. All right. So a night's reflection had convinced him to put the skids on the hunger that had almost gotten out of control again? So he was already regretting his suggestion she remain in the city for the entire week? One of them had to exercise some common sense. Or so she was telling herself when he offered an apology.

"Alex will be a few minutes. He got stuck on a phone call from Madrid."

"Oh." Belatedly, she noticed the absence of the small scar. A totally ridiculous relief bubbled through her. "Not a problem. I'm in no hurry. How are you this morning, Blake?"

"Good so far," he replied with a crooked grin. "We'll see how long that lasts after brunch with mother."

"Oh, sure! Make me more nervous than I already am."

"Alex warned you about Delilah, did he?"

"Not in so many words. But one of my partners knows her, or knew her way back when your folks first started in the business."

"From what Mom's told us, those were pretty wild days. 'Course, I'm sure the stories she related were highly edited versions."

He was really nice, Julie decided as she responded to his smile. Calm, comfortable, and easy to talk to despite those show-stopping good looks.

Unlike his brother, she gulped when the door opened at the other end of the hall. Just the sight of Alex Dalton's electric blue eyes and strong, square chin made her pulse stutter.

She pondered her reaction to the two men during the short drive through the bright Oklahoma morning. She was darned if she could understand why charming, handsome Blake stirred only mild feminine interest while his twin brought out her wild side. Bad enough that the uncharacteristic side of her had conquered common sense and a lifetime of caution last year. She'd come within a breath of letting it do the same thing last night. Even worse, she silently, contrarily, idiotically regretted that she hadn't!

She'd fallen asleep with the taste of Alex Dalton on her mouth and the undeniable realization he was the real reason for her jaunt to Oklahoma City. Not the lucrative business deal he'd offered. Not Dusty's solemn promise to behave. Just sitting here in the Jag's butter-soft leather seat, with his thigh so close to hers and his tanned hand resting on the gearshift mere inches away, raised little pinpricks of awareness.

She was still feeling their prickle when they pulled into the curved drive leading to a Italian renaissance masterpiece. Her eyes widening, Julie took in a three-tiered fountain a good twenty feet high, a profusion of marble columns and a facade decorated with elaborate cornices.

Alex pulled up at a shallow flight of steps leading to the monster front door. Blake was out of the backseat and holding out a hand to assist Julie before she got her seat belt undone. The Dalton boys were nothing if not courteous.

"Welcome to Casa Delilah," Blake said with a rueful smile.

She gave the sumptuous facade another sweep. "Not Casa Dalton?"

"Alex and I had struck out on our own before our mother went, uh, formal."

"Thank God," Alex muttered as he keyed in a code on a discreetly disguised keypad.

The code must have triggered a silent signal because they'd barely stepped into a soaring, two-story foyer before an honest-to-God butler materialized. Complete with frock coat and white gloves, no less! He crossed the black-and-white tiles in a stately tread and bent an approving nod on the Dalton brothers.

"You're right on time. Madam will be pleased."

"Wouldn't do to keep her majesty waiting."

Alex's drawled reply upped Julie's pucker factor by several degrees. The unabashedly curious glance the butler sent her way only added to it. Alex supplied the introductions.

"Louis, this is Julie Bartlett. Julie, meet Louis. He was major domo to Prince Albert of Monaco until my mother's last jaunt to Europe."

Hmm. How do you acknowledge an intro to a butler? Nod? Shake hands? Julie took her cue from Louis, who smiled and said politely, "A pleasure to meet you, Miss Bartlett."

"Same here."

"Madam is in the green salon," he informed them. "She's expecting you, so I won't announce your..."

"I'm right here."

The voice boomed through the cavernous foyer. The woman it belonged to was tall and slender and showed nothing of the hardscrabble roots she'd come from. At first. Once Julie got past the piles of gloriously upswept black hair and five or six carats of sapphires in the woman's ears, she got a glimpse of the hard-packed Oklahoma clay beneath Delilah Dalton's glittering surface.

"So you're the woman my son hooked up with in Mexico last year," the matriarch said, cutting straight to the chase.

Since there wasn't a whole lot to say in response, Julie merely nodded.

"Are you Molly's mother, Ms. Bartlett?"

The blunt question provoked instant and irate responses from her sons.

"Oh, for God's sake!"

"Back off, Del!"

"That's okay." Julie's reply was cool and level. "I understand your concern, Mrs. Dalton. I've provided Alex with the answer to that question."

The woman's glance whipped to her son. "Well?"

"Julie says she's not Molly's mother," he replied.

"And you believe her?"

"Yes."

His mother hissed, clearly dissatisfied with that simple response, and Julie waited for Alex to explain that she'd supplied evidence last night to confirm matters. He surprised her by withholding that bit of information.

"Now how about you retract your fangs?" he said instead. "The issue of Molly's parentage aside, Julie's our guest and future business partner. And I believe you invited us for brunch."

Louis faded discreetly away while Delilah matched Alex stare for stare. Her earrings caught a stray sunbeam filtering through the fanlight above the door. The sapphires' brilliant hue was the exact color of her sons' eyes, Julie realized, almost as dazzled by the square-cut studs as she was confused by Alex's reticence concerning the DNA sample she'd provided.

Evidently there was more going on between mother and sons than she was privy to. Somehow she'd managed to land squarely in the middle of whatever it was. She didn't care for the sensation of being caught between these two powerful personalities. Three, if you counted Blake. He might be more restrained than his twin but Julie suspected all three Daltons would close ranks immediately if they perceived a threat from outside their circle.

She was seriously considering departing the scene and leaving them to sort out their own mess when Delilah led the way to a sitting room decorated to resemble a soft, misty garden. The green salon, obviously. A silver coffee service occupied place of honor on a coffee table set with inlaid marble. With an obvious attempt at graciousness, Delilah gestured to the tray.

"Brunch will be ready shortly. Would you care for coffee while we wait, Miss Bartlett?"

"Yes, thank you. Just black."

She started to tack on a suggestion that they dispense with formalities and use first names but before she could frame the words, footsteps sounded in the hall. A moment later all eyes turned to the young woman who appeared at the door with a baby in her arms.

"Ahh," Delilah crooned, the stark planes and angles of her face softening. "Here's Grace with our little angel."

Grace being the nanny, Julie guessed. Or *au pair,* they called them these days. She looked to be in her midtwenties, maybe, with silvery blond hair and liquid brown eyes that smiled shyly at Alex and Blake.

Julie registered the details only briefly before her gaze dropped to the squirming infant in the nanny's arms. As an only child, Julie had no nieces or nephews to compare the baby to. Nor had she spent much time around other folks' kids. Yet even she could see this particular infant was a heartbreaker in training. Especially when the baby lifted a head topped with pale peach fuzz, gurgled happily and treated everyone present to a toothless grin. Julie was instantly and completely charmed.

"Isn't she beautiful?" Delilah asked with an unmistakable challenge.

She'd get no argument there.

"She certainly is."

The matriarch's glance sharpened but before she could follow that thrust with another, both of her sons moved toward the baby. Alex got there first. The hands that had sent ripples of delight down Julie's spine last night were incredibly careful as he transferred the infant to his arms.

"Hello, Mol." He brushed a knuckle over the baby's cheek. "How are you this morning, sweetheart?"

The weirdest sensation inched over Julie as Molly wrapped her tiny fingers around his thumb. For a moment— just a moment—she let herself imagine that this *was* her child and Alex's...

Whoa! No point in weaving fantasies of a nonexistent

family, or wishing she had one to come home to. So she'd lost her parents while she was still in high school? Only she knew that was the reason she'd spent so much time out of the country over the years, grabbing every crappy job that came her way. It still hurt too much to go back to the small Oklahoma town that had bred her. It was also why she'd yielded to Dusty's suggestion she throw in with him and Charlie. They were the closest thing to a family she had left.

She brought herself up short when she looked up to find Alex's mother watching her with the intensity of a hawk. Gauging her reaction to the baby, obviously. Looking for a sign, some flicker of the anguish or guilt a mother might exhibit at the sight of the child she'd abandoned.

Frowning, Delilah started to say something. She was interrupted by an audible burp from Molly. The baby followed that with a stream of regurgitated yuk that landed mostly on Alex's shirtfront. Julie's opinion of the Dalton matriarch inched up a reluctant notch when Delilah laughed and preempted the nanny.

"I'll take her. You go clean up, Alex." Still chuckling, Delilah dabbed at the baby's chin with a corner of her blanket. "Big Jake—my husband—used to say all babies did was eat, sleep and emit noxious substances from both ends."

Julie's grudging admiration for this display of grandmotherly devotion didn't last long. Only until Alex returned with a wet splotch on his shirt and the butler following on his heels.

"Brunch is served, Madam."

"All right."

"Here," the nanny said, holding out her arms for the now sleepy infant. "I'll take her upstairs."

Delilah dropped a kiss on the baby's head before relinquishing her, then led the way into a dining table decked in creamy linen, fresh flowers and Baccarat crystal. As soon as they were all seated, she resumed her attack with no holds barred.

"I understand your mother died of ovarian cancer," she said to Julie as she handed the son seated to her left a platter of delicately fluted quiches.

"Back off," Alex warned while Julie's hands fisted in her lap.

"I don't see any reason to beat around the bush," Delilah returned in response to his growled warning. "Julie may claim she's not Molly's mother but until we know for sure I see no reason to…."

"Back off, I said."

The sapphires flashed blue fire as Delilah faced down her son. Or tried to. You could almost hear the thunderbolts booming through the air as two iron wills clashed.

"You'll have to excuse us," Blake said in a quiet, steady voice that suggested he'd spent a good part of his life defusing situations like this one. "Molly's unexpected arrival has thrown us all off stride."

Julie's shrug fell into the "if you say so" category. Why hadn't Alex made it clear she played no role in this Dalton family drama? Why didn't *she?* Feeling more uncomfortable by the moment, she worked her way through a generous wedge of mushroom and goat cheese quiche, baby asparagus drizzled with hollandaise sauce and a fresh fruit compote.

Thankfully, Alex insisted on departing right after brunch. His mother protested but he stood firm in his intent to provide Julie some insight into Dalton International's operations. Delilah yielded, although the look she gave her son suggested she wasn't done with him—or Julie—yet.

Blake opted to stay and discuss some legal issue with his parent. Molly, they discovered during a quick trip to the nursery, had fallen asleep. She lay on her stomach with her bottom poking up. When Alex stroked the baby's back with a gentle hand, Julie got that funny ache again but couldn't hold back a sigh of relief after the mansion's massive front door closed behind them.

"Well," she murmured, sinking into the Jag's passenger seat, "that was interesting."

Alex grimaced and slid behind the wheel. "That's one way to describe my mother."

She angled to face him. "All right, Dalton, clue me in. Why didn't you tell Madam that I provided proof Molly isn't my baby? Why leave things hanging?"

"I didn't intend to," he admitted with a rueful grin. "Then it hit me. She's far more likely to keep her claws sheathed if she thinks there's a chance, however slim, that you are, in fact, Molly's mother. And that, Ms. Bartlett, gives us the rest of the week to pursue our own agendas."

An agenda that included an inside look at the mega-corporation that might fold Agro-Air into many layers of operations. Julie was still trying to convince herself that was her main reason for staying the rest of the week when Alex put the car in gear and swept down the curved drive.

Six

Dalton International's scope of operations left Julie swinging between awe, excitement and doubt. The corporation was so humongous and so diversified she worried that a small-time outfit like Agro-Air would get lost in the shuffle.

Still, she couldn't help but be impressed by Alex's detailed knowledge of every facet of DI's operations. Even more by his hands-on management style. She saw that up close and personal when the chiefs of DI's major divisions convened at a high-tech nerve center and gave her an overview of their areas of responsibility. Manufacturing, subsidiary operations, marketing, sales, distribution…each director presented their latest stats and initiatives. She noted with interest how frequently they turned to Alex for confirmation, validation or encouragement.

But it wasn't until he drove Julie out to DI's sprawling manufacturing plant on the outskirts of the city that she understood how close he was to the grass-roots of the business his parents had launched almost forty years ago.

The plant foreman met them at the entrance to the facility. He was dressed in sharply pressed coveralls and stood at least six-five. "I'm Hector Alvarez, Ms. Bartlett. Glad to hear you and Agro-Air may be joining the DI family."

"Thanks, and please, call me Julie."

"I understand you just had a bucketful of marketing and sales stats thrown at you. Now I'll show you what generates a good portion of them. Here, you need to put these on."

She took a set of ear protectors and one of the yellow hard hats he carried with him. He gave similar gear to Alex. Then the three of them entered what looked like a mile-long building and stood for a moment on a platform overlooking a vast assembly floor.

The noise hit like a sledgehammer. Even with ear protectors, it seemed to come at her from all directions. Computer-aided precision saws screeched through metal, fitters riveted joints, welders in protective suits sent sparks hissing into the air. Her nostrils twitched with the sting of acetylene and the distinctive tang of acid etching steel.

Gesturing, Alvarez nudged her toward an enclosed balcony overhanging the assembly floor. Inside the noise level dropped from a roar to a rumble. Following the example of Alex and the foreman, Julie removed her ear protectors and looked around with wide-eyed interest. Although the rows of cubicles were populated by individuals in jeans and tank tops or work shirts with sleeves rolled up, the equipment they worked on was clearly the best money could buy. Just the 26-inch high definition monitors on the workstations were enough to make Julie drool. The computers feeding them were all state-of-the-art.

"I'm going to walk you through our design, test, production scheduling and quality control units," Hector advised. "Then we'll go down on the floor and follow a product from initial cut to final assembly. Sound okay to you?"

Julie nodded, although Hector glanced from her to Alex for the real go-ahead. He gave it, and they began the tour.

Despite the carefully scripted agenda, they almost didn't make it past the first stop. To Julie's surprise and delight, Alex had already detailed a team of two engineers to look at Agro-Air's aerial spray system. One of the engineers was a lean, ropy Oklahoma native. The other, a recent UCLA grad with a double major in mechanical and polymer engineering, introduced herself as Lisa Wu and was clearly thrilled to have the lead on this, her first project for Dalton International.

"Alex said to take your spray system apart piece by piece and look for possible design improvements that might increase spread ratios. Dean and I are just getting started, but I think you might be interested in what we've done so far regarding nozzles."

A click of a mouse filled the monitor on her work station with a dazzling color array.

"Since the system has to deliver a variety of products from pest control to fertilizers, we looked at several variations. These…" she said, aiming the pointer at the top row of gleaming, stainless steel nozzles, "…incorporate the latest USDA Agricultural Research Service's spray drift reduction technology. The ARS used their High Speed Wind Tunnel Facility to measure droplet size at different airspeeds, spray pressures and orientation with a Sympatec Helos laser diffraction instrument."

"Hey, I read about that test!" Julie leaned in closer to squint at the display. "Didn't the ARS verify that some of the tested nozzles can reduce drift by seventy to eighty percent?"

"They did." Lisa beamed her approval. "And we think we can adapt one of those nozzles to the system you're currently using with only minor modifications."

"No kidding?"

"No kidding! Here, take a look at our initial drawings." She dragged up another desk chair. When Julie dropped into it eagerly, Alex and Hector Alvarez exchanged wry glances. The project's second engineer merely grinned.

Julie was bubbling with enthusiasm when she and Alex exited the facility three hours later.

"That was amazing!" She raked her fingers through hair pancaked by heat and the hard hat. "And this is just one of your production facilities."

"It's the largest, although our operation in Mexico runs a close second."

Yet he'd known the names, family situations and skill sets of a good portion of the several hundred employees working here. Julie was impressed. More than impressed. Alex Dalton was as technologically savvy as he was gorgeous. A fatal combination, she admitted as she settled gingerly on the hot leather of the Jag's passenger seat. She wouldn't be the first woman to succumb to his mix of sex and smarts. She'd seen the evidence of that in all those photos of elegantly gowned females gazing adoringly up at him.

Suppressing a grimace, she glanced down at her trusty black slacks and now wrinkled blouse. Elegant she wasn't. But for the rest of this week, at least, she had Alex's full attention. Along with Molly. And his mother.

She hid another grimace. Delilah had insisted they come for dinner tomorrow night. A family cookout, she'd promised. Very informal. Julie looked forward to it with as much enthusiasm as a spinal tap.

At least she had a whole twenty-four hours to psych herself up for the next clash with the redoubtable DD. And she had this evening. With just Alex. The thrill that raced through her at the thought should have warned her. Should have set off those internal alarms again. It didn't, however, and later she could only blame what happened on the high she was riding from her visit to DI's production facility... and the call Alex took on the way home.

His cell phone pinged just as they passed the I-40 exit for

Garth Brook's hometown of Yukon. He palmed the phone, glanced at the caller ID and sent her an apologetic smile.

"Sorry. I need to take this."

It was probably one of his plant managers with some critical production issue, she guessed, or DI's contracts division in the final, crisis throes of a multi-million dollar bid. Judging by Alex's end of the conversation, however, the call concerned a new construction project.

"No, we want to keep it to a single level." He listened a moment, frowning, then shook his head. "Sorry, Dave, I'm having a hard time visualizing it. Hang on."

He aimed another smile Julie's way. "Do you mind if we take a short detour? My architect's on site and wants to show me a possible modification to the building plans."

"No problem."

He went back on the phone with a promise to be there in twenty. When he'd disconnected, curiosity got the better of her.

"What are you building?"

"A house. Or more hopefully, a home. I don't want to raise Molly in a downtown high-rise. Providing, of course, she's actually my daughter. If not, Blake will take it from here."

Julie blinked, wondering why the heck his future plans came as such a surprise. Maybe because she'd been so focused on the here and now. So caught up in the question of Molly's birth that she never thought beyond it. She'd just sort of assumed Delilah would continue her role as Molly's guardian and/or nurturer. The realization that Alex fully intended to take over child-rearing responsibilities shifted her mental composite of this busy executive. She was still trying to adjust to the altered Alex when they pulled up to a gated community on the north side of town. The brass sign beside the gate welcomed them to Cottonwood Creek.

Alex clicked the gates open and drove into an obviously well-planned development. The homes were mostly native stone and brick...and nowhere near as huge as Delilah's

Nichols Hills mansion. Scattered skateboards and basketball goals suggested this was a family-oriented enclave, with
wide sidewalks for kids to skate or bike on safely. That impression was confirmed when they passed a clubhouse with
tennis courts, a full basketball court and a sparkling swimming pool filled with laughing, splashing kids.

Julie had loved growing up on a farm. Her parents had
worked hard. Had worked *her* hard from the time she was
old enough to pull part of the load. She'd never minded being
an only child because she kept so busy and had so many
friends at school. But this... Her gaze roamed the houses set
on either side of wide, tree-shaded streets. This would be an
ideal place to raise children. It was protected, but not iso-
lated. Close to schools, churches, malls. Populated by families with young, growing broods.

Julie's glance slid to the man beside her. Damned if he
hadn't messed up her mental composite of him yet again.
Alex Dalton could have afforded any home in any part of
town. Bought an estate to rival his mother's. Built on an exclusive, members-only golf course. Instead, he'd chosen to
make a home for his daughter here, where she'd have plenty
of friends to play with. If she *was* his daughter. It wasn't
looking likely at this point. Alex had indicated Julie was the
last possible on his list. The uncertainty had to be eating at
both him and Blake.

She shifted her gaze back to the wide, tree-lined street.
She could make a home for a child here, she thought on an
unexpected stab of envy. The little jab surprised her as much
as the thought. Her biological clock hadn't started to annoy
her yet. She'd been too busy, too caught up in her flying. But
seeing this... Thinking of Alex living here with Molly...

"Here we are."

He pulled into a cul-de-sac containing one of the few
empty lots left in the development. A pickup was parked at
the curb with two men conferring over a set of plans rolled

out across the hood. They looked up and greeted Alex with obvious relief.

"Thanks for swinging by."

"Not a problem," he responded. "Julie, meet Bob Dyer, my builder, and Dave Hanscom, the architect who's trying to design and site a one-level house on a lot that drops some fifteen degrees."

"That's the problem in a nutshell," the architect concurred with a wry grin. "We planned to sink steel beams to reinforce the slope we'll have to build up. Now I'm thinking we might want to use that space for a safe room instead of positioning it here, in the center of the house where I'd originally put it."

"Safe" meaning a reinforced concrete storm shelter, Julie knew. Born and bred here in the heart of Tornado Alley, she wouldn't build a house for herself without a safe room or storm cellar.

While the men conferred, she wandered down toward the creek lined with the trees that gave the development its name. Silvery green and pretty with their dark, twisted trunks, cottonwoods could be pesky as hell when they produced their fluffy white seeds that floated through the air like snowballs and clogged air-conditioning filters. They liked water, though, which is why they grew so thick along creek banks. And why so many of the pioneers crossing the Great Plains on the Santa Fe or Oregon Trails had desperately scanned the horizon for these signposts to water and firewood and shade. This particular creek was hardly more than a trickle now, but Alex would have to watch Molly to make sure she didn't tumble in once she started walking.

"I thought about that," he acknowledged when she mentioned it to him. "I started to build on a dry lot, but I figure that if Molly's anything like me, she'll find ways to get in trouble no matter where we live."

"You did that a lot, huh?"

"Like you wouldn't believe."

"Blake, too?"

"He was the good twin," Alex replied cheerfully. "Still is, for that matter. Although Saint Blake can surprise even me occasionally. Next time he downs a few drinks and loosens up a little, ask him about Singapore."

The pure devil in his blue eyes made her laugh. "I will."

It wasn't until they were on the way back to his car that reality hit. She wouldn't be around long enough to wait for Blake to loosen up. Singapore would most likely remain an untold tale. That fact took some of the shine from what had otherwise been a terrific afternoon.

It also, Julie realized later, contributed to the idiocy that followed.

She knew as soon as Alex asked where she'd like to go for dinner that she was treading dangerous ground. Her impressions of this man had undergone so many rapid-fire changes she hadn't had time to sort through them. The hunger was still there, though, compounding exponentially with every smile, every casual touch.

She'd wanted him before.

She ached for him now.

"It's been a busy day," she said, taking the coward's way out. "All I'm up for tonight is a long, cool shower and a chance to review the notes Lisa Wu gave me."

"You haven't eaten since brunch," he countered. "Aren't you hungry?"

She wasn't about to touch that one. "The DI guest quarters come well stocked. I saw some microwave popcorn in the cupboard. It's my second favorite food group."

"After?"

"First place is a tie between pizza and Tex-Mex."

"So you're a carb addict."

"By choice as much as by necessity," she admitted without the least remorse. "Not many of the places I flew in and out of these past few years dished up Dover sole or carrots au gratin."

"That covers food preferences. What about music?"

"My top three are all female jazz greats. Allison, Etta and Ella. You?"

"Garth, Toby and Bartok."

"Bartok?" She screwed up her nose. "The classical composer who did all that atonal stuff?"

"He's an acquired taste. Favorite authors?"

Funny, she thought as she fired back with Patterson, Roberts and Grisham. Most couples shared these tidbits of knowledge over several days or weeks of casual give-and-take. Usually *before* they tore off each other's clothes and acquired an even more intimate knowledge.

Her glance dropped like an anchor. The birthmark she now remembered with blazing clarity had almost been hidden by Alex's thatch of dark gold pubic hair. Julie had discovered it by accident when she'd slithered down his sweaty body and...

"Your turn."

She brought her head up with a snap. "Huh?"

"Movies. Top three."

"Aviator, Top Gun, Independence Day."

"Why am I not surprised, Flygirl?"

"Okay, smartass. Name yours."

The back-and-forth on top threes carried them off the interstate, through the city streets, and up to the penthouse. Alex leaned a forearm against the jamb and waited while she keyed the guest suite door.

"Sure you don't want to go out to eat?"

Hell no, she wasn't sure. Not when he leaned so close she could pick up the faint tang of shirt starch and healthy male sweat.

"I'm sure."

He searched her face. Whatever he saw there had him backing off. Dust and grime and the cottonwood fluff in her hair, most likely.

"I have a conference call with our Czech office that will

eat up most of tomorrow morning. How about I get Blake to go over some of the legalities of our merger with you then? I'll meet you afterward for lunch."

"That'll work."

"Okay."

He tipped her face to his and covered her mouth. Easily. Naturally. No pressure at all, other than the fireball that exploded in Julie's belly. Then, damn him, he gave her the early night she'd asked for.

"Later, Bartlett."

She delivered a series of mental kicks in the butt as she headed for the bathroom, shedding her clothes as she went. A long, cool, pulsing shower doused most of the fire his careless kiss had generated. An ice cold beer soaked the residue. The ashes were just about stone-cold dead when the front door buzzer sounded. Frowning, Julie secured the towel turbaned around her hair and the belt to the inch-thick terry cloth robe DI provided its guests before padding barefoot to the door.

Alex stood in the hall, his damp hair glistening dark gold, a clean shirt hanging open above jeans slung low on his hip, and a pizza box balanced high on one palm.

"It's later," he announced. "And there's no charge for delivery."

She warred with her better self for as long as it took him to stroll in and deposit the pizza on the coffee table. When he turned and let loose with one of his crooked grins, she gave up the struggle.

Slamming the door, she stalked across the room, smacked her palms against his just-shaved cheeks, dragged his head down, and locked her mouth on his.

Seven

Julie's first thought was that he tasted every bit as delicious as he had last night. Her second, that the man exhibited a take-charge attitude she might object to in other circumstances. A mere heartbeat or two after she'd covered his mouth with hers, he morphed from kissee to kisser.

She couldn't summon a single objection at the moment, however. Not one. On the contrary, the swift torque of his muscles as he crushed her against his chest sent an atavistic thrill through every inch of her. He was the elemental male. Strong, confident, eager to leap into the fray, more than ready to take what she offered.

His arm tightened around her waist. His stance widened. He used his free hand to tug the towel away from her hair and raked his fingers through the still-wet mass, anchoring her head for the controlled mayhem he wreaked on her lips. With her height and stubbornly independent nature, Julie couldn't remember ever feeling dominated. By anyone! Nor would she ever have imagined she would enjoy the sensation. But something deep and primal in her reveled in Alex's fast, hot surge of testosterone. Like every female of every species, she'd instinctively sought a mate who could match her in every way that counted.

Scratch that. *Mate* wasn't the right noun. Not as humans defined it, anyway. That term implied some kind of commitment beyond the purely sexual. And…

Oh, hell! Like she gave a hoot about semantics when Alex's tongue had worked past her teeth and his body had gone iron hard? Her senses spiraling almost out of control, Julie locked her arms around his neck. She'd barely gotten a grip before he bent and swooped her up in his arms.

"I was going to wait until after the pizza to make my move," he confessed, his voice low and rough.

"We'll make that dessert," she promised.

"But first," Alex murmured as he deposited her feet beside the bed and reached for the sash of DI's luxuriant terry cloth robe, "we'll treat ourselves to a six-course banquet."

"Six courses?" She had to grin. "Pretty sure of yourself, aren't you, Bubba?"

"Oh, yeah."

He yanked on the sash, let the robe fall open. If the hunger rampaging through Julie hadn't already puckered her nipples, the air-conditioned chill that hit them at that point would have done the trick. Then, of course, there were Alex's busy, busy hands.

He used them to tug the robe off her shoulders and down to her elbows. She was naked underneath, a fact he seemed to deeply appreciate. A growl sounded low in his throat. His eyes went laser blue.

"Now you," she said on a husky note.

She dragged off his unbuttoned shirt, tossed it aside, and splayed her hands on his lean, tanned torso. Golden chest hair tickled her palms. Warm skin and hard muscle played havoc with her senses. She let her hands glide down. Slowly, so slowly. Found the snap to his jeans. Then the zipper. Felt the size and urgency of his erection against her palm.

The feel of him generated a brief moment of sanity. She remembered the last time she'd touched him like this. Remembered how big he'd been, how rock hard and throbbing, before her eager fingers had helped his roll down the condom...one of several they'd gone through that night.

As if reading her mind, he dug into the front pocket of his jeans and produced a handful of foil packets. "I told you I was using the pizza to soften you up before I made my move. I came prepared."

"So I see."

Another all too vivid memory surfaced. Those little suckers weren't foolproof, as she'd reminded herself during those tense days after she'd discovered she was late. She'd kicked herself over and over again for trusting her future to a little scrap of latex and went back on birth control pills immediately. She was on them now, although condoms were still a good idea for that extra layer of protection from life's other unpleasantnesses.

"I also see you weren't kidding about that six-course banquet," she drawled, eyeing the half-dozen or so packets he tossed on the table beside the bed.

"A man can only hope."

Grinning, he heeled off his shoes and shucked his jeans. His shorts followed. Julie had only a moment to admire the perfect symmetry of tanned skin and taut muscle before he took her horizontal on the king-size bed. In a flash, the hunger Julie had banked during those few moments of banter came roaring back to life. Mouth and hands greedy, she gave herself up to the feast that was Alex.

Her soaring senses recorded the faint, leathery-lime scent of the aftershave he'd slapped on after his shower. Her fingers danced over slick muscle and bumpy spine. One of her knees slipped between his, and the soft prickle of his hair made the skin of her sensitive inner thighs tingle.

Every touch, every taste made her crave more. As the heat rose, she realized the hunger he stirred in her now was different from the lust he'd generated the first time they'd met. They'd barely gotten past first names then. She'd been attracted by his gorgeously packaged exterior and flat-out seduced by his smile. She'd had no grasp of the man behind the smile. Hadn't *looked* beyond his broad shoulders and handsome face.

Now...

Now he'd shown her glimpses of a complex, compelling personality. Smart, funny, authoritative. Maybe a little too authoritative at times. As when he'd all but blackmailed her into spending this week in the city. She couldn't work up much of a mad about it at the moment, though. Not with Alex nipping at the cords in her neck. And contorting to reach her breasts. And tormenting one aching nipple with his tongue and teeth.

"God, you're beautiful," he breathed against her skin. "All silky smooth and soft in just the right places."

Beautiful she wasn't. Julie knew that. But why disillusion the man by pointing out her many blemishes? Speaking of which....

She got a leg under her and rolled until she tipped Alex onto his back. Then it was her turn to nip and kiss and otherwise work her way down his long, muscled length. She found what she was looking for on the lower plane of his belly, just above his groin.

"I remembered this," she murmured, dropping a kiss on the small birthmark.

A thought occurred. She raised her head to find Alex regarding her through a screen of gold-tipped lashes.

"Just out of curiosity, does Blake have a matching birthmark?"

His mouth quirked. "Damned if I know."

"Your mother didn't put you both in the tub at the same

time when you were kids? You never compared, er, endowments as boys?"

"Sure we did. We just didn't get all that up close and personal in our comparisons. Now if you're finished with your examination..."

He reached for one of the foil packets and tore it open. When he was sheathed, Julie rolled with him again, welcoming him eagerly him into her body.

And into her heart. She had time for that one, fleeting thought as her pulse accelerated. Alex filled her. Rocked with her. Took them both to the edge and back again. She locked her calves around his and rode the wild, surging waves, her mouth and her hand as urgent as his.

She thought she was ready for the climax. Fully expected it to leave her limp. What she didn't expect was that it would arch her back and rip a ragged groan from the back of her throat that seemed to go on forever. She was still riding the crest when Alex gave a low, strangled grunt and thrust into her a final time.

The pizza was cold, the cheese congealed when they finally got around to it several hours later. They'd worked up such an appetite by then, however, that Julie would have downed hers half cold and blobby. But Alex coaxed her out of bed and into her robe. Re-bundled, she sat at the kitchen counter while he put the pizza in the oven and poured them both cold beers.

"This is good," she muttered after downing a big bite of a reheated slice. "Very good."

"We aim to please," he said around his own bite.

Julie couldn't resist. Her eyes dancing, she fed his ego. "You did. Believe me, you did."

When he treated her to a smug grin, her heart tripped.

Uh-oh! She could love this man. Already did, a little. She had no clue what she would do about it, though. Nothing right now, except scarf down pizza and beer and almost mewl with pleasure when he finished his share and started to nibble on her instead.

The rest of the night proved as pleasurable as the first part.

Boneless with pleasure and totally depleted, Julie finally fell asleep in Alex's arms. She barely stirred when he eased out of bed just after dawn the next morning. She did manage to surface for a few groggy moments when he brushed aside her tangled hair to drop a kiss on her nape.

"Call Blake when you're ready to go over those contracts. I'll leave his number by the phone."

She buried her face in the pillow. "Unnngh."

"And don't forget, we're doing dinner tonight at my mother's."

"Double unnngh."

Just moments after she heard the front door close, she was out again.

She met with Blake in his office a little past 9 a.m. He had coffee waiting, thank God, and a draft of the contracts merging Agro-Air into Dalton International's vast conglomerate. If Alex had mentioned to his brother that he and Julie had picked up last night where they'd left off a year ago, Blake gave no sign of it.

"The terms are pretty much as Alex described to you and your partners."

He sat next to her on the hunter-green leather sofa grouped with matching armchairs in one L of his office and spread the contracts on a brass-and-glass coffee table. She caught a whiff of his aftershave, a more subtle scent than Alex's leathery lime. The rest of him was more conservative, too. Pleated charcoal slacks, gleaming black leather belt, button down shirt, Italian tie. The spiffy look went with the framed law degree she'd spotted on the wall behind his desk.

"We're prepared to purchase a used Lane AT-602 that

should allow you to double your current business base. We'll also have our engineers look at ways to increase spread capacity."

"Alex has already done that. I met with them yesterday. I have to say I was impressed with what Lisa Wu and her partner have come up with in such a short time."

His mouth tipped in a smile so similar to his brother's that Julie did a double take. The personalities were definitely different but unless they were standing side by side, the physical similarities made it tough keeping them separate and distinct.

"Lisa's a great new hire," Blake agreed. "We snatched her right out from under the nose of Haliburton. Back to the contracts... As noted here, DI will take fifty percent of Agro-Air's profits until we've recouped the cost of the initial aircraft, after which we'll negotiate a profit-share percentage for the purchase of additional aircraft. As for the design and possible manufacture of a new application system, we'll bear the R&D costs. Agro-Air will provide technical input and flight testing. Is that what you and Alex agreed to?"

"Pretty much."

"Good. Why don't you take this copy of the contract with you? We can arrange a formal signing once your partners have had a chance to review and approve the clauses."

Before she made any move to take the papers, she took a final swig of coffee. Carefully, she replaced the cup in its saucer and eased into the issue that had been bugging her since she wrapped several strands of hair around Alex's shirt button.

"Did your brother tell you that I volunteered a DNA sample the first night I got here?"

"He did."

"Well?"

"I appreciate you being up front with us, Julie." His mouth quirked. "But I sure hate to strike you off our list. I was really hoping our search would end with you."

"I know. You're all anxious to ascertain Molly's heritage."

"We are, certainly. But you miss my meaning. I was hoping you specifically were the one."

"Me specifically? Why?"

"You're just what Alex needs. Someone smart, independent, more than able to give as good as she gets."

"Guilty as charged," she said, flattered by his assessment but secretly wishing he'd tacked on a few of the adjectives she would have used to describe the women she'd studied clinging to Alex's arm in the society photographs. Like glamorous. Sultry. Sophisticated.

Then again, Alex had called her beautiful last night. He'd been up to his eyeballs in lust at the time, she reminded herself ruefully. Still...

"Alex indicated I was the last possible on his list. What about you, Blake? Don't you have any viable candidates left on yours?"

"No."

A shadow darkened his eyes, come and gone so quickly she almost missed it.

"You do!" she exclaimed. "You've still got a possible on your list."

He smoothed his palms down his thighs. Slowly. Deliberately.

"C'mon, Blake. Give! Why haven't you gone after her?"

"She's dead, Julie. She died some months before Molly was born."

"Oh. I'm sorry."

"Yeah. Me, too."

He rolled his shoulders as if to dislodge an unwelcome burden and forced a smile. "So you understand why I'm no more eager than Alex to have Mother sharpening her claws again. Molly's distracted her."

"Still, I feel like a fraud for not telling her that I'm out of the baby stakes."

"Good Lord!" A look of acute dismay crossed Blake's face. "If you have an ounce of kindness in your heart, don't!

Tell her, I mean. As long as she thinks you're a viable candidate, she'll lay off Alex and me."

"Oh. Right. In the meantime, she continues to consider me several rungs lower than a whore for jumping into bed with your brother and refusing to accept the consequences of my slutty behavior."

He had the grace to look chagrined. "I didn't say Alex and I were clean in all this. If you knew what Delilah's put us through the past few years, though, you wouldn't resent granting us this small period of relative peace."

"I hesitate to state the obvious. But you and Alex *are* fully grown males well past the age of consent."

"You're right." Laughing, he spread both hands and hunched his shoulders in a gesture of surrender. "I don't know how it was in your family, but I *can* tell you this. Alex and I learned early on you can only stand up to an F-5 tornado like Mom for so long without getting blown off the planet."

A point Julie kept front and center in her mind when she and Alex arrived at Delilah's place that evening. The ubiquitous Louis answered the door, bowed, and informed them madam was on the upper terrace.

"Upper terrace?" Julie murmured to Alex. "Didn't your mom bill this as a backyard cookout?"

"Well," he said as he escorted her down the hall and through a set of wide double doors, "we're cooking out and this is the backyard."

"Right," she muttered, sweeping her gaze over the landscaped terraces that stair-stepped down to a gorgeously tiled swimming pool adorned with marble statues. "We should all have backyards like this."

A wrought-iron pergola interwoven in honeysuckle vines provided relief from the early evening sun. Their rich, sweet scent perfumed air cooled by a refreshing mist released at intervals from hidden nozzles. As Julie drank in the scene, her hostess emerged from inside the house. She had to admit Delilah looked almost human in a loose cotton blouse and well-worn jeans that emphasized her trim figure. She'd done her hair back in a fat braid that swished almost girlishly as she crossed the patio to greet them.

"Blake's in the kitchen, seasoning the steaks," she advised. "Alex, you're in charge of drinks. I'll have one of your patented margaritas." Her cool gaze moved to Julie. "You should try one. Alex has a special touch. Or did you get your fill of tequila during all those months in Mexico?"

Julie dodged the thinly veiled demand to know whether she'd swilled alcohol during her possible pregnancy. "Actually, I spent more time in South than in Central America. Margaritas aren't as popular in Chile as they are in Mexico."

"But Chile does produce some remarkable wines," Delilah persisted with bulldog tenacity.

"Yes, they do."

With a roll of his eyes, Alex stepped in to end the unsubtle inquisition. "Is Molly awake, Mom?"

The diversion worked. "I heard her stirring a few minutes ago."

"Why don't you have Grace bring her down while I mix up the drinks?"

"I'll go get her."

While Delilah was gone Alex busied himself at an outdoor kitchen crafted of stacked stones and gleaming appliances. A built-in refrigerator provided ice. Under-counter cabinets yielded a blender. The overhead bar opened to an array of bottles.

"Would you prefer something other than a margarita?" he asked. "I've been known to mix up a mean banana daiquiri."

"Ugh! I hate bananas. Just the smell of them makes me ill. My mother couldn't stand them, either."

He paused with a bottle in hand, an arrested expression on his face.

"What?" Julie demanded.

"We're just discovering what Molly will and won't eat in the baby food department," he replied slowly. "She spits out anything with so much as a hint of banana."

"Oh, no! Don't start down that road again."

She wasn't Molly's mother. She hadn't passed on any aversions, inherited or otherwise.

"Lots of people don't like smelly, mushy fruit," she protested.

"Yeah, I guess."

But the doubt was still in his face when he turned back to the bar.

Sighing, Julie let her gaze roam the formal garden on the terrace just below. Roses bursting with color, neatly trimmed boxwood hedges, a multi-spherical bronze sundial positioned to catch the eye as well as the sun. Delilah Dalton had certainly spared no expense having her grounds landscaped.

As if conjured up by the thought, the matriarch re-emerged from the house. A pink cheeked and bright-eyed Molly rode her hip. Until the baby spotted Alex, anyway. With a sound halfway between a coo and a gurgle, she seemed to twist right out of Delilah's grasp.

"Look out!"

Julie lunged forward, but the older woman had already tightened her hold on the squirming infant. The look Delilah sent Julie through narrowed lids telegraphed two distinct messages. One, she knew how to handle babies. Two, such apparent concern from a mother who may have abandoned her child was suspect at best.

Alex's broad shoulders intervened, cutting off the unspoken communication. "Come here, sweetheart."

While he settled the baby in the crook of his arm, Molly's nanny appeared with a bottle. "She needs feeding, Mr. Dalton."

"I'll do it. Unless..."

His eyes met Julie's with a question in their blue depths. She gave a small shake of her head. Much as she would enjoy holding the baby, she didn't want to underscore Delilah's sus-picions. More important, there was no point forming an at-tachment she would only have to sever in less than a week.

"Your drink's on the table, Mother."

The ice-cold margarita seemed to mellow Delilah. She downed it with unabashed gusto, then sipped a second more leisurely. Conversation ranged from Julie's impressions of her visit to the plant yesterday to some of the Dalton twins' more colorful escapades as boys. Yet Julie remained on full alert during a dinner of chilled cucumber salad, potatoes baked in the hot coals, and steaks grilled to perfection.

Grace joined them for dinner. The nanny kept a close eye on the baby but had little to do except enjoy her meal while Molly gleefully transferred from Alex to Blake to Delilah's lap, and back again. The infant might have lost her mother, but she certainly wouldn't lack for love.

A familiar pang snuck in under Julie's guard. Resolutely, she quashed it. She'd been in high school when she lost her parents. She'd had their love and guidance and support for more than half her life. She refused to feel sorry for herself or wish, even for an instant, that she could insert herself into this cozy family scene.

Nor would she blow what happened between her and Alex last night all out of proportion. They were both active, healthy and in their prime. Proximity and opportunity had reignited the sizzle that had sparked between them their first meeting all those months ago. In a few days they'd go their separate ways again. No harm, no foul.

Not much harm, anyway. As she watched the play of the light from the slowly setting sun on Alex's dark gold hair, Julie chewed her lower lip. She was falling for the man. She knew it. The question now was how far she'd let herself drop before…

"…plans for the weekend?"

Delilah's cool voice sliced into her thoughts.

"Sorry," Julie murmured. "I missed that. What did you say?"

"I asked whether you had plans for the weekend."

Her glance caught Alex's. The gleam in his eyes telegraphed an unmistakable message, but Julie didn't figure Delilah would appreciate hearing that she'd formulated no plans other than rolling around in bed with the woman's son. Repeatedly. All day Saturday and most of Sunday. Instead, she reverted to the agenda she'd mapped out for herself when she'd decided to make this little jaunt to the city.

"I want to do some shopping. And I saw that *Jersey Boys* opens at the Civic Center this weekend. I haven't seen it and…"

"Perfect," Alex interjected. "Mother's hosting a big fundraiser for her favorite charity prior to Friday's opening night performance. She's been trying to strong-arm Blake and me into escort duty. We can make it a foursome."

Delilah exercised too much self-control to let her annoyance show, but it was there in her cool reply. "The fundraiser is a black-tie affair, Alex. Julie may not wish to get all gussied up."

Wish to, or afford to? Julie knew which way those scales tipped. She'd pretty much depleted her bank account to buy into Agro-Air. She'd planned to hit the summer sales and do some serious bargain-hunting. But the idea of playing dressup and moving among Alex's circle of well-heeled friends grabbed on and wouldn't shake loose.

"That sounds like fun," she informed Delilah with a saccharine-sweet smile. "I'd love to join you."

Eight

Julie regretted her nasty impulse to one-up Delilah almost as soon as she'd given in to it. She wasn't into rubbing elbows with the rich and famous. Her milieu tended more toward the gritty and grease-stained. She waited to admit the error of her ways until after dessert, however, when the matriarch waved Grace back into her chair and insisted on taking Molly up for a bath herself.

Alex excused himself to take a call and Blake disappeared inside the house for a few moments, leaving Julie alone with the nanny. The sounds of summer wrapped around the two women. Cicadas buzzed in the bushes. A dove cooed to her mate in slowly gathering dusk. Down by the pool, fireflies flickered on and off, mirroring Julie's rapid on-again, off-again thoughts concerning the Friday evening bash.

"I may have jumped into this fund-raiser soiree a little too quickly," she confessed to Grace ruefully. "I don't have anything to wear to a fancy function like that."

"The age-old predicament of all females," the blonde commiserated with a sympathetic grin.

"And very accurate in this case. I don't really get many occasions to glam up in my line of work."

"But you said you wanted to do some shopping."

"I was thinking more along the lines of some new tops, shorts and work boots. I don't even know where to look for designer shoes and gowns."

"I accompanied Delilah to a couple high-end boutiques last week. She wanted to show off her grandbaby to her personal shoppers. I could jot down the names of the stores for you." She paused a moment before adding a kicker. "They'll poke a monster hole in your pocketbook, though."

"It's already got too many holes."

"There's another alternative." Grace hesitated again. "I helped Delilah bundle up some of her things a couple of days ago. She's sending them to a secondhand shop operated by one of her favorite charities. From what I gathered, she regularly harasses, harangues or otherwise browbeats her friends and acquaintances into keeping the place stocked."

"Surprise, surprise," Julie drawled.

Grace laughed and lifted her hair off her neck to let some air circulate. "As I've learned in my two short weeks with my employer, harassing and haranguing constitute Delilah's primary method of operation. I have no complaints, though. She's been darned good to me, and Molly's a joy."

Julie found no fault with the second half of that statement. The first had her lifting her brows in polite disbelief.

"It's true," Grace insisted. "Her bark is a whole lot worse than her bite. Most of the time."

"If you say so."

"Back to this stuff we bundled up. It was gorgeous, Julie. A Chanel suit and Viktor Russo handbag, among other things. Not your style, maybe, but I bet the shop has some things that are."

"I'm not sure I want to show up at a fancy dress ball wearing a gown one of Delilah's acquaintances discarded."

"Oh. Right." Grace chewed on that dire possibility for a while before offering another suggestion. "I'm pretty good with a needle. If you did find something you liked, we could alter and accessorize so that not even the original designer would recognize his creation."

The generous offer moved Julie. She'd enjoyed a wide circle of girlfriends during her younger years, but most had dropped off the radar after her parents' death and Julie's subsequent necessity of holding two or three jobs while working her way through college. Even the few she'd held onto had slipped away during the years she'd spent flying down in South and Central America. So the obvious sincerity behind Grace's suggestion warmed a corner of her heart.

"Thanks," she said with real gratitude. "I appreciate the offer, but you wouldn't have time to do alterations."

"Sure I would." A dimple appeared in the nanny's right cheek. "As you may have noticed, Delilah tends to preempt many of my duties. And tomorrow's my day off. I'd enjoy hitting the shops with you. Unless you and Alex have other plans," she tacked on as he reappeared.

"I don't know." Julie turned the question over to him. "Do we? Have plans for tomorrow?"

"We did," he answered with a small grimace as he slipped his cell phone into its case. "I wanted to take you to the airfield so you could scope out DI's air ops center. Looks like I have make a quick trip to Tulsa instead. One of our major customers has a problem that requires my attention. Sorry."

"No need to apologize. I didn't expect you to spend every day with me."

Or every night, although she sincerely hoped she wouldn't have to alter the agenda she'd formulated for later this evening. First priority was to get Alex alone. Second, to get him naked. Then... Well, three, four and five would take care of themselves.

Which begged the question—what came after five? Or six? Or seven? She didn't bother to kid herself any longer. Sometime in the past few days what she felt for Alex Dalton had slipped past attraction and plain old-fashioned lust. She was now flying dangerously close to unfamiliar territory, with no charts or instruments to guide her. She was wondering just where they would land when Blake emerged from the house.

"I heard Mom over the baby monitor," he announced with a grin. "She was informing Molly that good little girls probably shouldn't poop in their bathwater."

"Uh-oh." Grace pushed out of her chair. "I better get up there. So Julie, are we good for tomorrow?"

"I am if you are."

"Great. I'll pick you up at ten. We can have lunch out." She waved to the men. "'Night, Alex. See you, Blake."

Blake's gaze followed the nanny as she retreated into the house before turning back to Julie. "You and Grace have something planned for tomorrow?"

"We're going to hit the shops."

"Good. I'm glad she's getting out for a while. Mother's kept her jumping for the past two weeks. What's on your schedule, Alex?"

"I've got to go to Tulsa."

The brothers shared a look.

"No problem," Blake said in his easy way. "I'll spend the day here with Molly and Mom."

"But…" Guilt and confusion tagged Julie. "Grace said it was her day off."

"It is. And mother's more than competent to take care of Molly. What's more, she'll have Louis and the other staff close at hand. Alex and I just like to provide a little, uh, backup."

"Make that a little 'parental oversight'," Alex clarified as he and Julie drove through the star-studded night. "And not necessarily of Molly."

"Good grief! What do you imagine your mother could do with a six-month old in tow?"

"Whatever she decides *needs* doing," he returned with some feeling. "She had Blake and me crawling through pipe sections and swinging from oil rigs before we could walk. Hauling us out to the fields with her was a necessity back then. Times have changed, although you'd have a hard time convincing our mother of that."

Julie didn't comment but she suspected whichever of the Dalton men proved to be Molly's father would have their hands full riding herd on a small daughter and a super-charged mother. She pitied the poor woman who landed in the middle of that triangle. Any Dalton bride would have to fight tooth and nail to keep from getting mowed down in the scuffle.

Which brought her back full circle to the question of where this…this *thing*…between Alex and her could go. If, in fact, it went anywhere. A wave of sudden doubt hit her when she keyed open the door to the guest suite and he paused on the threshold.

"I've been thinking about us, Julie."

So there was an "us." The plural gave her a small thrill, although Alex looked way too serious for her peace of mind. Especially considering the agenda she'd privately mapped out for the rest of the evening.

"I've been pushing you since the day I showed up unannounced at Agro-Air," he said slowly.

"True, although I would probably use a stronger verb than 'push' to describe blackmail and the sneaky ploy of turning my stated weakness for pizza against me."

"So I'll back off," he continued, "if you want me to."

"Let me think about that for a moment." Crossing her arms, she gave the issue the serious consideration it deserved. "One, I didn't *have* to agree to the deal you offered me and my partners. Two, I didn't *have* to make this jaunt to the city.

Three, I certainly didn't *have* to grab you by the ears and drag you to bed last night."

"That's not quite how I remember it," he said as a grin slipped out, "but go on."

Okay, she needed to be honest here. Not a real problem, since she'd never learned to do coy. Still, she couldn't bring herself to voice the emotions she hadn't quite sorted through yet. The best she could do was a stripped-down version of the truth.

"Four, I seem to have a lamentable case of the hots for you, Dalton. So all things considered, I'd say no. I don't want you to back off."

That was all Alex had been waiting for. He'd been aching for this woman all evening. Listening to her spar with his mother... Seeing the moonlight glint on the dark red of her hair... Remembering how she'd moaned and arched under him last night... He'd damned near doubled over with wanting her.

His conscience had jabbed right through the wanting, though. More than one competitor had accused him of steamroller tactics. And it was true. He tended to go all out when he desired something. Or in this case, someone. Except desire didn't begin to describe the hunger he felt for Julie Bartlett. As a consequence, he'd spent most of the ride home telling himself to throttle back and let whatever this was between them develop gradually, naturally. Thank God she'd seen his brief spurt of nobility for the BS it was!

His conscience now conveniently out of the way, he covered the mouth she tipped up to his. Hunger ripped into him, swift and fierce. This time, though, he was determined to take things slow. He wanted to explore every inch of Julie's long, lithe body. Savor the strength in the sleek muscles she'd developed from jenking a two-ton aircraft into hard turns.

That was the plan, anyway. Right up until they stumbled into the guest suite, still locked together and feeding ravenously off each other. Her hands attacked his shirt buttons.

His tugged at the hem of her blouse. The moment Alex found smooth skin and warm woman, he jettisoned the last of his good intentions and backed her to the wide leather sofa.

She tumbled onto the cushions. He followed her down. Breathless and awkward with their bodies tangled at odd angles, she laughed up at him with those mesmerizing eyes. He could lose himself in them. In her. Might already have done just that. The realization hit while Alex could still form a semi-coherent thought, just nanoseconds before his blood rushed south, his mind shut down, and he channeled all his energy to the task of baring Julie to his hands and tongue and teeth.

He woke at his usual 6 a.m. the next morning. Julie lay sprawled beside him in glorious abandon, the top sheet tangled and twisted around her naked form. Smiling, Alex tucked his hands behind his head and let his gaze roam lazily over her curves and hollows.

He didn't have to hit the road for Tulsa until nine. That left them plenty of time for the slow, easy session he'd originally planned for last night. Yet as much as her sleek curves and cloud of tangled hair stirred him, Alex was content to just lie beside her and watch her sleep.

A first for him, he admitted wryly. He hadn't felt the urge to simply share the same airspace with the lawyer he'd dated on and off for almost six months. Barbara Hale was as energetic as she was driven. No lazing around in bed on weekends for her. No evenings just zoning out in front of the TV. Alex had admired her restless energy until their heavy work schedules combined with her insatiable need to see and be seen at an endless stream of social events had just flat worn him out.

This was nice, he mused as he thumbed a silky auburn tangle. Very nice. The background data he'd gathered on Julie suggested she just was as powered as Barbara and every bit as good at her job. Stubborn, too. Stick-it-in-your-eye stubborn. Yet she wasn't sharp or hard at the edges. Not hard at all, he thought, smiling as he eased downward and hooked an arm over her waist to nest her against him for a few more minutes.

Alex bumped up against the stubborn part when they shared a breakfast of coffee and toaster waffles that Julie consumed with real gusto and he left pretty much untouched. She was bundled into the robe again, her hair clipped carelessly atop her head as she perched on a barstool across the counter from him. Shaking his head, Alex watched as she stabbed the last, syrup-drenched morsel.

"Beats me how you can consume cardboard with such apparent enjoyment."

"I've eaten worse." She waved her fork in an airy circle. "Besides, cardboard is pretty much in the eye of the beholder."

"Can't argue with that." He checked his watch and downed the last of his coffee. "I've got to go. Grace is picking you up at ten, right?"

"Right. She's going to help me rig out for your mom's big bash tomorrow evening."

"Speaking of which…" He warned himself to tread carefully. "I know you didn't plan on that kind of expense. How about I call the stores mother shops at and…?"

"Don't say it!" she warned. "Don't even think it."

"Be reasonable, Julie. There's no need to drain your savings for a one-time event."

"Who says I'll wear what I buy just once?" she shot back, bristling. "I *do* have a life. Or I did before Agro-Air," she added under her breath.

Alex cursed his slip and tried to recover. "Look, if it makes you feel better, we can add whatever charges you run up today to the tab you insisted I keep for you."

That approach didn't work, either. If anything, it seemed to add fuel to the fire. Eyes shooting sparks, she slapped her fork onto the counter.

"I suggest you back off, Dalton. Now. Before you piss me off royally."

"I'm just trying to…"

"Trying, hell! What you're *doing* is coming across like a satisfied customer who wants to pay for services rendered."

He looked like she'd hauled off and taken a swing at him. Which she had. With malice aforethought.

"You know better than that."

"I do, huh? Then why do you keep making such an issue of money? Offering me a thousand dollars for a wad of spit. An all-expense paid week in the big city. Now the rich Mr. Dalton wants to deck his bed-partner out for an evening of hobnobbing with his high-class pals." She fluttered her lashes. "Gee, what's a girl supposed to think?"

"That the rich Mr. Dalton is looking out for his *partner*," he corrected tersely. "That I don't want her to… Oh, hell!"

As irritated now as she was, he rounded the counter and fisted his hands in the robe's lapels.

"Do what you want to today."

"I will," she retorted.

"Just keep this in mind while you're racking up the bills. I don't care what you wear. Or don't wear. You've had me tied in knots from the moment I spotted you in those baggy coveralls."

"Ha! I saw your face when you checked me out. You looked like you couldn't believe you'd ever hooked up with someone sporting a quart of grease under her nails."

"I'll give you that. The grease did set me back a step. You made up for it the next day when you sashayed in wearing those cut-offs. I damned near swallowed my tongue."

"Oh. Well." She could feel her bristles smoothing down. "You just regained some of the headway you lost, Dalton. Keep paddling."

"I would, but I've got to go. Just believe me when I tell you I'll take you any way I can get you. In jeans and boots. Dressed to the nines. Naked. Preferably naked."

He kissed her, hard, and headed for the door. When it thudded shut, Julie sat unmoving as one chaotic question after another chased through her mind like a dog chasing its tail. What the heck had Alex meant? What kind of spin should she put on that bit about taking her any way he could get her? Had she really kicked his chocks out from under him that first day, grease and all?

And where did she fit in with his quest to find Molly's mother? What if the mother came forward? What if it was someone Alex had connected with but had denied giving birth to his child for reasons of her own?

Geesh! This was hurting her head! Grimacing, she slid off the barstool and padded to the bedroom. She needed a long, hot run to work the kinks out of her mind, followed by an equally long and very cool shower.

When she hopped into the gas-saving Civic that Grace pulled up to the curb some two hours later, Julie had settled at least some of the issues that had rattled around in her head like loose lug-nuts. Foremost among them was a decision to take Alex at his stated word.

He wanted her any way he could get her? Fine. Time he saw what the other end of the spectrum looked like. The one where she wasn't dripping sweat and splattered with engine oil.

"Change of plans," she announced as she slid in beside Grace and snapped her seatbelt. "Forget the secondhand boutique. Take me to wherever Delilah shops when she wants to pull out all the stops."

"You're kidding, right?"

"No, ma'am."

Grace hooked slender wrists over the steering wheel. "We're talking big bucks here, Julie. Extremely big."

"So we look, we try on a few things, and we walk if the price tags make us gag. Or," she postulated as Grace put the Civic in gear, "we could get lucky and catch a sale."

"It'll have to be an end-of-season, going-out-of-business, one-time-only sweep to the walls," the nanny warned.

It wasn't quite a sweep and Julie didn't actually gag, but she did choke back a gasp when she saw the price tags on the gowns at the exclusive boutique on Western Avenue. And those were the markdowns! No way she was going to blow three thousand dollars for a handful of sequins and a few yards of silk.

The second boutique they hit was smaller and more intimate but just as pricey. Sighing, Julie fingered several of the heavily beaded creations before coming down to earth with a thud.

"Much as I would like to shine at Delilah's big do," she murmured to Grace, "I can't afford something like this. We'd better..."

"Excuse me."

They turned to find a petite brunette regarding them with curious eyes. Exquisitely attired in layers of soft aqua linen pinned up on one hip with a crystal-studded dahlia the size of a dinner plate, she cocked her head.

"I couldn't help overhearing you mention Delilah. Were you by any chance referring to Mrs. Delilah Dalton?"

"Yes, I was."

"May I ask? Are you looking for something to wear to her fund-raiser tomorrow evening?"

"Yes again. But I'm afraid I can't afford your stuff, as gorgeous as it is."

The brunette tipped her head to the other side. Her bright, bird-like black eyes measured Julie from neck to knee in one, comprehensive sweep.

"The gowns you were looking at are all couture, from well established designers. I've got some things in the back by a new young designer. She drove through last month and left some samples with me in the hope I would help her break into Oklahoma City's big money oil crowd. May I show them to you?"

"Well…"

"They're far more reasonably priced than the couture gowns you were looking at. And there's one that's perfectly suited to someone with your height and coloring."

"Go on," Grace urged, digging an elbow in Julie's ribs. "What have you got to lose by looking?"

Only her share of Agro-Air's almost non-existent profits for the next six months. Oh, what the hell!

"I'm all for giving new, young designers a break."

"Good. My name's Helen, by the way. Helen Jasper. This is my shop."

"I'm Julie Bartlett, and this is Grace Templeton."

"A pleasure to meet you both. Please, have a seat and I'll show you what I have."

What she had was a stunning two-piece in shimmering gold silk. The skirt was arrow straight and slit to the thigh on one side. The strapless bodice was reinforced, cut to a deep V, and hooked in front with crystal-studded fasteners shaped like the sun, moon and stars. At least Julie hoped they were crystal. But she knew as she hooked the last, glittering star that she had to have this dress.

When she stepped out of the dressing room, Grace seconded her decision. "Oh, Julie. It's perfect! Simple, yet elegant and daring. Now all you need are some strappy sandals…."

"Like these." The boutique owner lifted a pair of gold thong sandals with killer, four-inch stiletto heels from their box. "And this for your hair."

The comb she slipped from a velvet drawstring bag glittered with the same zodiac signs as on bodice and was obviously crafted to wear with the dress.

"I would suggest catching your hair up on one side, like this." Helen demonstrated, deftly anchoring the comb at Julie's left temple. "See how it draws all eyes to your face? You don't need earrings or a neckless. Any additional jewelry would be overkill."

Good thing, as Julie didn't have any pieces that came close to the sparkle in those suns and stars.

"Well?" Helen stood back and viewed her efforts a smug smile. She had her customer hooked and knew it. "What do you think?"

"I think we need to negotiate a down payment and monthly installments."

The boutique owner laughed and shook her head. "I'll sell you the entire ensemble for five hundred and your promise to drop the name of my shop at least a dozen times tomorrow night."

Julie didn't hesitate. With only a small pang, she bid farewell to the little that was left in her bank account.

"Done."

Nine

Julie and Grace celebrated the success of their expedition with a late lunch on the tree-shaded patio of a Mexican restaurant. While a fountain gurgled in the background, they dug fresh-baked tortilla chips into bowls of salsa and Grace satisfied Julie's curiosity about her career choice.

"Actually, I'm not a professional nanny," the blonde confided hesitantly. "I teach junior high social studies, or did until my…my dad got sick and I quit my job to take care of him."

"He okay now?"

"He passed away."

"I'm so sorry."

"So am I." Grace crumbled a chip and didn't look up as she continued. "I was at loose ends for a while after that, then Delilah heard I was sending out resumes and offered me this temporary position."

Okay, so DD wasn't the wicked witch of the west. Julie

hadn't gotten a glimpse of her good side yet, but apparently she had one.

Brushing the crumbs, Grace steered the conversation away from a subject that was clearly still painful to her. "I know you don't need any additional jewelry. You do need a bag, though. Want to check that secondhand shop for a little beaded number?"

What the hell. Her bank account was already mortally wounded. Might as well put it out of its misery.

"Sure."

After another successful foray, Grace pulled her Civic up at the curb outside the DI building just past 4 p.m.

"Delilah insisted on signing me up for a guest membership to the Oklahoma Country Club's health spa," she said as Julie gathered her purchases. "I'm going for a swim and a sauna later. Sure you don't want to join me?"

"Thanks, but Alex said something about dinner tonight."

Julie glanced up to find Grace regarding her with an odd look in her eyes.

"What?"

"Nothing."

"What, Grace?"

"It's none of my business."

"*What* isn't?"

"Well…" Her mouth tipped up at the corners. "You and Alex seem to have, uh, reconnected."

"Uh-oh. Is it that obvious?"

"Only to someone who's seen how stressed he's been the past few weeks."

Like his child's caretaker, Julie thought, and his brother and—big groan here—his mother.

"I can understand how discovering after the fact that you might be a father could stress a guy out." She paused with her hand on the car's door latch. "I'm not Molly's mother, Grace."

"I know. Delilah said you told Alex so up front. She's not completely convinced," the nanny cautioned.

"That's her problem, not mine."

Sincerely hoping that blithe assertion was true, Julie headed for the elevator with her purchases. She was zinging up to the guest suite when her cell phone buzzed. A glance at caller ID kicked up her pulse several notches.

Oh, for pity's sake! What was she? Eleven?

Still, she couldn't keep the smile from her voice when she answered Alex's call. "Hey, you."

"Hey to you, too."

"Where are you?"

"Still in Tulsa. We've pinpointed the problem but not the fix. Looks like I'm stuck here the rest of the day and most of the evening. I've got a few more of my people on their way over to join us. If our team doesn't come up with a solution in the next four or five hours, we might have to overnight."

"Hope you work it out."

"Me, too."

His husky reply echoed her own heartfelt sentiments.

"How did the shopping go?"

"Good." She hugged the dress bag draped over her arm. "Grace and I found some terrific bargains."

Bargain being a relative term, of course. Resolutely, Julie reminded herself that her gown was a steal compared to what Delilah and her circle would spend for one.

"I talked to Blake a little while ago," Alex was saying. "He'd like to take you to dinner."

"He's spent his day babysitting Molly. He doesn't have to spend his evening doing the same for me."

"He wants to."

"That's nice of him, but please call him and tell him he's off the hook. I've got some things I need to do this evening."

* * *

Checking in with Dusty topped the list. Then she needed to boot up her computer to take a look at their schedule for next week. She also wanted to make sure they had enough in reserve to cover the additional chemicals Dusty had ordered without her knowledge. Alex had kept her so occupied the past few days she'd let Agro-Air business slip to the back of her mind.

The second and third tasks proved far easier than the first. The fact that Dusty didn't answer either the office phone or his cell tied a small knot of tension in the pit of her stomach. Nor did Chuck Whitestone know his present whereabouts. Since the mechanic couldn't be bothered with hauling around a mobile phone, it took five calls before she located him at the Highway 21 Diner.

"Do you know where Dusty is?" she asked after he'd ambled over to the diner's pay phone.

"Said he was takin' off for the weekend."

"Off where?"

"Didn't ask."

"He's not hitting the slots, is he?"

"Didn't ask," Chuck repeated in his economical way.

"Tell him to call me if he contacts you, okay?"

"Will do."

Julie hung up and chewed on her lower lip. She could think of several reasons why Dusty didn't answer his cell phone. The most worrisome was that he couldn't hear it ring over the clamor of a busy casino. Or he might have heard it but checked caller ID, saw it was Julie, and didn't want to clue her in to his whereabouts.

At least he'd paid for that last batch of chemicals. Agro-Air's bottom line was almost as flat as Julie's eviscerated personal account now. She just hoped Dusty wasn't borrowing against the promise of future income springing from their partnership with Dalton International. No contracts had been signed yet. The Daltons could still back out of the deal if a debt collector drove up and towed away all their equipment.

The distinct possibility ate at Julie's pleasure in her purchases. She eyed the zippered bag hanging on the closet door, wondering how she could have been crazy enough to plunk down five hundred dollars for a dress, shoes and a spangly comb. Even the thirty dollars she'd shelled out at the second-hand store for a rhinestone-studded evening bag pinged her conscience.

She seriously considered returning the gown tomorrow and backing out of the fund-raiser. Might have done exactly that if Alex hadn't sabotaged her half-formed resolution by leaning on the doorbell to the guest suite mere moments after Julie rolled out of bed at her usual oh-dark-thirty the next morning.

She was barely awake. She'd slapped some water on her face and attacked the night fuzz on her teeth before making coffee, thank goodness, but she was still in the OSU Cowboys athletic T she wore as a sleepshirt and her hair could do double duty as a crow's nest.

Alex didn't seem to mind, however. Either that, or he needed a vision check as he swooped in for a quick kiss. "'Morning, beautiful."

Now he, Julie thought when he un-swooped, looked like every woman's secret fantasy come to life. All dark gold hair and wide shoulders and white squint lines at the corners of smiling blue eyes and...

"Get dressed."

The preemptory command interrupted her inventory. "Huh?"

"I've got a surprise for you."

"What is it?" she asked warily.

"Wouldn't be a surprise if I told you." Turning her by the shoulders, he aimed her at the bedroom. "Get dressed."

"All right, already."

Julie complied with the order, more than a little disappointed that this surprise involved putting on clothes instead of peeling them off. When she trudged back into the living room in jeans and a tank top and hinted as much, however, he just laughed.

"Later," he promised. "Let's go."

Once in the garage, he steered her to the Jag parked in its reserved slot. Two minutes later they were wheeling through the still-empty streets of downtown Oklahoma City.

Fifteen minutes after that, Alex turned into the approach to a small airport on the west side of town. The Dalton International symbol prominently displayed on the gate and the sleek executive jet visible through the open doors of one of the hangars suggested Alex was making good on his promise to show her DI's aeronautical operations center.

Then she caught sight of a just-washed aircraft parked on the tarmac. Water droplets still glistened on its canary yellow fuselage accented with a wide, jet-blue stripe.

"It's the Lane 602!"

"I had it flown in yesterday," Alex told her. "Thought you might want to take it for a test drive before we finalize the buy."

She was out of the Jag almost before it rolled to a stop, her avid gaze raking the Air Tractor from its single prop to its rear dispersal system. The present owner turned out to be an air-ag pilot operating out of Nebraska, who introduced himself as Jim O'Connor.

"Good to meet you, Dalton. And you, Ms. Bartlett." His gaze conveyed curiosity and something close to sympathy. "So you're partnered up with Dusty Jones, are you?"

"Two months now," Julie confirmed.

She kept her voice pleasant but flashed an unmistakable warning. *She* could criticize and carp at her partner but no one else better do so in her hearing.

O'Connor got the message. "Ole Dusty's one of the best ag pilots in the business," he said hastily. "I've seen him damn near stand his Pawnee on its tail."

Julie nodded her agreement, and O'Connor slapped a hand on the Air Tractor's fuselage.

"So, you want me to check you out on this baby?"

"Let me review the specs and owner's log first."

Excitement licked at her as she poured through the 602's vital statistics. Its Pratt & Whitney turboprop engine was a workhorse of the industry. The engine powered aircraft performing such diverse mission as transporting business passengers, dropping cargo in the Antarctic darkness at seventy-five degrees below zero, and performing fire suppression over blazing forests. The plane itself had a fuel capacity of more than two hundred gallons and its hopper could carry more than six hundred gallons of chemicals.

The dispersal system, she saw with a hastily suppressed thrill, could be easily modified along the lines Lisa Wu had suggested. With an intense exertion of willpower, Julie played down her excitement. No point letting O'Connor see how much she ached to get her hands on the throttle while there was still wiggle room in the sale negotiations.

Julie's almost instant grasp of the 602's capabilities impressed the hell out of Alex. With some notable gaps, the private investigator he'd hired to do a background check had provided a fairly detailed run-down on her background and flying experience. Still, she climbed into the cockpit after what felt to him like a *very* brief familiarization session.

He was used to the more sophisticated Gulfstream. It took longer to check out on highly instrumented twin-engine executive jets than single-seat air transports. Which is what he used to sop his pride until she taxied, lifted off, and made a few experimental passes.

Her first wing-over sent Alex's heart jumping into his throat. She made the climbing/descending turn at such a steep ninety degree bank that he didn't breathe easy again until she brought the 602 skimming back at thirty feet off the deck. Then she hopped over a stand of trees and pitched up in a hammerhead. The vertical maneuver was one of the first taught in flight schools. Pilots learned to pitch straight up, stomp on the rudder, and roll into a one-eighty to reverse course. Performing a hammerhead in a simulator or while he was at the controls himself was one thing. Watching Julie perform one at near stall speed squeezed his chest so tight Alex was sure he'd cracked a couple of ribs.

"Christ," he muttered when she climbed out of the cockpit and strutted over to where he leaned against the Jag, sweating bullets. "You pull stunts like that every day?"

"Pretty much." Her smile was smug. "It's called flying, Dalton."

She was good. She'd just demonstrated exactly *how* good. Yet when she and O'Connor put their heads together again, Alex couldn't shake the contrary wish that she piloted big, honkin' passenger jets with multiple back-up systems instead of what now seemed to him like little more than a fertilizer can with a prop.

The antsy feeling stayed with him while he gave Julie a tour of DI's hangars and ops center, followed by lunch at his favorite barbecue joint. It was still with him when he had to return for a hastily-called 3 p.m. meeting with Blake and DI's marketing director.

He stepped out of the elevators on the tenth floor and escorted her to the guest suite, sincerely regretting this change in plans.

"We'll have to move 'later' back a few more hours," he said at the door.

Her blank look made him grin and remind her of his promise when he rousted her out to see the plane early this morning instead of tumbling her back into bed.

"Oh, right. *That* later." She heaved a heavy, theatrical sigh. "It'll be tough, but I guess I can cool my jets awhile longer."

His kiss promised to more than make up for the additional delay.

"You all set for tonight?"

Julie chewed on a corner of her lip while she conducted a swift internal debate. She'd decided to return her purchases and back out of Delilah's big bash tonight. Paying so much for a gown went against her grain. On top of that, her inability to reach Dusty had started to gnaw at her.

On the other hand, the 602 had more than lived up to her expectations. With the additional plane and the improvements in spread ratio already being worked out by DI's engineering team, Agro-Air should turn a healthy profit this coming season.

Oh, for Pete's sake! Why was she overthinking all this? She'd never had trouble making a decision before. Had never been this wishy-washy about anything, much less a silly dress. What had gotten into her?

All she had to do was look into a pair of smiling blue eyes to know the answer. Alex Dalton. He'd gotten into her... heart, mind and body.

"Yes," she answered, slamming the door on any further debate, "I'm set."

"Good. The fund-raiser starts at six, but we don't need to be there that early. And it's just a few blocks from here, so how about I pick you up at six-thirty?"

"That works for me."

She made good use of the interval.

Her first priority was to contact Dusty. She was itching to tell him about taking the 602 up for a test spin and how sweet the plane was to maneuver. When she got no answer, she tried Chuck again. The mechanic still hadn't heard from his partner but evinced little concern about the lack of communication.

"Dusty'll get ahold of us sooner or later."

Better be sooner. Julie's nerves were wound tight as it was.

They coiled even more the closer it got to six-thirty. She killed part of the time with a long soak in mango-scented bubbles. A half bottle of conditioner took the 602's wind whip from her hair. Subsequent sessions with a blow dryer and curling iron made the thick mane almost manageable.

She fiddled with the jeweled comb, experimenting with different arrangements. She could pile the loose curls atop her head and anchor them with the comb. Or she could try for sleek and sophisticated by pulling her hair back in a smooth bun. In the end she decided to go with the boutique owner's recommended style—a smooth sweep on one side that brushed her shoulder, the other side caught back at the temple.

Her hair out of the way, she stepped into the narrow sheath of a skirt. Even with a lining, the gold silk was so thin Julie gave fervent thanks for the boutique owner's foresight in insisting Julie include a pair of seamless panties with her other purchases. No requirement for a bra, though. The bodice was cut to a deep V but fit tight and plumped her otherwise modest curves up nicely.

Very nicely, if Alex's reaction when she opened the door a little while later was any indication.

"Wow!"

The muttered exclamation was low but fervent enough to put a Cinderella smile in Julie's heart. The sight of her golden-haired prince in black tie and tux sparked an equally fervent response.

"Right back at you, Dalton."

"Turn around, let me see the full effect."

The four-inch stiletto heels made pirouetting on the plush carpeting a challenge but she pulled off a creditable turn without falling on her butt.

"The back view is great," Alex announced. "Superlative. But the front... Oh, sweetheart."

Julie couldn't remember the last time she'd blushed. If ever! She could feel a slow heat sneak into her cheeks now, though.

She knew darned well that at least part of the heat

stemmed from the profound feminine satisfaction that came with Alex seeing her in something other than coveralls, jeans or her trusty black slacks.

But most of it, she admitted on a silly, fluttery sigh, was a direct result of that murmured "sweetheart." The casual endearment didn't necessarily mean anything. Men—and women—used it all the time in this part of the country. Still, it warmed her enough to steal Julia Roberts's line from *Pretty Woman*.

"In case I forget to tell you later, I had a nice time tonight."

"I won't let you forget." His eyes gleamed with hot promise. "And just so you know, 'later' ranks at the top of my agenda for tonight."

Hers, too, although she didn't get a chance to say so before his glance made another slow sweep.

"Sure you want to go mingle with rich and not-so-famous?"

"Are you kidding? After I went to all this trouble to... How did your mother put it? Get all gussied up?"

"Okay, but when the small talk has you wanting to scream with boredom, don't say I didn't warn you."

Laughing, she slipped her hand into the crook of his arm. "I won't."

Ten

Given Alex's prediction of jaw-cracking boredom, Julie didn't really expect to enjoy Delilah's big bash. She'd never learned the art of small talk. Never practiced pasting on a polite smile to cover acute disinterest. Aside from Alex and Blake and their mother, she wouldn't know a soul at the fund-raiser.

Satisfaction over Alex's reaction to her spiffed-up persona and the sledgehammer effect of *his* tuxedoed persona on her senses had her so buoyed, however, that she almost floated into the limo he had waiting at the curb.

"I thought you said the party's only a few blocks from here," she commented as she wiggled her hip-hugging skirt into place.

"It is, but a princess should arrive in style. Besides, I doubt you could navigate the city streets in those shoes."

"They're not my usual style," she admitted, stretching out a leg to admire the lethal heels. "Might prove useful if

I have to fight off a mugger, though. I could put out his eye with one thrust."

Thankfully, no muggers intercepted them when they exited the limo and entered the Oklahoma City Museum of Art. Alex cupped a hand under Julie's elbow to escort her inside, where they were greeted by the museum's three-story glass masterpiece by Dale Chihuly. According to Alex, the brilliantly colored tower comprised more than two thousand twisting, turning pieces.

"They had to ship them from the artist's studio in sections."

She craned her neck to take in the sculpture's complexity and enormity. "How in the world did they ever put it together again?"

"Very carefully," Alex deadpanned.

Delilah had reserved the museum's rooftop terrace for her fund-raiser. The party was already in full swing when Alex and Julie stepped out of the elevator. Women glittering with jewels and men in hand-tailored tuxes sipped champagne and chattered against the backdrop of Oklahoma City's skyline lit to brilliance by the early evening sun. A forest of gently whirling fans and cool misters tamed the July heat, thank goodness, while an army of servers drifted through the crowd with trays of canapés and crystal champagne flutes.

A linen-draped table strategically placed close to the elevator displayed the "donations" Delilah had strong-armed for the silent auction. Julie almost choked when she spotted the starting bids for some of the items. Fifteen grand for two weeks at a private villa in the south of France? Twenty for a photographic safari in Kenya, led by one of National Geographic's foremost wildlife photographers? Neither of which included airfare, she noted, although the CEO of a major international airline had donated a pair of first-class tickets to any destination in the world for the bargain basement price of eighteen thou. But it was the gold pendant nested on black velvet that riveted her attention.

"Look! It's Viracocha, the Incan sun god."

"I'll have to take your word for that," Alex said with a smile.

"The Inca believe Viracocha rose from Lake Titicaca in the time of darkness to create the sun, the moon and the stars."

The pendant was at least three inches high and had to be crafted of solid gold. It depicted an incredibly elaborate god who wore the sun for a crown, clutched thunderbolts in his hands, and wept tears representing the life-giving rain that fed crops at high, dry altitudes.

"I saw a piece just like this in Chile," Julie exclaimed, mesmerized by the magnificent piece. "This is an amazing replica."

Or so she thought until she noted the starting bid.

"Whoa! This can't be a reproduction. Not at this price. What'd your mother do, Alex? Commission someone to heist the original from the Santiago Museum?"

A not-quite-amused voice drifted from behind them.

"I've been accused of a lot of things in my time. Not without some justification, I'll admit. I don't count robbing museums of priceless works of art among my many sins, however."

Julie sucked air. A low, hissing lungful. But when she looked to Alex for help, the wicked amusement on his face didn't offer an out. Resigned to her fate, she turned to face her nemesis.

A single glance told her Delilah had pulled out all the stops tonight. Diamonds dripped from her ears, her throat, her wrists and sparkled on at least three of her fingers. Her jet black hair was swept up in style a that added inches to her already impressive presence. Her still slender body was encased in an off-the-shoulder gown of shimmering jet that probably cost more than the Viracocha pendant.

"Sorry," Julie said. "I didn't mean to accuse you of stealing."

"Oh?" The older woman arched an aristocratic brow. "Sure sounded like it to me."

Julie deflected the barb the only way she could. "You throw one heck of a party, Delilah. This is a truly a magical setting. And you look fantastic," she added with genuine sincerity.

Delilah proved no more immune to flattery than any other woman. Her expression softening, she preened a bit before returning the compliment with only a hint of reluctance.

"So do you. Where did you get that dress?"

Cued by that auspicious opening, Julie segued into her assigned task. "At Helen Jasper's boutique. She stocks really gorgeous stuff. You should check out her shop."

"I will," Delilah promised as she linked her arm through that of her son's guest. "Let me introduce you to some of the other people here."

Much to Julie's surprise, she thoroughly enjoyed herself for the next hour. She'd figured she wouldn't have anyone to converse with except Alex and his brother and had worried about holding her own in the rarified atmosphere of megamillionaires. Contrary to her expectations, she found plenty to talk about with a good number of men whose roots still went deep into Oklahoma's red dirt.

The women not so much. Most of the females she was introduced to didn't profess the slightest interest in crop yields or the futures market, although she suspected those markets funded their rubies and emeralds. Their conversations tended more toward kids, schools and charity work. And clothes, which gave Julie plenty of opportunity to slip in the promised references to Helen Jasper's shop.

Naturally, the Daltons' recent acquisition of a new family member formed a topic of avid interest. Most of the women couched their questions in polite terms, asking how little Molly was adjusting or whether she'd started to crawl yet.

One or two dropped more pointed comments obviously designed to confirm the baby's parentage.

Alex answered the questions he chose to and dodged the others with practiced ease. Julie couldn't dodge the speculative looks, though. More than one set of assessing, mascara'ed eyes turned her way.

One pair was particularly penetrating. Thick black lashes framed the startlingly bright turquoise eyes. Had to be tinted contacts, Julie decided, as the owner sauntered in their direction.

"Hello, Alex."

The voice was low and sultry. The body that produced it had been poured into a strapless aqua sleeve.

"Hello, Barbara. Have you met Julie Bartlett?"

"Not yet."

"Julie, this is Barbara Hale. She's an attorney with Power, Davis and Cox."

The hand the attorney extended was tipped with blood-red nails, but its grip was strong and brisk.

"I understand you're a pilot, Ms. Bartlett. Or may I call you Julie?"

She phrased the request pleasantly enough but her voice seemed to have an underlying edge to it that Julie couldn't quite interpret.

"Julie's fine," she replied, "and yes, I am a pilot."

"I'm guessing that's how you and Alex must have met. He spends almost as much time in the air as he does in his office." Her liquid gaze shifted, smiled, caressed. "Don't you, darling?"

"Not quite."

The attorney slewed her aqua eyes back to Julie. All right. Point made and understood. She and Alex had enjoyed something more than a business relationship.

Maybe still did.

The thought punched through the evening's rosy glow. Why, Julie wasn't sure. Alex had made no bones about playing the field. He'd stated up front that she was the last candidate on his list of potential Molly-moms.

She couldn't help wondering where Barbara Hale had placed on the list. Near the top, she'd bet. The attorney was smart, sophisticated, obviously part of the same circles Alex and his family moved in. She'd probably never gotten a single drop of grease under those blood-red talons.

Was she hoping to take up where they'd left off before Molly entered Alex's orbit? If so, she had to be less than thrilled with Julie's appearance—or reappearance—in Alex's life.

Hale confirmed as much just a few hours later.

With the bids closed and the silent action over, Delilah announced they'd raised almost a hundred thousand dollars to benefit the summer camp she supported for children with terminal illnesses. The guests then downed the last of their champagne and moved from the museum's rooftop terrace to the Civic Center less than a block away.

Julie had attended a handful of performances at the Civic Center as a youngster. Then, as now, its gray granite facade and ornate ironwork evoked its Art Deco past. The facility had been built in the 1930s with a partial grant from President Roosevelt's Public Works Administration, and reopened in 2001 after a massive, three-year renovation. The complex now served as a prime venue for touring companies of Broadway hits like *Jersey Boys*.

They took their seats just moments before the curtain went up. The Daltons, of course had a private, first-tier box that gave an up-close view of the stage and orchestra pit. No fold-down auditorium seats for them. These armchairs were wide and plush and could be positioned for maximum enjoyment. Delilah and Blake spent the few moments before the lights dimmed chatting with friends in the next box, while Alex popped the cork on the bottle of champagne that sat waiting in a silver ice bucket.

Cristal, Julie noted, eyeing the label. She wasn't a wine connoisseur by any means but knew this particular brand of bubbly could run upward of five hundred dollars a pop. The realization she was sipping something that cost as much or more than her gown generated a prickly sensation.

She'd started out feeling like Cinderella, but all the money being thrown around tonight brought home just how far out of her league these people were. Until the lights dimmed, that is, and Alex stretched his arm across the back of her chair.

The smooth satin of his sleeve pressed against her bare shoulders. She leaned into its warmth, felt the muscle beneath the cloth. Relaxing, she gave herself up to the music of Frankie Valli and the Four Seasons.

The rags-to-riches story of four blue-collar toughs who climbed their way from the back streets of Newark, New Jersey, to glittering stardom enthralled her and the rest of the audience. So much so that Julie's hands hurt from applauding long and loud after each of the songs in the first act. When she mentioned the sting to Alex when they stretched their legs during the intermission, he lifted first one palm, then the other, for a kiss.

"All better?"

"Much," she murmured, all too conscious of Delilah's narrow-eyed stare.

It wasn't Alex's mother who approached when he made a trip to the men's room, however, but Barbara Hale. The attorney wore a smile that didn't quite reach her eyes.

"I'm sorry we didn't get to chat longer at the fund-raiser," she commented in her throaty drawl.

Suuuuure, she was.

"Have you and Alex known each other long?" the lawyer asked with a lift of one delicately penciled brow.

There were two ways Julie could go here. Return a vague answer or go with the truth. She opted for the one she suspected would get the most rise.

"We met last year."

"I see."

Julie just bet she did. She could almost see Hale counting backward.

"So you're in the baby stakes, too," the lawyer said, the gloves off now. "The front-runner, judging by the interchange I just witnessed between you and Alex."

"I really don't think that's any of your business."

"Oh, but I beg to differ. Alex and I had quite a thing going before this mess with Molly hit."

"Mess?"

Hale realized her slip and made a swift mid-course correction. "Certainly it's a mess. Just the legalities involved in obtaining legal parental custody could tie the Daltons up in court for months, if not years. Unless," she added after a deliberate pause, "they induce the mother to relinquish all legal rights."

"Induce being another term for bribe, buy or flat out extort?" Julie drawled.

She realized too late she'd left herself open to a swift jab. Hale wasted no time landing it.

"We both know there are all kinds of inducements in addition to money. Being wined and dined and made love to by someone who's very, very good at it, for example. A combination of all the above would be almost impossible to resist, wouldn't it?"

Julie'd had enough. Shrugging, she turned the barb back on the slinger. "For you, maybe."

Hale blinked at the blunt reply but before she could get off another shot the lights dimmed.

"Intermission's over. See you around, counselor."

With a cool nod, Julie walked away. Some of her irritation must have seeped through, though, as Alex looked a question at her when she joined him at the ramp to their box.

"I saw you talking to Barbara."

"She talked, I mostly listened."

"Hmmm." He cocked a brow. "I'm getting a sense there's a problem."

"If there is, it's nothing I can't handle."

She spent the second act trying to convince herself of that. Unfortunately, Hale's nasty insinuations held more than a grain of truth.

While Frankie and the boys belted out "Big Girls Don't Cry", Julie mulled over the fact that Alex *had* offered monetary inducement in the form of an extremely lucrative business deal. And he *had* wined and dined and made very, very skillful love to her. None of which would make the least difference in a parental custody suit, however, since Julie had no claim, parental or otherwise, on Molly.

Unless…

Good grief! Was she coming at this from the wrong end? Had the Daltons given up on finding Molly's real mother and decided to go with a substitute?

The wild thought sent Julie's emotions ping-ponging all over the damned auditorium. So many came at her from different directions she had trouble distinguishing righteous indignation from flat-out dismissal to the niggling little voice that whispered so what if she *was* a stand-in?

In one fell swoop she would gain a husband and daughter. A brother-in-law, which was good. A mother-in-law, not so good. A whole passel of folks besides Dusty and Chuck to care and worry and fuss over. Folks who would fuss over *her* for a change. The sticking point was Alex, of course. Would she marry him just to acquire a ready-made family?

The absurdity of that hit her at the same time Frankie's falsetto baritone slid up almost three octaves to hit the opening notes of "Sherry".

She and Alex weren't anywhere close to thinking exclusive, let alone permanent. Were they?

* * *

Delilah appeared to have the same question on her mind when she cornered Julie after the performance. They were standing on the steps of Civic Center, waiting while Alex and Blake summoned their separate vehicles. Night had blanketed the city in soft heat and bright lights. Ignoring the summer nightscape, Delilah pinned Julie with one of her penetrating stares.

"What are you doing tomorrow morning?"

"I haven't firmed up my plans."

"It's Saturday. Alex and Blake have a standing eight o'clock tee time at the Country Club whenever one or both of them are in town."

"Alex hasn't mentioned golf."

Or anything else at this point.

"Do you play?" Delilah wanted to know.

Like she had time to whack little white balls for three or four hours on Saturday mornings? She spent most of her weekends working on the Pawnee or mixing chemicals for the following week's runs.

"No, I don't."

"Good. You can spend the morning with Molly and me."

"I, uh…"

Delilah rode roughshod over her half-formed objection.

"We'll go to the zoo. We need to go early, though, before it gets too hot."

"Why don't I check with Alex and…"

"Alex is why I want some face time with you. Him and Molly."

Ooooh, boy! Julie couldn't think of anything she'd rather do than spend the morning at the ape house being grilled by Delilah.

"We'll pick you up at eight-thirty."

"I'll get you out of it," Alex promised when she informed him of the command performance.

They were in the limo, following a stream of red taillights through the city streets. Julie surprised herself as much as him by shaking her head.

"No, I need to go. It's time *someone* set your mother straight."

"Good luck with that," Alex said, laughing.

"I'm serious! We can't let her go on thinking there's a chance that I'm, ah…" She threw a glance at the driver and ended with an indistinct, "You know."

"When you know Delilah better, you'll discover she's going to think what she wants to. Period. End of story."

"C'mon, Alex! You're almost as bad as Blake when you talk about your mother. She can't be that intransigent."

"Want to bet?"

She might have argued the point further if he hadn't entwined his fingers in hers and lifted her hand to brush a kiss across her knuckles.

"Go one-on-one with the tigress tomorrow if you want. I've got something else in mind for you tonight."

Thrills shooting up her spine, Julie banished all thoughts of the mother and gave the son her full, undivided attention.

Eleven

A storm rumbled through during the night. As a result Saturday morning dawned bright and relatively cool. Still, Julie slathered on sunscreen and poked her hair through the back opening of a ball cap to get it off her neck. Loose and comfortable in cargo shorts and a short-sleeved T-shirt, she pushed through the glass door to the Dalton International building just as Delilah pulled up in a gleaming, cherry red Cadillac SUV.

Delilah popped the door lock and Julie slid into the passenger seat, blinking a little at the driver's accoutrements. Delilah wore crops, a sleeveless linen overblouse, wide bangle bracelets and sandals—all in eye-popping lemon accented with a profusion of daisies. Even the bright yellow diaper bag propped against the center console sported a field of flowers.

"Morning," Julie got out, blinking a little at the sartorial splendor.

Delilah returned a noncommittal grunt and took a swig from the travel mug she plucked from its holder.

Refusing to let the less than enthusiastic reply daunt her, Julie twisted to smile at the baby strapped into a rear seat carrier. Daisies adorned Molly, too, from her little floppy brimmed hat to her cloth sandals, one of which she'd kicked off so she could play with her foot.

"Hello, Mol."

The baby was busy with her toes but paused long enough to gurgle. Or maybe that was a burp. Hard to tell, but the gummy smile that accompanied the sound tugged at Julie's heart as she faced front and snapped her seat belt in place.

"So Grace isn't joining us?"

She made the observation casually, more as an ice breaker than anything else. Unfortunately, Delilah took instant exception to it.

"I'm fully capable of tending my granddaughter for a few hours without assistance."

Julie thought back to how Alex and Blake had conspired not to leave Delilah alone with Molly on Grace's day off, but decided discretion was the better part of valor. She couldn't quite keep the tartness out of her reply, though.

"Ooh-kay."

Delilah shot her a quick look. "You tryin' to be smart with me, girl?"

"I wouldn't say I'm trying."

The response elicited a huff of something that could have been smothered laughter. Flicking a glance at the rear and side view mirrors, Delilah pulled away from the curb.

"I'm not spoiling for a fight," she informed Julie.

"Good to know." She paused while Delilah negotiated a double row of orange barrels. "What *are* you spoiling for, exactly?"

"I told you last night. I want to talk to you about Alex. But let's wait 'til we get to the zoo and I'm not having to run an obstacle course."

Once clear of the downtown construction, it took only fifteen minutes to reach the sprawling hundred-acre Oklahoma City Zoo and Botanical Garden complex. Julie had visited the state's number one tourist attraction a number of times, either with her parents or on school field trips. This was the first time she'd made an entrance with one of the zoo's most generous benefactors, however.

The bronze "Donor Honor Roll" plaque mounted just inside the entrance attested to Dalton International's financial contributions. The effusive welcome Delilah received from both staff and volunteers suggested her interest was personal as well as financial—an impression Delilah confirmed when she steered Molly's stroller to the palatial new elephant habitat.

"Look at this," she exulted. "Nine and a half acres and the best facilities anywhere in the country!"

Their elevated viewing spot overlooked a sweeping vista of jungle, grassland and watering holes. In the hole directly below them, a shaggy pachyderm trumpeted ecstatically, snarfed up a trunkful of water, and threw spray over his back at the caretaker scrubbing his—her?—hindquarters with a long-handled brush.

"Did you help build all this?" Julie asked, as goggle-eyed as Molly at their proximity to the giant Asian grey.

"I'm on the fund-raising committee. We're at thirteen million and counting," she added with smug satisfaction.

Julie might not like the woman very much but had to admire her active involvement in her community. And, she conceded reluctantly when Delilah steered them to a tree-shaded bench, her mother's right to meddle in her sons' affairs.

Popping the seatbelt on the stroller, Delilah lifted out a squirming Molly. "Here, hold her while I fish out a bottle."

The baby fit perfectly in the crook of Julie's arm. Her still pale blue eyes peered up from under the brim of her daisy hat solemnly until Delilah produced a bottle from a cool pack inside the diaper bag. Fists waving, Molly demanded instant gratification.

Delilah passed Julie the bottle and waited until she had Molly sucking greedily before launching her attack.

"You and Alex sleeping together?"

Julie whipped her gaze from the baby's pursed, rosebud mouth and locked on Delilah.

"Yes."

"I thought so."

Her scowl suggested she wasn't particularly thrilled to have her suspicions confirmed.

"He's got more than just a bad case of the hots for you, you know."

Startled, Julie looked from her to the baby and back again. "No, I don't know. We, uh, haven't gotten around to dissecting our feelings for each other."

"Dissect 'em now. You just scratching an itch with Alex, or is it more serious?"

Well, she couldn't say she hadn't been warned. It was on the tip of her tongue to tell the woman to butt the hell out when Delilah preempted her.

"Don't get all hot and bothered with me, Julie. I love my son. I don't want anyone stomping on his heart."

"We're not to the stomping point, Delilah."

"You sure about that? I saw him getting kissy-eyed with you at the Civic Center last night. He never made that kind of public display with any of the women I've pushed at him these past couple of years."

"Probably *because* you pushed them at him."

"Probably," Delilah conceded grudgingly. "It's just…"

She paused while Julie hitched Molly a little higher in her arm.

"It's just I'm not getting any younger. I want to see Alex settled down. Alex and Blake both. With the right women."

The pointed addendum had Julie bristling again.

"I'm not sure how you define 'right', but I'll tell you this.

Whatever's between Alex and me has nothing to do with you. Or with Molly."

She glanced down at the child in her arms, and her heart gave a little lurch.

"Sorry, kiddo," she said softly. "I'm not your momma."

When she lifted her gaze and repeated that emphatically, Delilah flapped a wrist loaded with plastic yellow bangles.

"Oh, hell, I know that. I sent the water glass you used at brunch that first morning for DNA analysis. Shelled out big bucks to get the results the next day."

Julie's jaw dropped. Snapped shut. She had to wait until she could trust herself to utter something other than four-letter words to reply, however.

"You didn't have to shell out *any* bucks. I gave Alex a DNA sample the second night I was here. It's not my fault he chose not to tell you."

"Doesn't matter." The bangles flapped again. "A mother does whatever she considers necessary to protect her off-spring. Which brings us back to you and Alex."

"Delilah…"

Ignoring the irritated growl, the older woman gestured to Molly. "She needs burping."

She dove into the diaper bag, produced a folded pad, draped it over Julie's shoulder, and waited only until the baby was positioned and being patted to pick up where she'd left off.

"When I said I wanted my sons to settle down with the right women, I wasn't throwing stones at you. I was think-ing of what you do for a living."

Julie's hand paused in mid-pat. "How does that factor into the equation?"

"I'm Oklahoma born and bred, girl. I've been around enough crop dusters to know it's a dangerous occupation."

"Probably as dangerous as wrestling pipe with two small boys hanging on your arm," Julie retorted.

A satisfying belch put a temporary halt to their skirmish.

Hostilities resumed as soon as Molly was tucked back in Julie's arms, sucking happily.

"Big Jake and I did what we had to do to keep food on our table," Delilah argued. "If you and Alex connect, you sure certainly don't have to worry about where your next meal's coming from."

"I don't worry about that now!"

"No need to get huffy. I'm just telling it like it is."

Julie shook her head in mingled amazement and exasperation. "You're a piece of work, lady. A real piece of work."

Delilah brushed that aside as irrelevant and pressed ahead. "Alex told me how you took to the air in the Lane 602. Said you fly like you were born with wings. He also said his heart damned near stopped when you did wheelies in the sky."

"I'm a good pilot," Julie retorted, stung.

"Didn't say you weren't. But you and I both know it's not just the flying that makes what you do so dangerous. It's also breathing those chemicals day in and day out."

Julie bit back a hot retort. She could counter that she took every safety precaution in the book when she mixed fertilizers and pesticides—long-sleeved shirts, pants, boots, goggles, rubber gloves. Even a mask for her mouth and nose when she worked with particularly toxic liquids. But she couldn't deny that the risk was always there. One spill, one splash, one deep, unprotected breath could sear skin, eyes or lungs. Mouth clamped shut, she returned Delilah's unwavering stare.

"Have you thought about the effect those chemicals could have on your baby if you get pregnant?"

"Of course I've thought about it." Biting her lower lip, Julie let her glance drift to Molly's industriously working cheeks. "I'm not pregnant."

"Not now, maybe. But you want children someday, don't you?"

The answer came slowly, honestly. "Yes."

"Alex's children?"

"Christ, Delilah, don't you ever give up?!"

"No. You want Alex's children or don't you?"

"Okay! All right! Maybe I do. Someday."

Actually, she wanted *Alex*, pretty much any way she could get him. She looked up to find his mother watching her with a hawk's intensity.

"So it boils down to a simple question, Julie. Can you give up a career you obviously love to marry my son?"

Silence stretched out between them, broken only by Molly's contented slurping and the high-pitched bleat of an elephant calf calling for its mother. Julie considered long and hard before answering as truthfully as she could.

"Alex and I aren't anywhere near talking about marriage, but I promise you this. If we do reach that point, I'll think hard about what you and I just talked about."

"That's good enough for me."

To her astonishment, Delilah reached out and covered her hand.

"And I have to say, girl. My son would be damned lucky to have you."

Julie was still dealing with the shock of that pronouncement when Alex delivered another later that evening.

They'd joined Blake and Grace for dinner at Delilah's mansion. When they arrived at the Nichols Hills address, the ever-stately Louis informed them Miss Molly was already fed, bathed and asleep.

"Madam is waiting for you on the terrace," he added

Madam greeted her son with her usual brisk affection and Julie with noticeably less hostility. Alex and Blake noticed the altered atmosphere with obvious surprise. Grace merely smiled and asked how Julie had enjoyed her morning at the zoo.

"It was...interesting."

"I can imagine."

Delilah ignored the provocative remark and enlivened a

succulent meal of veal *roulade* served over egg noodles with a running recital of her twins' youthful exploits. The outrageous tales left the two women giggling helplessly and her sons pleading with her to stop, already.

When Julie said her good-nights after a surprisingly enjoyable evening, she saw Delilah slip something into Alex's pocket. That something, she discovered after he'd accompanied her back to the guest suite, was a small, square box. He waited until she'd tossed her purse on the living room coffee table to dig it out of his pocket.

"What is this?" she asked warily.

"Open it and see."

When she popped the lid, she gulped and stared for long moments in disbelief before she could wrench her gaze from the Inca sun god.

"Please tell me you didn't buy this for me!"

"Well…"

"Alex!"

Her mind scrambling, she tried to remember the last bid she'd seen on the piece. Almost twenty-five thousand, if she remembered correctly.

"I can't accept this!"

"Sure you can."

"This is an artifact. It belongs in a museum."

"So donate it to one of your choice."

With a smile that turned her knees to sludge, he lifted the gold amulet from its nest.

"I like the legend behind… What's this guy's name again?"

"Viracocha," she said weakly.

"I like the legend behind Viracocha." He angled her shoulders and fastened the amulet's black silk cord at her nape. "Didn't you say the Inca believed he created the sun and the moon and the stars?"

Hypnotized by the reflection thrown back by the night-darkened floor-to-ceiling windows, all she could manage was a distracted nod.

"At the risk of sounding like a complete ass," Alex murmured as he bent to nuzzle her neck, "I'm getting an inkling of what Viracocha must have felt when the stars emerged from darkness."

He turned her in his arms, and Julie's heart revved up to a couple of thousand beats a minute.

"Is it too soon to tell you I love you?"

Her throat closed. Her nails dug into her palms. Without much success, she fought to steady her wildly careening pulse.

"Not…"

The hoarse croak got stuck halfway out. She licked her lips and tried again.

"Not from where I stand."

"Good. Now let's see how it looks from a different angle."

They transitioned from vertical to horizontal with minimum fuss and maximum speed. Julie didn't even try to hold back her response to his taste and touch. She was just as voracious as Alex was, every bit as greedy. When he shoved a knee between hers, she wrapped eager fingers around his hot, pulsing erection.

The scent of him, the feel of him was so strong and so tantalizing she almost came at his first thrust. Teeth clenched, she fought against the rapidly increasing swirls of sensation as long as she could. When they built to a furious crescendo, she locked her legs around his thighs and rocked into him.

"Now, Alex. Now, now, now!"

He slammed into her, muscles cording, hips thrusting. With a raw, throat-closing groan, Julie rode the torrent of sensation. Her legs tightened around his thighs. Her nails dug into his back. She gasped out his name—a long, drawn out moan that twisted into a cry.

Vaguely, she heard his grunted response. Her mind spinning, she felt every muscle and tendon in his body lock. A heartbeat later, she shuddered on a wild tide of ecstasy. Moments, or maybe hours, later he poured into her.

A slow, delicious descent followed. A numbed corner of her mind registered the chest crushing hers. The moisture trapped between their bodies. The tang of sweat and musky scent of their lovemaking filled her nostrils.

Breathing in both, she lay in mindless lethargy until the creak of bedsprings and a sudden loss of body heat prodded her into semi-consciousness. She pried up an eyelid to find Alex—beautiful, studly, sweat-sheened Alex—propped on one elbow.

"Do you have any idea how you look wearing nothing but a gold amulet and a smile?" he said roughly.

"Tell me."

"Wild and pagan and *very, very* kissable."

To prove his point, he buried both hands in her hair and planted a *very, very* satisfactory kiss on her willing mouth. When he lifted his head, the lazy smile faded from his eyes.

"I meant what I said, sweetheart. I love you."

His words produced pretty much the same slam Julie had experienced when she'd thrown the 602 into a hammerhead yesterday morning. Her heart thudding, she slicked her tongue over suddenly dry lips.

"I love you, too. But…"

The hands buried in her hair tightened. "But?"

"Your mother and I had a long talk this morning, Alex."

Grimacing, he rolled onto his back and brought her with him. "I knew the sudden thaw between you two was too good to be true."

"She said…" Julie hesitated, knowing how much rode on the next few moments. "She said you mentioned being nervous about some of my maneuvers yesterday morning."

"Nervous, hell. You scared the crap out of me."

"Flying is what I do. What I am."

"I know that."

She framed his face with her palms. The day's growth of bristles tickled her palms. The dead seriousness in his eyes matched hers.

"Can you live with me going up every day?"

"I guess I'll have to," he said slowly. "Until you decide there's something more important you'd rather do."

Her breath hissed in. "Like playing Mrs. Alex Dalton and representing DI on the board of a half dozen charitable foundations?"

"Like taking over DI's air operations," he countered with a small crease between his brows. "Overseeing its soon-to-be-launched aero-agricultural division."

Overseeing, Julie echoed silently. Not doing. The women in his sophisticated world didn't get down and dirty. No sweat stinging their eyes as they wrestled with a frozen crankshaft. No grease in their hair or under their nails. The prospect of sitting on the sidelines for the rest of her life put a tight knot in her belly.

Alex caught the shift of emotions in her eyes, felt her withdrawal like a hard right to the jaw. He rolled with the blow, but a stubborn part of him wanted to ask why the future he offered wasn't enough. Why *he* wasn't enough.

And Molly! God, what about Molly? The way things stood now, they might never positively ID her mother. But the odds pointed seventy-thirty to Alex as her father. He was ready, more than ready, to go with those odds. Almost as ready as he was to put his brand on the woman staring up at him with her seductive, changeable eyes. Masking his fierce determination, he smoothed back her tangle of auburn hair.

"We don't have to decide all this right now. Just wear Viracocha for a few days. Let him, uh, shine his light," he finished with a sheepish grin.

Julie groaned. "That is *so* bad."

"Best I can do when you're all naked and sweaty," Alex returned, getting hard and hot again.

He eased out of bed the next morning while Julie sprawled in naked abandon, arms and legs flung out at ninety-degree angles. Her hair spilled across her pillow. The covers were tangled around her hips. Her soft, breathy snuffles told Alex she'd be out for a while yet.

He jotted a quick note saying he would return with breakfast and propped it on the bureau, leaning against the sun god's velvet box. He made a quick stop at his penthouse condo to shower and shave before walking the few blocks to Cecile's. Once there, he skimmed the chalked breakfast menu and reached for his cell phone to wake Julie and ask whether she preferred quiche or crepes.

"Great," he muttered when he discovered he'd left the phone at his condo. "Guess I'll have to choose for both of us."

He departed the bistro with two, lighter-than-air quiches and carry-out coffee containers brimming with rich, dark French blend. Anticipation thrummed in his veins as he let himself into the guest suite.

Silence greeted him, and emptiness. The purse Julie had tossed on the living room coffee table last night was gone. A half-downed cup of coffee sat on the counter of the kitchenette.

"Julie?"

The silence followed him into the bedroom. The tangled covers were thrown back. The open closet doors showed a row of bare hangars. Shoulders tensing, Alex spotted his note still propped on the bureau. Below his few lines was what looked like a hastily scribbled addendum.

Dusty called, he needs me.

Tried to reach you, couldn't.

I'll get back to you whenever.

Whenever? He appreciated Julie's loyalty to her partner,

sensed the urgency implied in her note, but whenever? The vague half promise, half brush-off stung.

Jaw-locked, he popped up the lid of the square box. Viracocha lay nested on his black velvet bed, raining tears of gold.

Twelve

Julie sped west on I-40, replaying Dusty's brief, garbled transmission over and over in her mind. He was in the Texas Panhandle. Some little town she'd never heard of. Floating in and out 'cause of the drugs they'd pumped into him.

They *who?*

She'd screeched the question twice, trying to pierce his drugged haze while a mental image materialized of two cement-jawed thugs sent to beat or otherwise extract retribution for unpaid gambling debts. The image disintegrated when Dusty mumbled something about swerving to avoid a mule deer. When that was followed by a slurred request for her to come spring him from this cussed hospital, Julie had kicked off the covers and grabbed her clothes.

As the miles whirred under her pickup's tires, she cursed Chuck Whitestone's stubborn refusal to let Agro-Air spring for a mobile phone. The mechanic was closer to the Panhandle, and could have gotten to Dusty faster. She'd briefly considered a quick detour to rev up the Pawnee, but she couldn't haul Dusty home in a single-seater if she got him released from the hospital as he'd begged.

Keeping a hand on the wheel and an eye on the endless stretch of highway rolling out ahead, she flipped up her cell phone and thumbed in Alex's number. Her thumb stilled in mid-jab. The blank screen said she had no service out here in the wide-open spaces.

Correction. She had no power. The solid red battery icon in the upper corner told her the damned thing was completely drained. And of course she didn't have her charger with her. It was back at the hangar, probably still plugged into the wall outlet after her last hurried charge.

With another curse, Julie tossed the phone onto the pick-up's dash and concentrated on the hundred and fifty miles of highway ahead.

She hit the Texas state line a little before 10 a.m. With her phone's MapQuest function as dead as the instrument itself, she had to pull into the Welcome Center for a map. The rectangular-shaped center sloped upward from an elevated berm, looking like a WWII bunker plunked down in the middle of nowhere. The place was crowded with weekend travelers going to or returning from summer vacations. Julie darted to the head of the line and snatched a Texas state map from the counter. After a quick pit stop she wrestled a cup of coffee from a bank of vending machines and hit the pay phone to dial Alex's number. He answered this time, thank goodness!

"Where are you?"

"In Texas. Dusty's been hurt. A car accident, I think. His message was kind of slurred."

"Why didn't you wait for me? I would've come with you."

"I didn't know how long you'd be."

It was a feeble excuse. Julie recognized that as soon as it came out of her mouth. The truth was that she'd learned to take care of herself—and her personal affairs—swiftly and independently. Charging to Dusty's side was a case in point. She'd rushed out of Oklahoma City fully prepared to provide whatever care or assistance he needed. It hadn't even occurred to her to do more than advise Alex of the situation.

He didn't seem all that pleased with her unilateral action. She could sense his irritation at being shut out. Sense him putting it aside, too, to offer help.

"I'm here if you need me, Julie. You or Dusty."

"I know. Thanks."

Taking her coffee with her, she climbed back into her pickup, and unfolded the map.

"Where the hell are you, Rockslide?"

She finally found the tiny dot in the northwest corner of the Texas Panhandle, less than a spit and a lick from the New Mexico state line. Groaning, she saw the only access was a county road that snaked like an angry diamondback around deep gulches and high mesas.

"What in God's name are you doing in Rockslide?" she asked her absent partner.

Resigned to a tortuous drive, she keyed the ignition and followed I-40 to Amarillo. A half hour after passing a twenty-foot Texan who offered a free six-pound steak to anyone who could gobble it down in less than an hour, she cut north Dalhart on 385. Ten miles out of Dalhart she turned onto the two-lane county road. Mere moments later, the high desert surrounded her.

Red-rock mesas carved by centuries of eroding winds thrust out of the sun-scorched earth. Tumbleweeds skittered across the road. Longhorn cattle grazed on God knew what or clustered around corrugated tin water tanks filled by rusted windmills turning lazily in the breeze. If she hadn't been so worried about Dusty, Julie might have enjoyed the starkly beautiful scenery.

Instead, she was a living, breathing bundle of nerves when she rolled into the cluster of ten or twelve adobe structures otherwise known as Rockslide, Texas. Slowing to a halt on the one road in and out of town, she hooked her wrists over the steering wheel.

"This place has a hospital?" she murmured in disbelief.

It didn't, as she learned during a stop at the town's quick-shop/feed-and-grain store. Apparently the only person with medical credentials within a fifty-mile radius was a retired-vet-turned-rancher the locals called in emergencies.

"I'm still licensed to practice," Dr. Hightower said with a shrug. "Comes in handy on occasion."

Julie could understand why. Out in these parts, the grizzled, gray-haired vet might well make the difference between life and death for two-and four-legged accident victims alike.

Dusty was a case in point.

"Damn fool crashed head-on into a stand of mesquite to avoid hitting a deer," Dr. Hightower advised as she led the way from her living quarters to the surgery. "I got him stabilized, kept a close eye on him until EMSA got here. They patched him up and wanted to haul him to the hospital down to Dalhart. He kicked up a fuss, said he didn't have insurance…"

"He does," Julie countered, her throat tight. "Our company policy covers personal injuries. The deductible's pretty hefty, though."

"Guess he didn't want to run that up. EMSA left him pretty sedated, and I kept him that way. He didn't know who or where he was for days after it happened."

"Will he…?"

She fought back a thick gob of fear. Dusty was the closest thing she had to family. Dusty and Chuck. Their lackadaisical approach to the business end of flying irritated the heck out of her at times. And Dusty's penchant for gambling raised a tight knot of worry. Yet her heart stuck halfway down her throat as she voiced the fear that had haunted her all the way from Oklahoma City.

"Will he be okay?"

"Should be. He's been in and out since it happened,

though. Don't be surprised if he doesn't recognize you," the vet cautioned.

After that dire warning, Julie sagged with relief when Dr. Hightower pushed through a door marked "Private" and a bandaged Dusty opened one bruiser of a black eye to glare at her.

"'Bout time you got here."

"I... I..."

Her throat closing, Julie astonished herself, the vet and her partner by bursting into loud, noisy sobs.

"Missy! I'm okay. Jest got a few busted ribs."

"And an ulna fractured in two places," Hightower put in, nodding to the plaster encasing his right arm.

"Not a problem. You got...me all fixed up, Doc." Punctuating his sentences with grunts and grimaces, Dusty pushed himself upright. "Soon's as Julie, uh, gets me home, I'll be right 'n—gol dang it!—tight."

The white lines that bracketed his mouth said just the opposite. Aching for him, Julie turned to the vet.

"Can he be moved?"

"Lord, yes! The sooner you get him out of my hair, the better. I'll send some horse pills with him for the pain. He swallows one of those, and he's out for the count."

With that dubious assurance, Julie helped the vet transfer her wobbly partner to a wheelchair.

She contacted Alex again after stopping for gas and purchasing another phone charger. His first query concerned Dusty's condition. His second, what her partner was doing in the Texas Panhandle.

"He got a call from a soybean consortium that wanted a bid on a job," she answered with a glance at her slumbering passenger. He had the seat tilted back and was filling the pickup's cab with heroic snores. "He couldn't fly the Pawnee, so he took his truck."

"Why couldn't he fly the Pawnee?"

"It's leaking oil again."

Concern sharpened Alex's voice. "You're not thinking about taking it up, are you?"

"Sure, when Chuck and I get it fixed."

"I'll send DI's chief mechanic down," he responded, all brisk executive. "Let him look at the engine, see if it needs a major overhaul."

"Whoa! Back off there, Bubba. Agro-Air's chief mechanic and I are perfectly capable of deciding what, if anything, needs overhauling on our aircraft."

Silence answered her swift retort, followed a moment later by a careful reply.

"You better re-read those contracts, Julie. When Agro-Air merges with DI's aeronautical operations division, I'll have final decision-making authority on major issues. Safety ranks number one in my book."

The sheer arrogance of it took her breath away. She forced herself to count to ten, then ten again, but still ground out her response.

"Safety is number one at Agro-Air, too. And you can bet your bippy I'll re-read those contracts. They're not signed yet, Dalton."

Alex hung up, feeling every bit as steamed as Julie had sounded. He'd mishandled her, dammit. Mishandled the whole conversation. He could see that now. His only excuse was that he wasn't used to having his decisions challenged. Especially by the woman he now wanted standing beside him as a whole helluva lot more than a business partner.

He tried to shrug off her last, ominous threat. Refused to believe she would convince her partners to back out of a merger that would take Agro-Air out of the red for the first time in a long time. But she was just stubborn enough, just independent enough to buck any attempt to exercise corporate oversight.

Tough! Signed contracts or not, she wasn't getting out of this deal.

Jaw tight, Alex glared at the phone. A handshake was as good as a signature in Oklahoma courts. DI had already expended a good number of engineering hours in Agro-Air's interest. He'd also had the 602 flown in at considerable expense and agreed to its purchase. All with Julie's tacit consent and approval.

Then there was the matter of the unsigned, unspoken contract between the two of them personally. Alex was damned if he'd let her back out of that, either. The woman had all but turned him inside out. No way he intended to just sit back and wait for her to "get back to him whenever."

Ms. Bartlett might not realize it yet, but she'd run smack up against a will even more intractable than her own. She was his, Alex thought with a fierce, primal possessiveness that surprised but didn't daunt him. Now all he had to do was convince her.

He'd give her time to sort through this situation with Dusty, he decided. Let her cool off after their unexpected flare-up. Then he'd yank whatever chain he had to get her back in his arms.

Who the hell did he think he was?

The terse conversation left Julie simmering for most of the way back to Dusty's place. If Alex Dalton thought he could override her need to go with her gut in the air—or on the ground!—he had another think coming.

Thoroughly ticked, she speared a glance at her snoring partner. The sight of his cast forced her to apply the air brakes to her temper.

If she'd been the only one at the other end of the DI-AA deal, she would have told Alex to stuff it. But she wasn't. Dusty and Chuck needed her more than ever now. Like it or not, she'd have to throttle back. Professionally, anyway.

Personally...

She'd have to throttle back there, too. Alex Dalton had more than he realized of his overbearing, overpowering mother in him. Only now that Julie had put some distance between herself and his charismatic personality did she see how close she'd come to letting it dominate her. Her! The same woman who could hold her own in the air or on the ground in any country in the northern *or* southern hemisphere.

The thought of pulling away from Alex carved a hole in the pit of her stomach but she had to face facts. Maybe love wasn't enough. Maybe neither one of them could blunt or shape or otherwise alter the basic character traits that made them who they were.

That gut-wrenching thought stayed with her in the days that followed. She spent a good part of those days force-feeding Dusty horse pills and the spicy tacos both he and his obese feline were addicted to.

In between, she and Chuck got the Pawnee airworthy again—which she relayed to Alex in a terse voice mail. Good thing, too, as word that Dalton International was folding Agro-Air into its corporate family had spread. Customers who'd shied away from a one-plane, shoestring operation the previous planting season now came knocking. Job offers poured in.

With Dusty out of commission, Julie had to take up the slack. She was in the air from dawn to late summer dusk. At the end of each grueling, sixteen-hour day, she crawled out the Pawnee's cockpit and barely made it to her apartment before falling face first onto the bed.

Even then she couldn't sleep. All she had to do was close her eyes and she could see Alex, almost hear his breath pacing hers in the stillness of the night. Over and over she tried to reconcile the ways they differed with the irrefutable fact that she ached for him. But could she change the woman she was to become the wife he wanted?

It didn't help that they continued to play an irritating game of telephone tag. She finally got through to him on Thursday morning. She had just come down from an early run. Dusty sat ensconced in a folding lawn chair with Belinda draped across his lap and his arm in a sling, grumbling nonstop about being so useless while Chuck refueled the Pawnee and reloaded its hopper.

A near exhausted Julie tuned out both partners. Grasping a can of Boost energy drink in one hand, she dialed Alex's private number with the other. His executive assistant chirped an acknowledgment.

"Ms. Bartlett! Mr. Dalton is anxious to speak to you. He's in a closed door meeting with Ms. Hale at the moment, but he left instructions to put you through whenever you called."

Julie couldn't help herself. She had to ask. "Ms. Hale?"

"Barbara Hale. She's an attorney here in Oklahoma City. Hang on, I'll connect…"

"Wait!"

A swift, mental image seemed to magnify tenfold the doubts she'd been playing with. She could picture the sleek, sophisticated Barbara with her dark head bent close to his. Hear again the lawyer's unsubtle reference to their previous, intimate relationship.

If Molly hadn't dropped into his life…

If Julie hadn't surged to the top of his list of possible mothers…

The ache she'd carried around for the past few days became a sharp, lancing pain. Molly. Sweet, bubbly Molly.

Oh, God! She was too tired to deal with this right now!

"Don't interrupt him," she said sharply.

"But…"

"I'm getting ready to go back up. Tell him I'll call him later."

"But…"

She snapped the phone shut, cutting the woman off in mid-protest, and tried to convince herself she'd done the right thing. Dusty and Agro-Air needed her. Whether or not the merger with DI went through, whether or not she and Alex worked out their personal stalemate, she couldn't leave her partners in the lurch. It would be weeks, maybe months, before Dusty was well enough to fly again. In the meantime…

The phone was still in her palm when it gave an insistent tweet. She stared at it, jaw tight, and let it ring. When it finally went to voice mail, she looked up to find Dusty and Belinda regarding her with identical, unwinking stares.

"Something happen between you and Dalton you want to tell me about, Missy?"

"No."

The curt reply raised his brows. "Well, something's sure got your tail feathers in a twist. If it's not Dalton, what is it?"

The empty Boost can crumpled in Julie's fist. She sent it arcing into the old oil drum that served as their recycling bin. The loud rattle when it hit made Belinda hiss and Dusty stare.

"Look," he said with a furrow between his bushy white brows, "if you're worrying 'bout that bill from EMSA, don't. We'll get it paid. Same for the new load of fuel we just had delivered. When the merger with DI goes through, we'll have more contracts than we kin handle."

Swallowing a sigh, Julie scrubbed a hand across her sweat-streaked forehead. They needed to talk about the contracts. Later. When she wasn't hot and grimy and nursing the mental image of Alex in a closed door meeting with Barbara Baby. Jaw tight, she yanked her long-sleeved work shirt from the back of the lawn chair.

"I'd better help Chuck with the mix."

Dusty pursed his lips, barely noticing when Belinda rolled over on his lap. He tickled her belly absently until Julie climbed back into the cockpit and taxied out to the grass strip for her third run of the morning. Then he used his good arm to push out of the chair.

* * *

Julie was too experienced a pilot to risk her life and her aircraft to bone-aching weariness. She could feel it pulling at her, though, as she swooped over a just-planted field to lay a wide stream of fertilizer. Although the sun was still well up in the sky, she wouldn't make another run today. Six had maxed her out. Her and the Pawnee both. The plane was putting out almost as much oil as fertilizer.

She checked her gas to make sure she had enough to make it back to base after dumping the last of her load. She did, barely, and came skimming in with the gauge nudging close to empty. Tail bumping on the grass strip, she was taxiing to the hangar when her radio cackled and a voice pierced the static.

"Agro-Air, this is Delta Indigo six-six-niner. I have your strip in sight."

Delta Indigo?

DI!

Julie made the connection at the same moment Dusty acknowledged the transmission.

"Roger six-six-nine. You're cleared to land."

Swinging the Pawnee's tail around, she killed the engine and searched the horizon. A moment later she spotted a bright yellow speck winging through the blue sky. Speechless, she watched the Lane 602 put down in a smooth glide.

She was out of the Pawnee when the 602 rolled up. Still stunned, she waited while Alex shut down, folded back the canopy and climbed out.

Her first wild thought was that he looked as good as she did bad! No oil patches on *his* jeans. No sweat ringing the armpits of *his* shirt. Then all she could see was the cool determination in his eyes when they met hers.

"What are you doing here?" she demanded.

"Dusty called and told me to get my butt in gear. He seems to think we have some personal issues to settle."

She threw a fulminating glance at her partner. Dusty returned it with bland innocence.

"He's right," she admitted reluctantly, scowling as she tried to articulate the doubts that had gnawed at her. "I've had time to think since I got back from Oklahoma City, Alex. Not a lot of time, admittedly, but enough to know I don't fit into your world."

"What world is that?"

"C'mon, Dalton! Don't make this harder than it already is. You have a corporation to run and a child to raise. I have two partners and a business that requires my total concentration for the foreseeable future."

"Wrong."

She blinked at the hard, flat response. "'Scuze me?"

"You have three partners. Make that five, including Blake and Delilah. According to the terms of our contract they..."

"Agro-Air hasn't agreed to the contract yet!"

"Yeah, it has. Your senior partners faxed their concurrence this morning. You're outvoted, Julie."

"What!"

She spun around, eyes blazing, but Alex's next comment preempted her hurt, angry protest.

"They also faxed a blunt recommendation to get my head out of my ass."

He gripped her elbow, brought her back to face him.

"Dusty reminded me—very correctly—that DI's acquiring a helluva a pilot in this merger."

"You got that right," she spit. "And I..."

"Which is why we negotiated an additional clause to the contract."

Her brows snapped together.

"Agro-Air needs another pilot while Dusty's laid up," he continued, his eyes holding hers. "I need a better understanding of what you do. The ins and outs of the business, the tricks of the trade, the risks. So I fly as your back-up for the next few weeks. Learn from you. Trust your instincts. In the process, I hope you'll come to trust mine."

He held out a hand, palm up.

"What do you say? Do we have a deal?"

He was meeting her halfway. More than halfway. Could he actually rein in his take-charge personality? Listen and learn without butting heads?

Could *she?*

Maybe not completely. But she knew in that instant she'd be a dead fool not to try. An offer like this—a man like this!—didn't come around twice in a girl's life.

With a tremulous smile, she laid her hand in his. "We've got a deal."

"Whooeee!" The gleeful cackle erupted from the lawn chair. "When's the wedding?"

"You mean merger?" Julie corrected.

"Hell, Missy, I ain't blind. When's the wedding?"

"I... Uh, we..."

She threw Alex a helpless look. Grinning wickedly, he yanked her into his arms.

"As soon as possible."

The kiss bent her over his arm. When he tilted her upright again, she had to fight for breath.

"Now that we've got that settled," he said, still grinning, "you want to check out the new nozzles we welded on to the 602's dispersal system?"

She nodded, her legs as quivery as her heart, but couldn't get as jazzed about the nozzles as she had just a week ago. Delilah's caution still stuck like a burr in her head.

If she married Alex... Correction, *when* she married Alex, she would have to seriously limit her exposure to fungicides and pesticides. One, she couldn't risk bringing residue home on her clothing that might irritate Molly's tender skin. Two, she didn't need to be breathing even safe levels of toxins if she decided to get pregnant. That would come someday in the future. A year or so down the road. When Dusty was back in the cockpit and Agro-Air was turning a healthy profit.

She hadn't factored in Delilah's single-minded determination to see her sons settled. Within twenty minutes of being apprised of the pending mergers, the matriarch took charge. With a decisive snort she steamrolled any notion of a long engagement. Molly, she declared emphatically, needed a father *and* a mother.

A little more than three weeks later, she pulled off what every newspaper in the state would later gush was Oklahoma's version of a royal wedding.

Thirteen

The wedding of Julie Marie Bartlett and Alexander Dalton made the evening news on every local station. As the reporter for Channel 9 News informed her viewers, Delilah Dalton crowned her many social and philanthropical triumphs with a glittering affair attended by five hundred of her friends, business associates and any Dalton International employee with a yen to wish the bride and groom well.

Cameras panned the scene outside St. Stephen's, showing limos lined up for a full block, and zoomed in on the bride and groom as they emerged from the church. The bride wore a gown by a hot new designer sold exclusively by Oklahoma City boutique owner Helen Jasper, the reporter informed her audience. The square-cut neckline had supposedly been fashioned to showcase the bride's unusual engagement gift—an intricately worked gold medallion representing an Incan god. She carried a bouquet of white gardenias accented with gold lace and was given in marriage by her friend and business partner, Josiah "Dusty" Jones. Ms. Grace Templeton was the bride's maid of honor. Blake Dalton served as his brother's best man.

The scene then cut to the front facade of the Dalton mansion in Nichols Hills, where it was rumored the reception flowed through the first floor and spilled out onto the terraced gardens.

It was no rumor. Blake could verify that. More than four hours after the ceremony several hundred guests still thronged the house and gardens. The dozens of champagne fountains Delilah had ordered set up no doubt contributed to their staying power, as did the constant stream of servers who emerged from the kitchen with loaded silver trays.

Blake leaned against a pillar, taking a short breather while the indefatigable general moved among her troops. Delilah had held Molly all through the ceremony, slipping upstairs just moments before the guests began arriving to put the baby down for a nap. Now the baby was riding her hip again, decked out in a lacy dress the exact melon shade as her grandmother's.

Blake's chest twisted at the sight. He knew it would hit his mother hard when Alex and Julie got back from their honeymoon and set up housekeeping. It would hit him even harder. Although the odds pointed overwhelmingly to Alex as Molly's father, there'd been that niggling doubt, that small chance...

"One down," his brother's amused voice drawled from just behind his shoulder, "one to go."

Shaking off the ache at knowing he would be relegated to the role of uncle, Blake faced his twin.

"She's going to double the pressure on you now," Alex said with something less than sympathy.

"Tell me about it. Sure you didn't propose to Julie just to get Mother off your back?"

His brother's gaze went to a group one terrace below, where his bride made a family tableau with Grace, Delilah and Molly.

"I'm sure."

Another pang hit Blake. This one was too close to envy for comfort. Ashamed, he countered it by stating the obvious.

"Julie's the best thing that ever happened to you, you know."

"Yeah," Alex said softly, "I know."

"Then get your butt down there and…" He broke off, his glance caught by the figure standing half in, half out of the patio doors. "Did you invite Jamison?"

"Our private investigator?" Alex's brow creased. "No. Hell, do you think Delilah invited him?"

"I wouldn't be surprised."

Although…

The PI's rumpled brown suit and apparent reluctance to mingle with the other guests suggested he wasn't there to socialize, an impression he reinforced when he caught sight of Alex and Blake.

He tipped up his chin in an unmistakable signal and faded back inside the house. The brothers stood where they were, prey to sudden disquieting thoughts, before starting for the house. Their mother's imperious voice stopped them.

"Alex! You and Julie only have an hour until your flight. You'd better change out of that monkey suit and get to the airport."

The two brothers looked at each other, sharing the silent communication that had never yet failed them.

"I'll talk to him," Blake said quietly.

Alex trusted his twin implicitly. He knew without being told Blake would advise him if the PI had critical information to impart.

Apparently he didn't. Alex and Julie came back downstairs to a raucous chorus of shouts and well wishes. While Julie tossed her bouquet, Alex searched for his brother. Blake caught his eye over the heads of the crowd and gave a small shake of his head.

Alex nodded and turned to the woman who'd turned his world upside down. Hooking a hand under his bride's elbow, he escorted her to a limo and proceeded to put brother, mother and daughter out of his head.

Julie of the dark red hair and laughing eyes filled every corner of his heart.

* * * * *

THE SHEIK'S VIRGIN
Susan Mallery

One

The island of Lucia-Serrat glittered like an emerald in a bed of sapphires. Phoebe Carson pressed her forehead against the window of the small commuter plane and stared at the lush landscape below. As they circled in preparation for landing, she saw a snow-white beach, a rain forest, a crescent of blue, blue ocean, then a small city perched on a cliff. Her heart pounded in her chest and her ears popped.

The flight attendant announced that it was time to return seat backs and tray tables to their upright positions. What had seemed so strange when her journey had begun was second nature to her now. Phoebe tightened her seat belt and checked her tray table. She'd been too busy staring out the window to bother putting her seat back. She'd wanted to see everything as they approached Lucia-Serrat.

"Just as you promised, Ayanna," she whispered to herself. "So beautiful. Thank you for allowing me to spend this time here."

Phoebe returned her attention to the view out the window.

The ground seemed to rush up to meet them, then she felt the gentle bump of the airplane wheels on the runway. She could see lush trees and bushes, tropical flowers and brightly colored birds. Then the plane turned to taxi toward the terminal and her view of paradise was lost.

Thirty minutes later Phoebe had collected her small suitcase and passed through customs and immigration. The official-looking young man had greeted her, stamped her passport and had asked if she had anything to declare. When she said she did not, he waved her through.

As easy as that, Phoebe thought, tucking her crisp new passport into her handbag.

All around her families greeted each other, while young couples, obviously on their honeymoon, strolled slowly arm in arm. Phoebe felt a little alone, but she refused to be lonely. Not at the beginning of her adventure. She found the courtesy phone and called her hotel. The hotel clerk promised that the driver would arrive to pick her up within fifteen minutes.

Phoebe had started for the glass doors leading out of the airport when a small store window caught her eye. She didn't usually shop very much, but the display drew her. Bottles of French perfume sat in nests of satin. Designer handbags and shoes hung on barely visible wires from the ceiling of the display case. Everything looked beautiful and very expensive, yet she knew there was no harm in looking while she waited for her ride to the hotel.

Phoebe stepped into the coolness of the store and inhaled a cloud of perfume-scented air. Different fragrances blended together perfectly. Although she was intrigued by the bottles on display, the tall, chicly dressed woman behind the counter made her nervous, so she turned in the opposite direction, only to find herself in front of a case of jewelry.

Rings, earrings, bracelets and necklaces appeared to have been casually tossed into the velvet-lined case. Yet Phoebe suspected it took a long time to make everything look so artless. She bent to get a closer look. One of the center diamonds in a cocktail ring was larger than the nail on her little finger. Phoebe figured she could probably live well for a couple of years on what that one piece cost. If this was an example of shopping in Lucia-Serrat, she would restrict hers to looking in windows.

"I think that is too large for you."

The unexpected comment caught her off guard. She straightened immediately, pressing her hand to her chest.

"I was just looking," she said breathlessly. "I didn't touch anything."

A man stood in front of her. While she was tall—nearly five-ten—he was several inches taller. Dark hair had been brushed back from his handsome face. There were tiny lines by the corners of his amazing brown-black eyes, and a hint of a smile teasing at the corners of his mouth. She told herself to look away—that it was rude to stare—but something about his expression, or maybe it was the sculptured lines of his cheekbones and jaw, compelled her.

He looked like a male model in an expensive liquor ad, only a little older. Phoebe instantly felt out of place and foolish. Her dress had cost less than twenty dollars at a discount outlet, and that had been last year, while the man's suit looked really expensive. Not that she had a lot of experience with things like men's suits.

"The bracelet," he said.

She blinked at him. "Excuse me?"

"I thought you were looking at the sapphire bracelet. While it's lovely and the color of the stones matches your eyes, it is too large for your delicate wrist. Several links would have to be removed."

She forced herself to tear her gaze from his face, and looked at the jewelry case. Right in the center was a sapphire bracelet. Oval blue stones surrounded by diamonds. It probably cost more than a beachfront hotel back home in Florida.

"It's very nice," she said politely.

"Ah, you do not like it."

"No. I mean yes, of course I like it. It's beautiful." But wishing after something like that was about as realistic as expecting to buy a 747.

"Perhaps there was something else you were shopping for?"

"No. Just looking."

She risked glancing at him again. There was something about his dark eyes, something almost…kind. Which made no sense. Handsome gentlemen didn't notice women like her. Actually no one noticed women like her. She was too tall, too thin and much too plain. Nor had anyone ever made her stomach flutter as it was doing right now.

"Is this your first visit to Lucia-Serrat?" he asked.

Phoebe thought of the blank pages in her new passport. "It's my first trip anywhere," she confessed. "I'd never been on a plane until this morning." She frowned as she thought about the time zones she'd crossed. "Or maybe it was yesterday. I flew from Miami to New York, then to Bahania, then to here."

He raised one eyebrow. "I see. Forgive me for saying this, but Lucia-Serrat seems an unusual place to begin one's travels. Many people are not familiar with the island. Although it is very beautiful."

"Very," she agreed. "I haven't seen very much. I mean, I just arrived, but I saw it from the plane window. I thought it looked like an emerald. So green and glittering in the middle of the ocean." She inhaled deeply. "It even smells different. Florida is sort of tropical, but nothing like this. Everyone seems so cosmopolitan and sure of themselves. I don't even know what—"

She pressed her lips together and ducked her head. "Sorry," she murmured, wondering if she could have sounded more like a schoolgirl. "I didn't mean to blurt all that out."

"Do not apologize. I am enjoying your enthusiasm."

There was something about the cadence of his speech,

Phoebe thought dreamily. His English was perfect, but had a more formal quality. There was also a trace of an accent, not that she could place it.

He lightly touched her chin, as if requesting she raise her head. The contact was fleeting at best, and yet she felt the impact all the way down to her toes.

"What brings you to my island?" he asked gently.

"You live here?"

"All of my life." He hesitated, then shrugged. "My family has been in residence for over five hundred years. We came for the spices and stayed for the oil."

"Oh, my." That sounded so romantic. "I, um, wanted to visit because of a family member. My great-aunt was born here. She always talked about the island and how she hated to leave. She passed away a few months ago." Some of Phoebe's happiness bled away as a pang of loneliness shot through her. "She wanted me to see the world, but it was her request that I begin here, where she was born."

"You and your great-aunt were close?"

Phoebe leaned against the jewelry case. From the corner of her eye she saw two store clerks talking frantically in the corner. They gestured wildly, but didn't approach either her or the stranger.

"She raised me," she said, returning her attention to the kind man in front of her. "I never knew my father, and my mother died when I was eight. Great-Aunt Ayanna took me in." She smiled at the memory. "I'd been raised in Colorado, so moving to Florida was pretty exciting. Ayanna said it was the closest place to Lucia-Serrat she could find. I think she missed the island very much."

"So you honor her memory by visiting the island."

Phoebe hadn't thought of it that way. She smiled. "That's exactly right. I want to visit the places she liked to go. She even gave me a list."

The tall stranger held out his hand. Obviously he wanted

to read the list. Phoebe reached into the outside pocket of her purse and handed it to him.

He unfolded the single sheet of paper and read silently. She took the opportunity to study his thick hair and the length of his lashes, the powerful build of his body. They weren't standing very close at all, yet she would swear she felt the heat of his body. A crazy thing to be thinking, she told herself. But true. A warmth seeped through her as she watched him.

As he returned the list to her, he said, "All excel-lent choices. Are you familiar with the legend of Lucia's Point?"

Phoebe had long since memorized Ayanna's list. Lucia's Point was second from the bottom. "Not at all."

"They say that only lovers may visit. If they make love in the shade of the waterfall, they will be blessed all the days of their lives. So have you brought your lover with you?"

Phoebe suspected he was teasing her, but she couldn't stop herself from blushing. A lover? Couldn't the man tell from looking at her that she'd never even had a boyfriend, let alone a lover?

Before she could think of something to say—preferably something witty and charming and sophisticated—a uniformed man appeared at her side.

"Ms. Phoebe Carson? I am here to take you to your hotel." He bowed slightly and took her luggage. "At your convenience," he said, and backed out of the store.

Phoebe glanced out the window and saw a green van sitting at the curb. Gold lettering spelled out Parrot Bay Inn, where she would be staying for the next month.

"My ride is here," she told the stranger who had lingered to chat with her.

"I can see. I hope you will enjoy your time in Lucia-Serrat."

His dark eyes seemed to see inside her. Could he read her mind? She hoped not—if he could, he would figure out that she was an inexperienced fool who was completely out of her element with him.

"You've been very kind," she murmured when nothing more charming occurred to her.

"My pleasure."

Before she could turn away, he reached out and took her hand in his, then raised it to chest level. He bent his head and lightly kissed her fingers. The old-world gesture took her breath away, as did the tingling that instantly shot up her arm.

"Perhaps we will be lucky enough to run into each other again," he said.

Phoebe was incapable of speech. Fortunately he left before she did something really embarrassing like stutter or babble. After a couple of seconds she was able to draw in a breath. Then she forced herself to start walking. She left the store and stepped out into the warm afternoon. It was only when she was settled in the hotel van that she thought to look for the man she'd met in the store. She didn't even know his name.

But look as she might, she couldn't spot him. The driver climbed in and started the engine. Five minutes later they had left the airport behind them and were on a two-lane road that hugged a cliff above the sea.

The ocean stretched out to the horizon on her right, while on her left, lush foliage crept down to the side of the road. Flashes of color fluttered from branch to branch, proof of the wild parrots that made their home on the tropical island. Phoebe could smell that salty air and the rich, dark earth dampened by a recent shower. Excitement coursed through her—she was really here, she thought as the van arrived at the hotel.

The Parrot Bay Inn had been built nearly two hundred years before. The white building soared up several stories, with red and pink bougainvilleas covering the bottom two floors. The foyer was an open atrium, the reception desk hand carved with an elegance from an older time. Phoebe registered and was shown to her room.

Ayanna had made her niece promise to visit the island of Lucia-Serrat for a month, and to stay only at the Parrot Bay Inn. Phoebe refused to consider the expense as she was shown to a lovely corner mini-suite complete with a view of the ocean and a balcony worthy of Romeo and Juliet. She felt as if she were floating as she stepped out to watch the sun sink toward the west.

A reddish-orange bath colored the sky. The water turned from blue to dark green. She breathed in the scents of the island as she leaned against her balcony railing and savored the moment.

When it was dark, she moved back into her room to unpack and settle in for her stay. The four-poster bed looked comfortable and the bathroom, while old-fashioned, was large and contained every amenity. If the silence made her a little sad, she refused to dwell on her loneliness. She was used to making her own way. Here, on the island of her great-aunt's birth, she would connect with all that Ayanna had spoken of. She would feel her aunt's presence. She would begin to live her life.

Just before she went down to dinner there was a knock on her door. When she opened it, a bellman carried in a large spray of tropical flowers, touched his cap and left before Phoebe could tell him there must be some mistake. No one would be sending her flowers.

Even though she knew it was foolish, she couldn't help imagining the handsome stranger she'd met at the duty-free shop at the airport. No. Not him. He had to be at least thirty-three or thirty-four. He would think of her as a child, nothing more. Yet her fingers trembled as she opened the white envelope tucked among the blossoms.

"May your stay on the island be delightful."

No signature. Which meant that while they weren't from the man at the store, she could pretend they were. She could imagine that instead of awkward, she'd been funny and charming. Instead of dressed in something old and out of style, she'd been elegant and sophisticated and that he couldn't stop thinking about her. Much as she couldn't stop thinking about him.

The next morning Phoebe took the stairs instead of the elevator. She wore loose cotton trousers and sandals, a tank top covered by a matching short-sleeved shirt. While Lucia-Serrat was more forward thinking than many Arab countries, she didn't want to cause offense by dressing too immodestly. In her oversize straw bag she'd packed sunscreen, a few pieces of fruit from the bowl in her room, a bottle of water and a map. Today she would begin to tackle Ayanna's list, beginning with what was closest to the hotel. When she grew more familiar with her way, she would rent a car and explore the outlying areas. As for visiting Lucia's Point, well, she would deal with that problem when she had to.

Phoebe skipped down the last two steps and stepped into the foyer of the hotel.

"Good morning. I trust you slept well?"

She skittered to a stop, unable to believe what she was seeing. It was him—the man from the store the previous day. Oh, the suit was gone, replaced by casual trousers and a crisp white shirt. But she recognized his handsome features and the odd fluttering in her stomach. His teeth flashed white as he smiled at her.

"I see by your expression of surprise that you remember me. I hope the memory is pleasant."

She thought of how she'd gone to sleep remembering his light kiss on her fingers, and her dreams of a dark-haired stranger promising to show her the delights of Lucia's Point. A blush crawled up her face.

"Good morning," she whispered, thinking that response was a whole lot safer than discussing her memories of him.

"So you begin your tour of my island today. I remember—your aunt's list. What did you wish to explore first?"

Phoebe didn't know what to say. "I thought I would start with the Parrot Cove beach," she said hesitantly, not sure what brought him to the hotel, or why he bothered to speak with her. While thoughts of him had kept her occupied for hours last night, she couldn't have been a very interesting encounter for him.

"Not the beach," he said with a flick of his wrist. "While we have the most beautiful beaches in the world on the island, there is nothing extraordinary about sand. I have decided we will start with the banyan tree."

Phoebe resisted the urge to stick her finger in her ear to see if something was stuck there. She couldn't possibly have heard the man correctly. "I, um …" She took a deep breath. "I don't understand."

"Then I need to be more clear. I was charmed by what you told me yesterday and I have decided to assist you in fulfilling your late aunt's last request. Therefore I shall escort you to all the places on the list." He gave her a rakish smile. "Well, perhaps not *all* the places."

She instantly thought of Lucia's Point, which was no doubt what he wanted her to do. She thought the man might actually be teasing her. Was it possible? No one ever took the time to kid around with her.

And as tempting as his offer might be, there were a couple of things she couldn't forget. "I wouldn't want to be a bother, and even if you were willing to share your time with me, we've only just met. I don't even know your name."

He touched his fingertips lightly to his chest. "I am most remiss," he said, and swept her a low bow. He should have looked silly, but somehow he managed to look very elegant. "I am Mazin, a resident of the island, and your servant for as long as you command me to serve."

Phoebe couldn't believe this was happening—maybe in a movie, but not in real life and certainly not to her. She glanced around and realized that everyone in the lobby was watching them. She hesitated, torn between what she wanted to do and what she knew she *must* do.

"Miss Carson?" A man approached. The brass name tag said he was Mr. Eldon, the hotel manager.

"I want to assure you that, ah…" He glanced at the stranger. "That Mazin is a most honorable gentleman. No harm will come to you while you are in his presence."

"You see," Mazin said. "I have those who are willing to vouch for my character. Come, Phoebe. See the wonders of Lucia-Serrat with me."

She was about to refuse—because she prided herself on being sensible—when Ayanna's words came back to her. Her aunt had wanted her to live life to the fullest and never have regrets. Phoebe knew she would regret refusing Mazin's invitation, regardless of how foolish it might be to accept.

"The banyan tree sounds very nice," she said softly, and allowed Mazin to lead her out to his waiting car.

Two

The young woman cast one last tentative glance over her shoulder before slipping into the front seat of his Mercedes. Mazin closed the door and circled to the driver's side, all the while trying to figure out what he was doing.

He didn't have time to play games with children—and that's exactly what Phoebe Carson was. A child of twenty or so. Far too young and inexperienced to succeed at his kind of game. Why was he bothering? Worse, why was he wasting his time?

He slid onto the driver's seat and glanced at her.

She stared at him, her eyes wide—as if she were a cornered rabbit and he were some deadly predator. A perfect metaphor, he thought wryly. He should walk away—tell her that he was too busy to take her on a tour of the island. If he wanted a woman—*a woman*, not a child—there were dozens who would fly to his side at the first hint of his interest. They knew him and his world. They knew what was expected. They understood the rules.

Phoebe understood nothing. Even as he put the car in gear, he knew he was making a mistake. Because he was acting against his good sense—something he never allowed himself to do. His nature didn't allow him to take advantage of those who were not his equal. So why was he here with her?

Yesterday he had seen her going through customs. She had seemed both brave and terrified...and very much an innocent. At first he had kept track of her because he had been sure she was being met and he wanted to make sure she found her way. Later, when he had realized she was alone, he had found himself compelled to approach her for reasons he could not explain.

He had just returned from his own trip abroad. He should have been eager to go home. And yet he had taken the time to speak with Phoebe. Having spoken with her, he could not forget her.

Madness, he told himself. Simple madness.

"The weather seems very nice," she said, interrupting his thoughts.

Mazin glanced out the front windshield. The sky was blue and cloudless. "With only the occasional sprinkle, this is our dry season," he told her. "In the fall we have a rainy season, followed by several weeks of monsoons. Sometimes I am surprised that all of Lucia-Serrat doesn't wash away into the sea. But we survive and after the rains, everything grows."

Maybe it was her eyes, he thought as he turned onto the main road. So wide and blue. Trusting, he thought grimly. She was far too trusting. No one could be that innocent. He gritted his teeth. Was that the problem? Did he think she was pretending?

He wasn't sure. Did women like her really exist, or was this all an elaborate plot to get close to him? He glanced at her, taking in the long blond hair pulled back in a thick braid and her simple, inexpensive clothing. Was she trying to put him at his ease by appearing so far out of his league as to be beneath notice? Yet he had noticed. For reasons he could not explain, she intrigued him.

So he would play her game—whatever that might be—until he learned the truth, or grew tired of her. Because he would grow tired...he always did.

"You said your family had been here five hundred years," she said, glancing at him quickly, then returning her attention to the window. "I can't imagine having that much personal history."

"The island was first discovered by explorers setting out from Bahania nearly a thousand years ago," he told her. "It was uninhabited and considered sacred ground. The royal family claimed it for their own. As European sailors set out to conquer the New World, the king of Bahania grew concerned that his private paradise would be taken for Portugal, Spain or England. So he sent relatives to live here. Eventually the island became populated. A sovereignty was established. To this day, the crown prince of the island is a cousin of the king of Bahania."

Phoebe looked at him, her eyes wide. "I guess I knew about there being a prince, because that's how my great-aunt got in trouble, but I never thought about there being one right this minute. Does he live on the island?"

"Yes, he is a permanent resident."

She looked as if she were about to ask another question, when they drove past a break in the trees. Phoebe stared at the view of the ocean and caught her breath.

"It's so beautiful."

"Do you not see the ocean where you live?"

"Sometimes." She gave him a quick smile before returning her attention to the view." Ayanna's house is a few miles inland. I used to spend a lot of time by the water when I was in school, but after she became ill, I never had the time."

She pressed her fingers against the window. Her hands were as delicate as the rest of her. Mazin eyed her clothes. They were worn, although well cared for. In the right designer gown, with a little makeup and her hair styled, she would be a beauty. Like this, she was a plain gray dove.

While the fantasy of Phoebe as a femme fatale appealed to him, he found himself equally attracted to the little dove sitting next to him.

A dove who had no idea of his identity. Perhaps that was part of her appeal. He so rarely spent time with women who were not clear on who he was and what he could give them.

"There is a grove of spice trees," he said, pointing to his left. "People assume that spices come from seeds, but often they are found in the tree bark."

She turned to look. As she leaned toward his side of the car, he caught the scent of her body. Soap, he thought, nearly smiling. She smelled of the rose soap left for guests at the Parrot Bay Inn.

"Dozens of different kinds of spice are grown here," he said.

"What are those flowers?" she asked. "Are they growing out of the tree bark?"

"No. They're orchids. They're grafted into the branches of the trees and grown for use in flower arrangements. Some are used in perfume. Mango trees are the best hosts, but you will find orchids growing everywhere on the island."

"I haven't seen any oil pumps. You said there was oil on the island. Or is it out at sea?"

"Both."

He waited, wondering if this was where she would tip her hand. Interest in oil meant interest in money...specifically his. But Phoebe didn't even blink. She turned her attention to the passenger window, almost as if the oil didn't matter.

Now that he thought about it he realized that her enthusiasm for the island was far greater than her enthusiasm for him accompanying her. Was she really the shy tourist she claimed to be?

He couldn't remember the last time a woman hadn't hung on to his every word. It was almost as if she wasn't overly interested in what he had to say. If true, it was a unique experience.

They rounded a bend. The main bazaar stretched out on a flat stretch of stone-covered earth.

"The Lucia-Serrat marketplace has been in existence for nearly five hundred years," he said. "These outer walls are part of the original walls that surrounded the area."

Phoebe clapped her hands together in delight. "Oh, Mazin, we must stop. Look at everything they're selling. Those little copper pots and flowers and oh, is that a monkey?"

She laughed as a small monkey climbed across several open-air booths to snatch a particularly ripe slice of mango from a display. The owner of the monkey handed over a coin before the owner of the fruit stall could complain.

Mazin shook his head. "Not today, Phoebe. We will save the bazaar for another day. After all, you have a list and to see everything, we must proceed in an orderly fashion."

"Of course. Your way makes sense." She leaned back in her seat. "I've always been in favor of being orderly." She sighed softly. "Except something about this island makes me want to be reckless." She smiled at him. "I am not, by nature, a reckless person."

"I see."

Her innocent words, the light in her eyes and the way her smile lingered on her full mouth sent a jolt of desire through him. The arousal was so unexpected, Mazin almost didn't recognize it at first.

He wanted her. He *wanted* her. How long had it been since he had done little more than go through the motions of making love? His desire had faded until he could barely remember what it was like to ache with passion. He had bedded the most skilled, the most beautiful women of his acquaintance and none of them had stirred him beyond the desire necessary to perform. Yet here, with this plain gray dove, he felt heat for the first time in years.

The fates that determined his life were once again having a great laugh at his expense.

"What do you know of present-day Lucia-Serrat?" he asked.

"Not very much. Ayanna mostly talked about the past. What it was like when she was my age." Her expression softened with obvious affection. "She would describe glittering parties she attended. Apparently she was invited to the prince's private residence for several events. She talked about meeting visiting dignitaries from other countries. She even met the Prince of Wales—the one who became King Edward and then abdicated the throne for Mrs. Simpson. Ayanna said he was an elegant dancer."

She talked about other parties her great-aunt had attended. Mazin wasn't sure if her lack of knowledge about current events on Lucia-Serrat was real or pretense. If she played a game, she played it well. If not—

He didn't want to think about that. If Phoebe Carson was exactly what she appeared to be, he had no business involving himself with her. He was jaded and far too old. Unfortunately, with his body unexpectedly hard with desire, he doubted he was noble enough to walk away.

"Look," Mazin said, pointing out the window. "There are parrots in the trees."

Phoebe strained to see, then rolled down her window. The tall trees were alive with the colorful birds. Reds, greens, blues all blended together into a fluttering rainbow of activity. She breathed in the sweet air of the island and thought how it was a miracle that she was here at all.

Mazin turned left, heading inland. Mazin. Phoebe still couldn't believe that he'd actually come to her hotel that morning simply to show her around the island and help her with Ayanna's list. Men never noticed her. It was amazing enough that he'd bothered to speak with her yesterday, but to have remembered her through the night—who would have thought it possible?

She brushed her hands against her slacks. Her palms were damp. Nerves, she thought. She'd never met anyone like Mazin. He was so sophisticated and worldly. He made her nervous.

A sign up ahead caught her attention. A carving of a small creature standing on its back feet and staring toward the sky sat on top of the sign.

"Meerkats," she breathed. "Oh, look. It's the reserve."

"I suppose you're going to ask me to stop there, as well."

She wanted to, but thought the banyan tree was a better outing to share with her companion. At least staring at a tree wouldn't make her babble like an idiot. Being around adorable meerkats with their funny faces and charming antics would make her gush in a very embarrassing way.

"I'm determined to abide by the schedule," she said, trying to sound mature. "I'll see the meerkats another day."

"Quite sensible," Mazin murmured.

His tone of voice caught her attention. She glanced at him, taking in his strong profile and the air of confidence and power that surrounded him. She didn't know why he bothered with her, but she knew that whatever his expectations, he was destined to be disappointed. She had never been good at fitting in. She had no experience with the opposite sex—not that he was interested in her that way.

"You probably think of me as a child," she said before she could stop herself. Heat instantly flared on her cheeks and she had to resist the need to bury her face in her hands. Instead she pretended to be engrossed in the view out the passenger window.

"A child," he repeated. "Not that. A young woman. How old are you, Phoebe?"

She thought about lying, making herself sound older, but what was the point? People already thought she was much younger than her actual age.

"I'm twenty-three."

"So very grown-up," he teased.

She glanced at him. Their eyes met and she was relieved when she saw his expression was kind. "I'm not all that grown-up. I've seen little of the world, but what I have seen has taught me to depend on myself." She swallowed, then risked asking a question of her own. "How old are you?"

"Thirty-seven."

She did the math instantly. Fourteen years. Not such an impossible distance, although she didn't know what Mazin would think of it. No doubt his world was incredibly different from hers. They would have no experiences in common—which might make the age difference seem even larger.

Not that it mattered, she reminded herself. She didn't know why he'd taken time out of his day to show her around the island, but she doubted he had any *personal* interest in her.

She briefly wondered if he'd ever been married, but before she could gather the courage to ask, he turned down a narrow road. Trees and shrubs grew on both sides, their bright green leaves nearly brushing against the sides of the car.

"The banyan tree is protected by royal decree," Mazin said as he pulled into an empty parking lot. "It is considered a national treasure."

"A tree?"

"We value that which is unique to our island." His low voice seemed to brush across her skin.

Phoebe shivered slightly as she stepped out of his car. She glanced back once, noticing for the first time that he drove a *large* Mercedes. She recognized the symbol on the hood, but had no idea about the type of car, save that it was big and a silvery gray. Back home she drove a nine-year-old Honda.

Different worlds, she thought again.

"Is the park open?" she asked as they headed for a path leading to a covered patio with an information booth at the far end. She glanced both left and right. "There isn't anyone else around."

"This is not our busy season for tourists," Mazin told her

as he lightly touched the back of her arm to guide her up the stairs toward the information booth. "Plus it is early in the day for visitors. However, the park is open."

Phoebe studied the plants they passed. She didn't know any of them on sight. There were brightly colored blossoms everywhere. Lavender star-shaped flowers hung from spindly trees. Spine-covered pods in vivid red reached for the sun. A wild and sultry perfume filled the air as if the flowers conspired to intoxicate her. Even the air brushed against her body like a sensual caress. Lucia-Serrat was like no place she had ever been.

Mazin reached the information booth. He spoke quietly with the person inside. Phoebe glanced up and saw that the price of admission was three local dollars. She reached for the purse she'd slung over her shoulder, then hesitated. What was she supposed to do? It hadn't occurred to her that Mazin would pay, but would he be mad if she said anything?

She had barely fumbled with the zipper on her purse when he turned and looked at her. His dark eyes narrowed.

"Do not even consider insulting me, my dove."

There was steel behind his words. Phoebe nodded and dropped her hands to her side. Then she replayed his sentence, pausing at the very end. *My dove.* It didn't mean anything, she told herself as she mentally stumbled over the two words. No man had ever called her by anything other than her name. But it wasn't significant. He probably used flowery language with everyone.

She would store this memory away, she told herself. Later, when she was alone, she would pull it out and pretend that he had meant something wonderful. It would be a harmless game, something to hold the loneliness at bay.

He collected two tickets and they walked through an arch covered with blossoming bougainvillea.

"People think the pink and red on bougainvillea are the flowers," Phoebe said inanely before she could stop herself.

"Actually those are just leaves. The flowers are very small and often white."

"You know horticulture?" Mazin asked.

"Uh, not really. Just that. I read about it somewhere. I read a lot of things. I guess my head is full of obscure facts. I could probably do well on a game show."

She consciously pressed her lips together to keep from talking. Could she sound more stupid? The fact that Mazin made her nervous was of interest to no one save herself. If she continued to act like an idiot, he wasn't going to want to spend any more time with her.

The stone path had been worn smooth by years of use. They stepped from bright sun into shade provided by large trees. There were several formal gardens all around them. As they turned a corner, Phoebe caught her breath. In front of them stood the famous Lucia-Serrat banyan tree.

From where they were standing, they couldn't see the center of the tree. Branches spread out in all directions, some slender, some as thick around as a man. Sturdy roots grew down from the branches, anchoring the tree to the ground in hundreds of places. The tree itself stretched out for what seemed like miles. A small sign said that the circumference of the aerial roots was nearly ten acres.

"Is it the biggest in the world?" she asked.

"No. There is a larger tree in India. There is also a large one in Hawaii, although this one is bigger."

The leaves were huge and oval, tapering on each end. She stepped forward, ducking under several branches. There were paths through the aerial root system. She could see where others had walked. Reverently she touched the surprisingly smooth bark. This tree had been alive for hundreds of years.

"It feels like it's a living part of the structure of the island," she said, glancing back at Mazin.

He shrugged. "There is strength in the tree. Once it gets established, it can survive most any kind of storm. Even if one part is destroyed, the rest survives."

"I wouldn't mind being that strong," she said as she crouched down and picked up a fallen leaf.

"Why would you think you are not?"

She glanced at him. He stood within the shade of the tree. His dark eyes were unreadable. Phoebe suddenly realized she knew nothing about this man, that she was on a strange island and for all she knew, he made a habit of abducting female tourists traveling alone. She should be cautious and wary.

Yet she didn't want to be. Whatever had drawn her to Mazin continued to pull her to him today. She was foolish to trust him, and yet trust him she did.

"Strength requires experience and knowledge," she said. "I haven't lived very much. I never made it to college." She rose to her feet, still clutching the leaf in her hand. "My aunt got sick the summer after I graduated from high school. She wanted me to go live my life, but I stayed home to take care of her." She rubbed the leaf between her fingers, then dropped it to the ground. "I'm not complaining. I don't have any regrets. I loved Ayanna and would give up everything to have her with me again. I would rather be with her now than be here or—"

Phoebe broke off when she realized what she'd said. Embarrassment gripped her. "I'm sorry. I didn't mean to imply that I wasn't enjoying your company."

Mazin dismissed her apology with a wave of his hand. "It is of no concern. I am not insulted. Your affection for your aunt does you credit."

He stared at her as if she were some strange creature he'd never seen before. Phoebe touched her cheek with the back of her hand and hoped the shadows of the tree kept him from seeing how she blushed. No doubt he found her silly and boring.

"Are you hungry?" he asked abruptly. "There is a café nearby. I thought we could have lunch."

Her heart fluttered, her embarrassment fled and it was

as if the sun brightened the sky a little more than it had. Mazin held out his hand in invitation. Phoebe hesitated only a second before placing her trembling fingers in his hand.

Three

The café sat on the edge of the ocean. Phoebe felt as if she could stretch out her foot and touch the blue water. A soft breeze carried the scent of salt and island flowers, perfuming the air. The sun was hot, yet a large umbrella shielded them so that they felt only pleasantly warm.

She had the strongest urge to bounce up and down with excitement. She couldn't believe she was really here, on the island, having lunch with a very handsome man. If this was a dream, she didn't ever want to wake up.

Mazin was being so very kind. Her fingers still tingled from his touch when he'd held her hand as they'd walked to his car. She knew he hadn't intended the gesture to have meaning. There was no way he could have known how the heat from his hand had burned into her skin or made her heart race so delightfully.

"Have you decided?" he asked.

She glanced at the menu she held and realized she hadn't read it. She'd been too busy admiring the view.

"Maybe there's a local dish you would like to recommend," she said.

"The fresh fish. The chef here prides himself on his preparation. You won't be disappointed."

As she knew she wouldn't be able to taste anything, she didn't doubt that he was right. He could feed her ground-up cardboard and she would be content.

Their waiter appeared and Mazin gave him their orders. Phoebe picked up her iced tea and took a sip.

"This is such a beautiful spot," she said as she put down her glass. "I'm surprised it's not crowded for lunch."

Mazin seemed to hesitate. "Sometimes it is, but we're a little early."

Phoebe glanced at her watch. It was nearly noon, but she wasn't about to contradict her host. Besides, it might be fashionable to dine late on the island.

They sat on a patio that held about a dozen tables, all protected by umbrellas. In the distance she could see a grove of trees filled with parrots. Small lizards sunned themselves on the stone wall across from their table.

"What do you think of my island?" Mazin asked.

She smiled with contentment. "It's beautiful. Ayanna always talked about Lucia-Serrat being paradise, but I'm not sure I ever believed her. Everything is so clean. It's not just the absence of trash on the road, but the fact that plant life grows everywhere. Are there really other people on this island?"

He smiled. "I assure you, my dove, we are not alone."

Too bad, she thought wistfully.

"There has been much debate about the future of the island. We require certain resources to survive, yet we do not want to destroy the beauty that brightens our world."

"There's a lot of that kind of talk in Florida," Phoebe said, leaning forward slightly. "Developers want to build apartment buildings and hotels. They impact the infrastructure. Growth is good for the economy, but irresponsible growth can be bad for the land itself. It's a delicate balance. I worry about things like the rain forest. Part of me wants to come firmly on the side of whatever tree or animal is in need, but I know that people need to eat and heat their homes."

"I would have assumed you were a rabid conservationist," he said, his voice teasing.

She smiled. "I'm not the rabid type. I care and I do what I can. I don't think there are any easy answers."

"I agree. Here on Lucia-Serrat we seek to find a balance. We live in harmony with nature. Yes, we must dig for oil, but all precautions are taken to protect the sea and those creatures who live there. That adds to the cost. There are those who protest, who want more oil and less worry about the birds and the fish." His brows drew together. "There are those who would influence policy, but so far I have been—"

He broke off in midsentence, then shrugged. "So far I have been happy with the choices the prince has made."

Phoebe rested her elbows on the table. "Do you know the prince?"

"I am familiar with the royal family."

She turned that over in her mind. It was hard to imagine. "I've never even met the mayor where I live," she said, more to herself than to him. "Don't you like him?"

Mazin's eyebrows rose in surprise. "Why do you ask me that?"

"I don't know. The way you said you've been happy with his choices. There was something in your voice. I thought maybe you didn't like him."

"I assure you, that is not the case."

She sipped her iced tea. "Is there a parliament or something to keep the prince in line? I mean, what if he started making unfair rules? Could anyone stop him?"

"Prince Nasri is a wise and honorable ruler. To answer your questions, there is a form of parliament. They handle much of the government, but the prince is the true leader of the people."

"Is he well liked?"

"I believe so. He is considered just. Two days a month anyone may come to see him and discuss a grievance."

"What about you? What do you do?" she asked.

Mazin leaned back in his chair. "I am in the government. I coordinate oil production."

She had no idea what that might involve. If he was in the government and knew the royal family then he had to be a pretty important man. "Is it all right that you're here with me now?" she asked. "I wouldn't want you to get in trouble for taking the day off."

"Do not worry yourself," he told her with a slow smile. "I have plenty of vacation days available to me."

They walked along the beach after lunch. Mazin couldn't remember the last time he'd simply gone for a walk by the sea. Although he could see the ocean from nearly every window in his house, the view had ceased to be beautiful. He doubt he even saw it anymore.

Yet with Phoebe, all was new. She laughed with delight as waves rolled close and lapped at her feet. She'd rolled up the legs of her slacks, exposing her slender ankles. He studied the naked skin, amazed that he felt aroused gazing at her. She was completely dressed except for her bare feet and he *wanted* her.

Twenty-three, he reminded himself. She was only twenty-three. No younger than he had suspected, but younger than he had hoped.

"Is there a coral reef?" Phoebe asked.

"Not on this side of the island, but on the north end. The area is more protected there. Do you dive?"

She wrinkled her nose. "I'm assuming you mean skin diving. I've never done it. I don't know that I could. Just the thought of being trapped underwater makes me nervous."

As she spoke, she pulled her braid over her shoulder so the length of blond hair lay against her chest. She unfastened the ribbon, then finger-combed her hair so it fluttered loose around her face.

Sunlight illuminated the side of her face, highlighting her perfect bone structure. If she were any other woman of his acquaintance, he would have assumed she was going for an effect, but with Phoebe, he wasn't so sure. While he still thought she might be playing a game with him, several hours in her company had made him stop wondering about the sincerity of her innocence. She blushed too easily for someone at home in the world. And if she was as inexperienced as he suspected, then she was in danger of being taken advantage of by someone....

Someone like himself, he thought grimly. Someone who could easily pluck the flower of her womanhood, savor its sweetness, then discard it.

He did not consider himself a bad person. Perhaps Phoebe had been sent into his life as a test of that theory. Perhaps he was taking this too seriously. He should simply enjoy her company for the day, return her to her hotel that afternoon and forget he'd ever met her. That would be the wisest course of action.

"The ocean is very different here," Phoebe said as they continued to walk along the beach. "I don't have a lot of experience, but I know the color of the water is different than it is in Florida. Of course, the color is often a reflection of how shallow the water is. Around the gulf coast there are places you can wade out forever. Is it deeper here around the island?"

"Three sides are deep. The north end of the island is quite shallow."

Phoebe sighed softly to herself. Why couldn't she talk about something more interesting? Here she was strolling along a beautiful beach next to a charming man and she babbled on about ocean depth. *Be brilliant*, she ordered herself. Unfortunately she didn't have a lot of experience in the brilliant department.

"Would you like to have a seat?" he asked when they reached a cluster of rocks sticking out of the white sand.

She nodded and followed him to a flat rock warm from the sun. She dumped her shoes and purse on the sand, then slid next to him, careful to make sure they didn't touch. A light breeze teased at her hair and made goose bumps break out on her wet feet.

"Tell me about your great-aunt," he said. "What was her life like here on the island?"

Phoebe drew one knee to her chest and wrapped her arms around her leg. "Her mother owned a beauty shop in town and Ayanna learned to be a hairdresser there. When she was eighteen she went to work in the Parrot Bay Inn. Apparently back then it was an international hot spot."

Mazin grinned. "I have heard many stories about 'the old days,' as my father would call them. When people flew in from all over the world to spend a week or two in the Lucia-Serrat sun."

"Ayanna said the same thing. She was young and beautiful, and she wanted a great romantic adventure."

"Did she find it?"

Phoebe hesitated. "Well, sort of. There were several men who wanted to marry her. She became engaged to one or two, always breaking it off. One of the men insisted she keep the ring. It was a lovely ruby ring. She wore it often." She smiled at the memory.

"If she broke the engagements, then they weren't romantic adventures," he said.

"You're right. I know the great love of her life was the crown prince. Apparently they were in love with each other, even though he was married. Eventually people found out and there was a great scandal. In the end, Ayanna had to leave."

Mazin gazed out toward the ocean. "I remember hearing something about that. Despite being such an old man, I was not alive then."

"You're not so very old."

He nodded regally. "I'm pleased you think so."

She wasn't sure if he was teasing or not. "I don't think Ayanna ever heard from the prince again. She never admitted anything to me, but I have always suspected that in her heart of hearts she thought he would come find her. So her romance has an unhappy ending."

"She lived in your country for many years. Didn't she marry?"

Phoebe shook her head. "There were always men who wanted her, right up until she died. But although she enjoyed their company, she never loved any of them."

"Did they love her?"

"Absolutely. She was wonderful. Charming, intelligent, funny and so lovely in every respect."

He turned toward her, then placed his index finger under her chin. "I would imagine you look much like her."

Phoebe's eyes widened in surprise. "Not at all. Ayanna was a great beauty. I don't look anything like her."

How could he pretend to think she could even compare to Ayanna?

"You have a lovely face," he murmured, more to himself than her. "Your eyes are the color of the sea on a cloudless day, your skin is as soft as silk."

Phoebe felt heat flaring on her cheeks. Telling herself he wasn't really complimenting her didn't stop her from being embarrassed. She felt like some hick straight off the farm, with hay in her hair.

She pulled back slightly so that he wasn't touching her. "Yes, well, you're very kind, but it's hard to ignore facts. I'm too tall and too skinny. Half the time I think I look like a boy more than a grown woman. It's fairly disheartening."

Mazin gazed at her. His dark eyes seemed able to see into her soul. "I would never mistake you for a boy."

She couldn't look away. Her skin prickled as if she'd been

in the sun too long. Maybe she had. Or maybe it was the island itself, weaving a magic spell around her.

"Men don't find me attractive," she said bluntly, because she couldn't think of anything else to say. "Or interesting."

"Not all men."

Was it her imagination, or had he just moved a little closer? And was it suddenly really hot?

"Some men find you very attractive."

She would have sworn he didn't actually say that last sentence, because his lips were too close to hers to be speaking. But she couldn't ask, because she was in shock. Tremendous shock. She even stopped breathing, because at that moment he kissed her.

Phoebe didn't know what to think or do. One minute she'd been sitting on a rock by the ocean trying not to babble, and the next a very handsome, very sophisticated older man was kissing her. On the lips. Which, she supposed, was where most people kissed. Just not her. Not ever. In fact—

Stop thinking!

Her mind obeyed, going blank. It was only then that she realized his mouth was still on hers, which meant they were kissing. Which left her in the awkward position of having no clue as to what was expected of her.

The contact teased, making her want to lean into him. She liked the feel of his lips against hers and the way he placed one hand on her shoulder. She felt the heat of his fingers and the way his breath brushed across her cheek. She could see the dark fan of his lashes and the hint of stubble on his cheek. He smelled like sunshine, only more masculine.

Every part of her felt extra sensitive and her mouth trembled slightly.

He broke the kiss and opened his eyes, making her think perhaps hers should have been closed.

"You did not want me to do that," he said quietly. She blinked several times. Not want her first kiss?

Was he crazy? "No, it was great."

"But you didn't respond."

Humiliation washed over her. Phoebe slid off the rock onto the sand, then reached for her shoes. Before she could grab them, Mazin was at her side. He took her hands in his and somehow compelled her to look at him.

"What aren't you telling me?" he asked.

"Nothing." Everything, she thought.

"Phoebe."

He spoke in a warning tone that made her toes curl into the sand. She swallowed, then blurted the truth out all at once, or at least as much of it as she was willing to confess.

"I don't have a lot of experience with men. I never dated in high school, because I didn't fit in. Then Ayanna got sick and I spent the four years nursing her. That didn't leave time for a social life—not that I wanted one. The past six months I've been sad. So I'm not really good at the whole kissing thing."

She stopped talking and hoped he would buy her explanation without figuring out that no man had ever kissed her before.

She waited for him to say something. And waited. A smile teased at the corners of his mouth. His dark expression softened slightly. Then he cupped her face in his large, strong hands.

"I see," he murmured before once again touching his lips to hers.

It should have been the same kiss she'd just experienced. Weren't they all the same? But somehow this felt different. More intense. Her eyes fluttered closed before she realized what had happened. Oddly, the darkness comforted her. Her brain shut down as well, which was nice because in the quiet she could actually feel the contact of skin on skin.

He kissed her gently, yet with a hint of fire that left her breathless. Somehow she found the courage to kiss him back. Tiny electric tingles raced up and down her arms and legs, making her shiver. Mazin moved closer, until they were practically touching. He swept his thumbs across her cheeks, which made her want to part her lips. When she did, she felt the light brush of his tongue against hers.

The contact was as delightful as it was unexpected. The tingles in her arms and legs turned into ripples and she found it difficult to stand. She had to hold on to him, so she rested her hands lightly on his shoulders. They were kissing. Really kissing.

He stroked her lightly, circling her, exciting her. After a minute or so, she found the courage to do the same to him. Every aspect of the experience was amazing.

Of course, she'd read about this in books and seen passionate kissing in the movies, but she'd never experienced it herself. It was glorious. No wonder teenagers were willing to do it for hours. She found herself wanting to do the same.

She liked everything about it—the way he tasted, the scent of him, the heat flaring between them. Her body felt light, as if she could float away. When he released her face and wrapped his arms around her, pulling her close, she knew there was nowhere else on earth she wanted to be.

Their bodies touched. From shoulder to knee, they pressed together. She'd never been so close to a man, and was stunned to find every part of him was muscled and hard. She felt positively delicate by comparison.

At last he drew back and rested his forehead against hers.

"That was a surprise," he said, his voice low and husky.

"Did I do it wrong?" she asked before she could stop herself.

He laughed. "No, my dove. You kissed exactly right. Perhaps too right."

Their breath mingled. Phoebe felt all squishy inside. She wanted to stay close to him forever, kissing until the world ended.

Instead of reading her mind, Mazin straightened, then glanced at his watch.

"Unfortunately, duty calls," he said, then put his arm

around her. "Come. I will see you back to your hotel." She wanted to protest, but he'd already given her so much. In a single day she'd experienced more than she could ever have imagined.

"You've been very kind," she said, savoring the weight of his arm around her waist. He waited while she picked up her purse and shoes, then drew her close again.

"The pleasure was mine."

Oh, please let him want to see me again.

They walked to the car in silence. Once there, Mazin held open the passenger door.

Phoebe told herself not to be disappointed. One day was enough. She could survive on these memories for a long time. But before she slid into the car, he caught her hand and brought it to his lips.

"Tomorrow?" he asked in a whisper.

"Yes," she breathed in relief. "Tomorrow."

Four

Phoebe stepped carefully along the stone path through the center of the botanical garden. A light rain had fallen early that morning, leaving all the plants clean and sweet smelling. Overhead tall trees blocked out most of the heat from the midday sun. It was a pretty darned perfect moment.

"There are legends about ancient pirates coming to the island," Mazin was saying. "Archaeologists haven't found any evidence of raiders on the island, but the stories persist." He smiled. "Children are warned that if they don't behave, they'll be taken from their beds in the middle of the night."

Phoebe laughed. "That should scare them into doing what they're supposed to."

"I'm not sure they actually believe in the ancient pirates."

"Did you?"

He hesitated, then grinned. "Perhaps when I was very small."

She tried to imagine him as a little boy and could not. She glanced at his strong profile, wondering if his features had ever looked childish and soft. Her gaze lingered on his mouth. Had he really kissed her yesterday? It seemed more like a dream than something that had actually happened.

The hem of her dress brushed against a bush growing out onto the path. Drops of water trickled onto her bare leg. She tugged on her short-sleeved jacket and knew that, dream or not, she had been foolish to put on a dress that morning. Slacks would have been more sensible.

Only, she hadn't been feeling very sensible. She'd wanted to look special for Mazin—pretty. As she didn't wear makeup or know how to do anything fancy with her hair, a dress had been her only option. Now that she was with him, she hoped he didn't realize she'd gone to any effort. Yesterday he had said kind things about her appearance, but she wasn't sure she believed the compliments. Of course she'd had plenty of time to relive them last night, when she'd barely slept at all.

"Are there other stories about the island?" she asked.

"Several. Legend has it that when there is a lunar eclipse visible from Lucia-Serrat, there is magic in the air. Mysterious creatures are said to appear, and animals can talk."

"Really?"

He shrugged. "I have no personal experience with talking animals."

A branch stretched across part of the path. Mazin took her arm and led her around the obstruction.

His fingers were warm against her bare skin. Some time before dawn it had crossed her mind that he might be trying to seduce her. As she had no experience with the process, she couldn't be sure. If he was, should she mind? Phoebe couldn't decide.

Her plan had always been to go to college and become a nurse. She knew little of love and less of marriage. For years she'd had the feeling both were going to pass her by—hence her education-career plan. She wanted to be prepared to take care of herself.

But an affair was not marriage. She was on the island for

only a few weeks. If Mazin offered to teach her the mysteries between a man and a woman, why on earth would she say no?

They turned left at the next opportunity. Tall bamboo shared space with different kinds of bananas. Some were small, some large. Many were unfamiliar.

"I've never seen anything like this," she said as they paused next to a cluster of red bananas.

"Florida is tropical," he reminded her.

"I know, but where I live it's more suburban. There are some exotic plants, but nothing like this."

"You moved there when you were young, I believe?"

She hesitated. "Yes."

"You do not have to speak of your past if you do not wish to."

"I appreciate that. I don't have anything to hide." They began walking again. Phoebe folded her arms over her chest. She didn't mind talking about her life—she just didn't want him to think she was some backwater hick.

"I was born in Colorado. I never knew my father, and my mother didn't speak of him. Her parents died before I was born. She did…" Phoebe hesitated, her gaze firmly fixed on the ground. "She didn't like people very much. We lived in a small cabin in the middle of the woods. There weren't any other people around and we never had contact with the outside world. There was no electricity or indoor plumbing. We got all of our water from a well."

She cast a quick glance at Mazin. He seemed interested. "I did not know there were parts of your country without such amenities."

"There are some. My mother taught me to read, but didn't discuss much of the outside world with me. We were happy, I guess. I know she cared about me, but I was often lonely. One day when I was eight, we were out collecting berries. There was a lot of water from the spring snow runoff higher in the mountain. She slipped on some wet leaves, fell and hit her head. I found out later that she died instantly, but at the time I didn't know why she wouldn't wake up. After a few hours, I knew I had to go get help, even though she had always forbidden me to have anything to do with other people. There was a town about ten miles away. I'd stumbled across it a couple of times when I'd been out exploring."

Mazin stopped walking and grabbed her by her upper arms. "You had never been into the town before?"

She shook her head.

"You must have been terrified."

"I was more scared that there was something wrong with my mother, or that she was going to be mad when she woke up." She sighed, remembering how she'd been trying so hard not to cry as she explained what had happened to several strangers before one of them finally took her to the sheriff's office.

"They went and got her," she said. Mazin released her arms and she started walking. It seemed easier to keep moving as she talked. "Then they told me she was dead. I didn't know what it meant for a long time."

"Where did you go?"

"Into a temporary foster home until they could locate a relative. It took about six months, because I didn't know anything about my family. They had to go through all of her personal effects to get leads. In the meantime I had to adjust to a life that everyone else took for granted. It was hard."

Those three words couldn't possibly explain what it had been like, Phoebe thought. She still remembered her shock the first time she'd seen an indoor bathroom. The toilet had stunned her, while the idea of *hot* running water on demand had been a taste of heaven.

"I started school, of course," she said.

"You must have had difficulties."

"Just a couple. I knew how to read, but I'd had no education. Math was a mystery to me. I knew my numbers, but nothing else. Plus I'd missed all the socialization that most children undergo. I didn't know how to make friends, and I'd never seen a television, let alone a movie."

"Your mother had no right to do that to you."

She glanced at him, surprised by the fierceness in his voice. "She did what she thought was best. Sometimes I think I understand, other times I'm angry."

They stepped into the sun and Phoebe was grateful for the warmth.

They walked in silence for several minutes. There were things about her past that she'd never admitted to anyone, not even Ayanna. Her aunt had been so kind and supportive from the first that she hadn't wanted to trouble her.

"I didn't make friends easily," Phoebe whispered. "I didn't know how. The other children knew I was different and they stayed away from me. I was grateful when they found my aunt, not only to have a home, but to get away from the loneliness."

Mazin led her to a bench on the side of the path. She settled in a corner, her hands clasped tightly together, the memories growing larger in her mind.

"Ayanna drove out to get me. Later she told me it was because she thought the car trip would give us time to get to know each other." She smiled sadly. "Her plan worked. By the time we reached Florida, I was comfortable with her. And I did a little better making friends. I'd learned from previous mistakes. Unfortunately, I had more trouble in school. For a while the teachers were convinced I was retarded. I couldn't even score well on the IQ tests because I didn't have the frame of reference to answer the questions."

"Yet you were successful."

She nodded. "It took a long time. Ayanna took me to the library every week and helped me pick out different books so that I could learn about things. It's the little things, like knowing that the word *pipe* has two meanings."

She suddenly realized how long she'd been talking, and

groaned. "I'm sorry. I don't even remember what you asked me. I know you couldn't have wanted this long answer."

"I'm happy to hear about your past," Mazin told her, lightly touching the back of her hand. "I am impressed by your ability to overcome a disadvantage."

She supposed his answer should have pleased her, but it didn't. She wanted him to see her as someone he could find exciting, not as an example of a job well done. She wanted him to take her in his arms again and kiss her thoroughly.

With a fierceness that both shocked and frightened her, she found herself wishing that he *did* want to seduce her.

But instead of kissing her or even holding her close, he rose.

Reluctantly she got to her feet.

They continued to walk through the garden. Mazin was a most attentive host, pointing out plants of interest, inquiring about her state of well-being in the hot morning. As the sun rose in the sky, her spirits plummeted. She shouldn't have told him about her strange upbringing. She shouldn't have spilled her secrets. How could he think of her as anything but odd?

"You have grown silent," Mazin said when he realized Phoebe had stopped talking.

She shrugged.

He took in the slump of her shoulders and the way her fingers endlessly pleated her skirt. "Why are you sad?"

"I'm not. I just feel..." She pressed her lips together. "I don't want you to think I'm stupid."

"Why would I think that?"

"Because of what I told you."

She had told him about her past. From his perspective, the information had only made her more dangerous. Yesterday she had been a pretty woman who attracted him sexually. Their kiss had shown him the possibilities and the accompanying arousal had disturbed his sleep. Today he knew that she was more than an appealing body. He knew that she had a strong spirit and that she had succeeded against impossible odds. Why would that make him think she was stupid?

Women were complex creatures.

"Put it from your mind, my dove," he told her, taking her hand in his. "I admire your ability to overcome your past. Come, I will show your our English rose garden. Some of the rosebushes are very ancient, and still annoyed to find themselves so far from home."

The next morning Phoebe had almost convinced herself that Mazin meant what he said—that he admired her for her past. However, she couldn't quite embrace the concept, mostly because he hadn't kissed her goodbye. He'd kissed her on the first day, but not on the second. Didn't that mean they were moving in the wrong direction?

She stood in front of the bathroom mirror and pulled her hair back into a ponytail. As the dress hadn't created any magic the day before, she was back in slacks and a T-shirt. Maybe now he would want to kiss her.

She finished with her hair and dropped her hands to her side. After only two days in the company of a handsome man, her brain was spinning. It was probably for the best that there hadn't been any kissing. Except she'd really enjoyed how she'd felt in his arms.

"At least I'm having an adventure, Ayanna," she said as she smoothed sunscreen on her arms. "That should make you happy."

She was still smiling at the thought of her aunt's pleasure when the phone rang. Phoebe turned to look at it, her stomach clenching. There was only one person who would be calling her, and she already knew the reason.

"Hello?"

"Phoebe, this is Mazin. Something has come up and I will not be able to join you today."

She was sure he said more, that he kept talking, but she

couldn't hear anything. She sank onto the bed and closed her eyes.

He wasn't coming. He was bored with her. He thought she was a child, or maybe he'd been lying when he'd said he appreciated her past. It doesn't matter, she told herself, squeezing in the pain. This trip wasn't about him—it never had been. How could she have forgotten?

"I appreciate you letting me know," she said brightly, interrupting him. "I'll let you get back to your day and I must begin mine. There is so much to see on this beautiful island. Thank you, Mazin. Good-bye."

Then she hung up before she did something stupid like cry.

It took her fifteen minutes to fight back tears and another ten to figure out what she was going to do. Her aunt had specifically left her the money to visit Lucia-Serrat. Phoebe couldn't repay her by wasting time sulking. She read Ayanna's list and then studied the guidebook. The church of St. Mary was within walking distance. Next to that was a dog park. If the beauty of the architecture and stained glass didn't ease the disappointment in her heart, then the antics of the dogs would make her laugh.

That decided, Phoebe headed out on her own. She found the church, a stunning structure with high arches and cool interiors. She admired the carvings and let the silence and peace ease her pain.

She'd known Mazin only a little over two days, she told herself as she sat in a rear pew. He had been more than kind. It was wrong and foolish of her to expect more of him. As for the kiss and her fantasies that he might want to seduce her, well, at least she *had* been kissed. The next time, with the next man, she would do better. Eventually she would figure out how to be normal.

She left the church and walked to the dog park. As she'd hoped, there were dozens of dogs playing, running and barking. She laughed over the antics of several small dalmatian puppies and helped an older woman put her Irish setter in the back of her car.

By the time she stopped for lunch her spirits had risen to the point where she could chat with the waitress about the menu and not think about Mazin.

While waiting for her entrée, she made friends with the older English couple at the next table, and they recommended she try the boat tour that went around the island. The trip took all day and offered impressive views of Lucia-Serrat. As they were all staying at the Parrot Bay Inn, they walked back together and Phoebe stopped at the concierge desk to pick up a brochure on the boat trip. Then she headed up to her room, pleasantly tired and pleased that she'd gotten through the day without thinking of Mazin more than two or three dozen times.

Tomorrow she would do better, she promised herself. By next week, she would barely remember his name.

But when she entered her room, the first thing she noticed was a new, larger spray of flowers. Her fingers trembled as she opened the card.

"Something lovely for my beautiful dove. I'm sorry I could not be with you today. I will be thinking of you. Mazin."

Her throat tightened and her eyes burned as she read the card. She didn't have to compare the handwriting with that on the first card she'd received—she knew they were the same. The fact that he had just been trying to be nice didn't lessen her pain. Perhaps she was being foolish and acting like a child, but she missed him.

The phone rang, interrupting her thoughts. Phoebe cleared her throat, then picked up the receiver.

"Hello?"

"Here I had imagined you spending the day pining for me when in truth you were out having a good time."

Her heart jumped into her throat. She could barely breathe. "Mazin?"

"Of course. What other man would call you?"

Despite her loneliness, she couldn't help smiling. "Maybe there are dozens."

"I wouldn't be surprised." He sighed. "Aren't you going to ask me how I knew you weren't alone in your room, pining for me?"

"How did you know?"

"I've been calling and you have not been there."

Her heart returned to her chest and began to flutter, even though she knew she was a fool. "I went to the church and the dog park. Then I had lunch. A lovely couple told me about the boat tour around the island. I thought I might do that tomorrow."

"I see."

She plowed ahead. "You've been more than kind, but I know you have your own life and your own responsibilities."

"What if I wish to see you? Are you telling me no?"

She clutched the receiver so hard, her fingers hurt. Tears pooled in her eyes. "I don't understand."

"Nor do I."

She wiped away her tears. "Th-thank you for the flowers."

"You are welcome. I am sorry about today." He sighed. "Phoebe, if you would rather not spend time with me, I will abide by your wishes."

Tears flowed faster. The odd thing was she couldn't say exactly *why* she was crying. "It's not that."

"Why is your voice shaking?"

"It's n-not."

"You're crying."

"Maybe."

"Why?"

"I don't know."

"Would it help if I said I was disappointed, as well? That I would rather be with you than reading boring reports and spending my day in endless meetings?"

"Yes, that would help a lot."

"Then know that it is true. Tell me you'll see me tomorrow."

A sensible woman would refuse, she thought, knowing Mazin would not only distract her from her plans for her future, but that he would also likely break her heart.

"I'll see you tomorrow."

"Good. I will see you then."

She nodded. "Goodbye, Mazin."

"Goodbye, my dove. Until tomorrow. I promise to make the day special."

He hung up. She carefully replaced the phone, knowing that he didn't have to try to make the day special. Just by showing up he would brighten her world.

Five

"Where are we going?" Phoebe asked for the third time since Mazin had picked her up that morning. They'd already toured the marketplace, after which he had promised a surprise.

"You will see when we arrive," he said with a smile. "Be patient, my dove."

"You're driving me crazy," she told him. "I think you're doing it on purpose."

"Perhaps."

She tried to work up a case of righteous indignation, but it was not possible. Not with the sun shining in the sky and the beauty of Lucia-Serrat all around them. Not with Mazin sitting next to her in his car, spending yet another day with her.

She had known him little more than two weeks. They had spent a part of nearly every day together, although not any evenings. So far they'd worked their way through a good portion of Ayanna's list. Phoebe had seen much of the island, including a view from the ocean on the tour boat.

"Is it a big place, or a small place?" she asked.

"A big place."

"But it is not on my list."

"No."

She sighed. "Did my aunt visit there?"

"I would think so."

They drove toward the north end of the island, heading inland. Gradually the road began to rise. Phoebe tried to picture the map of the island in her mind. What was in this direction? Then she reminded herself it didn't really matter. She had memories stored up for her return home. When she was deep in her studies, she would remind herself of her time on Lucia-Serrat, when a handsome man had made her feel special.

She glanced at him out of the corner of her eye. He was concentrating on his driving and did not notice her attention. Although he was unfailingly polite, he had yet to kiss her again. She wasn't sure why, and her lack of experience with men kept her from speculating. She thought it might have something to do with the fact that she was inexperienced, but couldn't confirm the information. Asking was out of the question.

They rounded a corner. Up ahead, through a grove of trees, a tall house reached up toward the sky. She squinted. Actually it was more of a castle than a house, or maybe a palace.

A palace?

Mazin inclined his head. "The official residence of the prince. He has a private home, but that is not open to the public. Although this is not on your Ayanna's list, I thought you might enjoy strolling through the grounds and exploring the public rooms."

She turned to him and smiled with delight. "I would love to see it. Thank you for thinking of this, Mazin. My aunt came here often to attend the famous parties. She danced with the prince in the grand ballroom."

"Then we will make sure we see that part of the castle."

They drove around to a small parking lot close to the building. Phoebe glanced at the larger public lot they had passed on their way in.

"You forget I have a position of some importance in the government," he said, reading her mind as he opened his car door. "Parking here is one of the perks."

He climbed out of the car, then came around to her side and opened the door. Phoebe appreciated the polite gesture. Sometimes she even let herself fantasize that he was being more than polite, that his actions had significance. Then she remembered she was a nobody from Florida and that he was a successful, older man simply being kind. Besides, she had her life already planned. Okay, maybe her plan wasn't as exciting as her imaginings about Mazin, but it was far more real.

"This way," he said, taking her hand in his and heading for the palace. "The original structure was built at the time of the spice trade."

"You told me that the crown prince is always a relative of the king of Bahania. He was probably used to really nice houses."

Mazin flashed her a grin. "Exactly. Originally the prince lived in the palace, but as you can see, while it is a beautiful palace, it is not especially large. Quarters were cramped with the prince's family, his children and their children, various officials, servants, visiting dignitaries. So in the late 1800s the prince had a private residence constructed."

Mazin paused on the tree-lined path and pointed. "You can see a bit of it through there."

Phoebe tilted her head. She caught a glimpse of a corner of a building and several windows. "It looks nearly as big as the palace."

"Apparently the building project grew a little."

She returned her attention to the graceful stone palace in front of them. "So official business occurs here? At least the prince doesn't have much of a commute."

"I'm sure he appreciates that."

They crossed the ground around to the front of the palace. Phoebe still felt a little uneasy about trespassing, but as Mazin wasn't worried, she did her best to enjoy the moment. He was a knowledgeable host, explaining the different styles of architecture and telling her amusing stories from the past.

"Now we will go inside," he said. "Our first stop will be the ballroom."

They headed for the main gates overlooking the ocean. As they crossed the open drawbridge, a distant call caught Phoebe's attention. She looked toward the sound. A small boy raced toward them, down the length of the drawbridge. Dark hair flopped in his face, while his short, sturdy legs pumped furiously.

"Papa, Papa, wait for me!"

Phoebe didn't remember stopping, but suddenly she wasn't moving. She stared at the boy, then slowly turned her attention to Mazin. Her host watched the child with a combination of affection and exasperation.

"My son," he said unnecessarily.

Phoebe was saved from speaking by the arrival of the boy. He flew at his father. Mazin caught him easily, pulling him close into an embrace that was both loving and comfortable. They obviously did this a lot.

A tightness in her chest told her that she'd stopped breathing. Phoebe gasped once, then wondered if she looked as shocked as she felt. She knew Mazin was older. Of course he would have lived a full life, and it made sense that his life might include children. But intellectualizing about a possibility and actually meeting a child were two very different things.

Mazin shifted his son so that the boy sat on his left forearm. One small arm encircled his neck. They both turned to her.

"This is my son, Dabir. Dabir, this is Miss Carson."

"Hello," the boy said, regarding her with friendly curiosity.

"Hi." Phoebe wasn't sure if she was expected to shake hands.

He appeared to be five or six, with thick dark hair and eyes just like his father. She had been unable to picture Mazin as a child, but now, looking at Dabir, she saw the possibilities.

Mazin settled his free hand at Dabir's waist. "So tell us what you're doing here at the castle. Don't you have lessons today?"

"I learned all my numbers and got every question right, so I got a reward." He grinned at Phoebe. "I told Nana I wanted to see the swords, so she brought me here. Have you seen them? They're long and scary."

He practically glowed as he spoke. Obviously viewing the swords was a favorite treat.

Phoebe tried to answer, but her lips didn't seem to be working. Mazin spoke for her.

"We were just about to walk into the castle. We haven't seen anything yet. Miss Carson is visiting Lucia-Serrat for the first time."

"Do you like it?" Dabir asked.

"Um, yes. It's lovely."

The boy beamed. "I'm six. I have three older brothers. They're all much bigger than me, but I'm the favorite."

Mazin set the boy on the ground and ruffled his hair. "You are not the favorite, Dabir. I love all my sons equally."

Dabir didn't seem the least bit upset by the announcement. He giggled and leaned against his father, while studying her.

"Do you have any children?" he asked.

"No. I'm not married."

Dabir's eyes widened. "Do you like children?"

Phoebe hadn't thought the situation could get more un-comfortable, yet it just had. "I, ah, like them very much."

"Enough," Mazin said, his voice a low growl. "Go find Nana."

Dabir hesitated, as if he would disobey, then he waved once and raced back into the castle. Phoebe watched him go. Children. Mazin had children. Four of them. All boys.

"He's very charming," she forced herself to say when they were alone.

Mazin turned toward her and cupped her face. "I could read your mind. You must never try to play poker, my dove. Your thoughts are clearly visible to anyone who takes the time to look."

There was a humiliating thought. She sighed. "You have lived a very full life," she said. "Of course you would have children."

"Children, but no wife."

Relief filled her. She hadn't actually allowed herself to think the question, but she was happy to hear the answer.

"Come," he said, taking her hand in his. "I will show you the ballroom where your Ayanna danced. As we walk, I will tell you all about my sordid past."

"Is it so very bad?"

"I'm not sure. Your standards will be higher than most. You will have to tell me."

They walked into the castle. She tried to catch a glimpse of Dabir and his Nana, but they seemed to have disappeared.

"Some of the tapestries date back to the twelfth century," he said, motioning to the delicate wall hangings.

She dutifully raised her gaze to study them. "They're very nice."

Mazin sighed, then pulled her toward a bench by the stone wall. "Perhaps we should deal with first things first, as you Americans like to say."

He sat on the bench and pulled her next to him. She had the brief thought that actually sitting on furniture in the royal castle might be punishable by imprisonment, or worse, but then Mazin took her hands in his and she couldn't think at all.

"I am a widower," he told her, staring into her eyes. "My wife died giving birth to Dabir. We have three boys. And I have another son from a brief liaison when I was a young man."

That last bit of news nearly sent her over the edge, but all she said was, "Oh."

Four sons. It seemed like a large number of children for one man. No wonder he hadn't been spending his evenings with her; he had a family waiting at home. If they were all as charming as Dabir, he must hate being away from them.

"I've been keeping you from them," she said softly. "I've told you that you don't have to keep me company."

"I choose to be here."

She wanted to ask why, but didn't have the courage. "You must have help with them. Dabir mentioned Nana."

He smiled. "Yes. She is a governess of sorts for my youngest. The two middle boys are in a private boarding school. My oldest is at university in England."

She tried not to show her shock. "How old is he?"

"Nearly twenty. I am much older than you, Phoebe. Did you forget?"

"No, it's just…" She did the math. He'd had a child when he'd been seventeen? She was twenty-three and had been kissed only once. Could they be more different?

"I know you say you choose to be here," she said, "but you have a family and work obligations. I must be a distraction. Please don't be concerned. I'm very capable of entertaining myself. How could I not enjoy my time on this beautiful island?"

"Ah, but if you remain alone, you will never be able to visit Lucia's Point."

She ducked her head as heat flared on her cheeks. Lucia's

Point—the place for lovers. It seemed unlikely that she would be visiting that particular spot on this trip.

A horrifying thought occurred to her. She tried to push it away, but it refused to budge. Then she found herself actually voicing it aloud as she risked looking at him.

"You have four sons, Mazin. Do you see me as the daughter you never had?"

He released her hands at once. She didn't know what that meant, but she was aware of his dark eyes brightening with many emotions. None of them seemed paternal.

"Do you see me as the father you never had?"

Her blush deepened. "No," she whispered. "I never thought of that."

"I do not think of you as a child, especially not my own. On the contrary. I see you very much as a woman."

"Do you? I want to believe you, but I've lived such a small life."

"It is the quality of one's life that matters."

"Easy to say when you had your first affair at seventeen," she blurted before she could stop herself. She pressed her fingers to her mouth, horrified, but Mazin only laughed.

"An interesting point. Come. We will walk to the ballroom. When we are there, I will tell you all about my affair with the ever-beautiful Carnie."

"She was an actress," Mazin said ten minutes later as they strolled through a vast open area.

Tall, slender windows let in light. Dozens of candelabras hung from an arched ceiling. There was a stage in one corner, probably for an orchestra, and enough space to hold a football game.

Phoebe tried to imagine the room filled with people dressed in their finest, dancing the night away, but she was still caught up in his description of his first mistress as "ever beautiful."

"*Was* she very lovely?" she asked before she could stop herself.

"Yes. Her face and body were perfection. However, she had a cold heart. I learned very quickly that I was more interested in a woman's inner beauty than her outside perfection."

His statement made her feel better. Phoebe knew that in a competition of straight looks, she wouldn't have a chance, but she thought her heart would stand up all right.

"We met when the film company came here to shoot part of a movie. She was an older woman—nearly twenty-two. I was very impressed with myself at the time and determined to have her."

She didn't doubt he'd achieved his goal. "What happened when you found out she was pregnant?"

He took her hand in his. The pressure of his palm against her, the feel of their fingers laced together nearly distracted her from his words.

"She was upset. I don't know if she'd hoped for marriage, but it was out of the question. My father..." He hesitated. "The family did not approve. We had money, so an offer was made. She accepted."

Phoebe stared at him. "Didn't you love her?"

"Perhaps for the first few weeks, but it faded. When I found out about the child, I wanted my son, but I didn't think Carnie and I had much chance at happiness. She stayed long enough to have the baby, then left."

"I could never do that," Phoebe said, completely shocked by Carnie's behavior. "I would never give up my child. I don't care how much money was involved."

Mazin shrugged. "I don't think my father gave her much choice."

"That wouldn't matter. I would stand up against anyone. I'd go into hiding."

"Carnie preferred the cash."

Mazin heard the harshness in his voice. Most of the time

he was at peace with his former lover, but occasionally he despised her for what she had done, even though it had made his life simpler.

"Is she still alive?"

"Yes, but she rarely sees her son. It is better that way."

He watched the play of emotions across Phoebe's face. She was so easy to read. She was outraged by Carnie's decision, yet it went against her nature to judge anyone negatively. Her wide mouth trembled slightly at the corners and her delicate brows drew together as she tried to reconcile harsh facts with her gentle nature.

She was a good person. He couldn't say that very often, not with certainty. She wanted nothing from him, save his company. Their time was a balm and he found himself in need of the healing only she could provide. Being with her made him quiet and content. Two very rare commodities in his life.

She had been startled by Dabir's sudden appearance. Mazin had been, as well, but for different reasons. He had seen something as he'd watched her. Over the past six years he had become an expert at judging a woman's reaction to his children. Some pretended to like them because they wanted to be his wife. Some genuinely enjoyed the company of children. He put Phoebe in the latter category.

He liked her. Mazin couldn't remember the last time he had simply liked a woman. He also wanted her. The combination caused more than a little discomfort. Because he cared about her, he refused to push her into his bed, which was exactly where he wanted her to be. Holding back was not his style, yet this time it felt right.

She was different from anyone he'd ever known. He suspected she would say the same about him.

"Phoebe, you must know I'm a rich man," he said.

She bit her bottom lip. "I sort of figured that out."

"Does that bother you?"

"A little."

She glanced at him. Her long blond hair fell down her back. He wanted to capture it in his hands and feel the warm silk of the honeyed strands. He wanted many things.

"I don't understand why you spend time with me," she said in a rush. "I like being with *you*, but I worry that you're bored."

He smiled. "Never. Do you remember yesterday when we went to see the meerkats?"

"Yes?"

"You fed them their lunch of fruits and vegetables. You were patient, feeding each in its turn, never tired."

She sighed. "They were wonderful. So cute and funny. I could watch them for hours. I love how they stand guard, watching out for each other."

"You told me you'd seen a show about African meerkats and how one was burned in a fire."

She stopped walking. He moved to stand in front of her. As they had the previous day, her eyes filled up with tears.

"It tried to stand guard, but couldn't," she whispered. "They all huddled around it. Then a couple of days later, it left the group and went off to die."

A single tear rolled down her cheek. Mazin touched it with his finger "Tears for a meerkat. What would you give to a child in need?"

"I don't understand the question."

"I know, but these tears are why I am not bored with you."

She sniffed. "You're making absolutely no sense."

He laughed. "You would find others to agree with you. So tell me, what do you want from your life?"

Her blue eyes widened slightly. "Me? Nothing special. I'd like children. Three or four, at least. And a house. But before any of that, I want to get my degree."

"In what?"

"Nursing. I like taking care of people."

He remembered her dying aunt. Yes, Phoebe would do well with the sick.

"I would like—" She shook her head. "Sorry. This can't be interesting. My dreams are very small and ordinary. Like I said, a small life. I'm not sure there's all that much quality there."

"On the contrary. You have much to recommend you."

Then, against his better judgment, he pulled her close.

She came willingly into his arms, as he had known she would. Her body pressed against him, her arms wrapped around him. She raised her head in a silent offering, and he did not have the strength of will to deny her.

He touched his mouth to hers. This time she responded eagerly, kissing him back. He kept the contact light, because if he took what he really wanted, they would make love here in the public rooms of the castle. So he nipped at her lower lip and trailed kisses along her jaw. He slid his hands up and down her back, careful to avoid the tempting curves of her rear.

Her breathing accelerated as he licked the hollow of her throat. She wore a dress with a slightly scooped neck. The thrust of her small breasts called to him. It would be so easy to move lower. He could see the outline of her tight nipples straining against the fabric of her clothing. Desire filled him with an intensity that made him ache.

Good sense won. He returned his attentions to her mouth. She parted in invitation. He might be able to resist her other temptations, but not that one. He had to taste her sweetness one more time.

He plunged into her. She accepted his conquest and began an assault of her own. Just once, he thought hazily, and slipped his hand onto the curve of her hip. She responded by drawing closer, pressing her breasts against his chest and breathing his name.

Mazin swore. Phoebe was very much an innocent, and she didn't know what she was offering.

He wanted her and he couldn't have her. Not only because she was a virgin, but because he hadn't told her the truth about everything. At first he'd withheld the information because it had amused him. Now he found he didn't want her to know.

He forced himself to pull back. They were both breathing heavily. Phoebe smiled at him.

"You've probably heard this a thousand times before," she said, "but you're a really good kisser."

He laughed. "As are you."

"If I am, it's because of you."

The blush of arousal stained her cheeks; her lips were swollen. Her beauty touched him deep in his soul. He wanted to see her in diamonds and satin.

He wanted to see her in nothing at all.

"What are you thinking?" she asked.

"That you are an unexpected delight in my life."

Her blue eyes darkened with emotion that he didn't want to read. Slowly, tentatively she touched his mouth with her fingertip. Her breath caught in her throat.

"What do you want from me, Mazin?"

He found himself compelled to speak the truth. "I don't know."

Six

Phoebe pulled a chair close to the balcony and stared out at the stars. The balmy night air brushed against her bare arms, making her tremble slightly, although she couldn't say why. It wasn't that she was cold or even fearful. She knew in her heart that nothing bad could happen while she was on the island.

Perhaps it was the memory of Mazin's kiss that made her unable to keep still. Something had happened that afternoon when he'd taken her in his arms. She'd seen something in his eyes, something that had made her think this might not just be a game to him. His inability to tell her what he wanted from her made her both happy and nervous. One of them had to know what was going on, and she didn't have a clue. Which left Mazin.

She pulled her knees to her chest and wrapped her arms around her legs. Her long white cotton nightgown fluttered in the breeze.

There had been a difference in his kiss today. An intensity

that had shaken her to her core. Did he want her that way? Did he want to make love with her? Did she want to make love with him?

He was not the man she had fantasized about. In her mind, Mazin had no life, save that time he spent with her. Now she knew that he had been a husband. He was a father, with four sons. He had a life that didn't include her, and when she was gone, he would return to it as if she'd never been here at all.

Were all his sons like Dabir? She smiled at the memory of the bright, loving little boy. Spending time with him would be a joy.

Several years of babysitting had taught her to assess a child very quickly. Dabir would no doubt get into plenty of trouble, but he had a generous heart and a sense of fun. She bit her lower lip. One child would be easy, but four? Worse, Mazin's oldest was only a few years younger than she was. The thought made her shiver. Not that Mazin's children were going to be an issue, she reminded herself.

Phoebe stared up at the stars, but the night skies didn't hint at how long until Mazin grew tired of her, nor did they whisper his intent. Instead of meeting her during the day tomorrow, Mazin had arranged for them to spend the evening together. Somehow the change of time made her both excited and nervous.

No matter what, she told herself, she would never have regrets. Just as Ayanna had made her promise.

Moonlight sparkled on the ever-shifting ocean. Phoebe breathed in the scent of sea spray and nearby flowers. Whatever else might happen in her life, she would remember this night forever.

Mazin sat across from her, handsome as always. Tonight he wore a suit, making her glad she'd spent more than she should have for a pretty blouse in the hotel boutique. Her slim black skirt had seen better days, but it was serviceable enough. After nearly an hour of fussing with her hair, she'd managed to pin it up into a French twist. She felt almost sophisticated. Something she would need to counteract the effect of Mazin's attraction by moonlight.

"I feel a little guilty," she said as the waiter poured from the wine bottle.

"Why?" Mazin asked when the waiter had left and they were alone. "Have you done something you should not have done?"

"No." She smiled. "But it's evening. You should be home with your family."

"Ah. You are thinking of my children."

Among other things, she thought, hoping he couldn't read her mind and know how many times she had relived their kisses.

"Dabir, especially," she murmured. "Wouldn't you rather be home, tucking him in bed?"

Mazin dismissed her with a shake of his head. "He is six. Far too old to be tucked in bed by his father."

"He's practically a baby, not a teenager."

Mazin frowned. "I had not thought he would still need that sort of attention. He has Nana to take care of him."

"That's not the same as having you around."

"Are you trying to get rid of me?"

"Not at all. I just don't want you to take time away from them to be with me. I know if I had children, I would want to be with them always."

One corner of his mouth turned up. "What of your husband's needs for you? Would they not come first?"

"I think he'd have to learn to compromise."

Mazin's humor turned to surprise. "It is the children and the wife who must compromise." He shrugged. "Most of the time. I was married long enough to have learned that on rare occasions the man does not come first."

"I should think not." She leaned toward him. "Tell me about your sons."

"Why do I sense you are more interested in them than in me?"

"I'm not. It's just…" She hesitated, then decided there was no point in avoiding the truth. "I find the subject of your children very safe."

"Because I am unsafe?"

Rather than answer, she took a sip of her wine.

He chuckled and reached forward, capturing her free hand in his. "I know you, my dove. I have learned to read you when you avoid my eyes and busy yourself with a task. You do not wish to respond to my question. Now my job is to learn why."

He studied her, his dark eyes unreadable. She wished she could know him as well as he seemed to know her.

"Why do you fear me?" he asked unexpectedly.

Phoebe was so surprised that she straightened, pulling her hand free of his. She clutched her fingers together on her lap.

"I'm not afraid." She bit her lower lip. "Well, not too afraid," she added, because she'd never been much of a liar. "It's just that you're different from anyone I've ever met. You're very charming, but also intimidating. I'm out of my element with you."

"Not so very far." He patted the table. "Put your hand here so that I may touch you."

He spoke matter-of-factly, but his words made her whole body shiver. She managed to slide her hand over to his, where he linked their fingers together. He felt strong and warm. He made her feel safe, which was odd because he was the reason she felt out of sorts in the first place.

"See?" he said. "We fit together well."

"I don't think that's true. I don't know why you spend so much time with me. I can't be anything like the other women in your life."

Now it was his turn to stiffen. He didn't pull his hand away, but ice crept into his gaze. "What other women?" he asked curtly. "What are you talking about?"

She sensed that she had insulted him. "Mazin, I didn't mean anything specific. Just that I can see that you're a handsome, successful man. There must be dozens of women throwing themselves at you all the time. I have this picture of you having to step over them wherever you go."

She wanted to say more, but her throat tightened at the thought of him being with anyone else, even though it probably happened all the time.

"Do not worry, my dove," he said softly. "I have forgotten them all."

For how long?

She only thought the question. There was no point in asking. After all, Mazin might tell her the truth, and that would hurt her.

"I can see you do not believe me," he said, releasing her fingers. "To prove myself, I have brought you something."

He snapped his fingers. Their waiter appeared, but instead of bringing menus, he carried a large flat box. Mazin took it from him and handed it to her.

"Do not say you can't accept until you have opened it. Because I know in my heart that once you see my offering, you won't be able to refuse it."

"Then I should refuse it before I see it," she said.

"That is not allowed."

Phoebe lightly touched the gold paper around the box. She tried to imagine what could be inside. Not jewelry. The box was far too big—at least eighteen inches by twelve. Not clothes—the box was too slender.

"You won't be able to guess," he told her. "Open it."

She slipped off the bow, then pulled the paper from the box. When she lifted the lid and drew back the tissue, her breath caught in her throat.

Mazin had given her a framed picture of Ayanna.

Phoebe recognized the familiar face immediately. Her great-aunt looked very young, perhaps only a year or two older than Phoebe was now. She stood alone, in front of a pillar. Behind her, open archways led to the ocean. She recognized the palace at once.

Ayanna wore a formal ball gown. Diamonds glittered from her ears, wrists and throat. With her hair pulled back and her posture so straight and regal, she looked as elegant as a princess.

"I've never seen this picture before," she breathed. "Where did you find it?"

"There are photographic archives. You had mentioned that your aunt was a favorite with the crown prince. I thought there might be pictures of her, and I was right. This one was taken at a formal party at the prince's private residence. The original remains in the archives, but they allowed me to make a copy."

She didn't know what to say. That he would have gone to all this trouble for her moved her beyond words. Still, she had to make an attempt to speak. "You're right. I can't refuse this gift. It means too much. I have a few pictures of Ayanna, but not nearly enough. Thank you for being so thoughtful and kind."

"My only motive was to make you smile."

She didn't care what his motive had been. There was no other present in the world that could have had so much meaning. Phoebe didn't know how to explain all the feelings welling up inside her. She wanted to go to Mazin and wrap her arms around him. She wanted to try to explain her gratitude, and she wanted him to kiss her until she couldn't think or speak or do anything but respond to him. Her eyes burned with unshed tears, her heart ached and there was a hollow place inside that she couldn't explain.

"I don't understand you," she said at last.

"Understanding isn't necessary." She wondered what was.

He sipped his wine. "In two nights there is a celebration of the heritage of Lucia-Serrat," he said.

"While we are a tropical paradise, our roots are in the desert of Bahania. Along with a special meal, there will be entertainment. Dancers and music. Although this event is not on your Ayanna's list, I suspect you would enjoy yourself. If you are available that evening, I would be honored if you would accompany me."

As if she had other plans. As if she would rather be with anyone but him. "Thank you for asking me, Mazin. The honor of accompanying you is mine."

He stared at her, his dark eyes seeing into her soul. "It is probably for the best that you cannot read my mind," he murmured. "All that is between you and the death of your innocence is a thin thread of honor that even now threatens to unravel."

Once again he left her speechless. But before she could try to figure out if he really meant what he said—and deal with the sudden heat she felt in her belly—the waiter appeared with their menus. The mood was broken. Mazin made a great show of putting the picture safely back in the box. They discussed what they would have for dinner. His comment was never again mentioned.

But Phoebe didn't forget.

Two days later, a large box was delivered to her room. Phoebe knew instantly that it was from Mazin, but what could he be sending her? She unfastened the large bow and ribbon holding it in place, then lifted the cover.

Moving aside several layers of tissue revealed a dark blue evening gown that shimmered as she lifted it up to examine the style. Her breath caught in her throat. The silky fabric seemed to be covered with scatters of starlight. The low-cut bodice promised to reveal more than she ever had before, while the slender skirt would outline her hips and legs. It was a sensual garment for a sophisticated woman. Phoebe wasn't sure she had the courage to wear it.

A note fluttered to the floor. She set the dress back in the box and picked up the folded paper.

She recognized the strong, masculine handwriting instantly. Besides, who but Mazin would be sending her a dress?

"I know you will try to refuse my gift," he wrote. "You may even call me names and chide me for my boldness. I could not face your temper—for the thought of your anger leaves me trembling with fear. So I am leaving this dress in secret, like a thief in the night."

Phoebe knew she couldn't possibly accept such an extravagant gift. However, Mazin's note made her smile and then laugh. As if anything about her could ever frighten him.

She made the mistake of carrying the dress over to the mirror and holding it up in front of herself. Then she tried it on.

As she'd feared, the sensual fabric clung to every curve. Yet something about the material or the style or both made her actually look as if she *had* something worth clinging to. Her breasts seemed fuller, her waist smaller. She had a vision of herself in more dramatic makeup, with her hair cascading in curls down her back. While she'd never believed that she looked anything like Ayanna, with a little help she might come close.

Still wearing the dress, Phoebe dashed for the phone. She called the beauty salon in the hotel. Luckily they had a cancellation and would be happy to assist her in her transformation. If she would care to come downstairs in a half hour or so?

Phoebe agreed and hung up. Then she returned her attention to her reflection. Tonight she would look like the best possible version of herself. Would it be enough?

Phoebe arrived first at the restaurant. Mazin had called at the last minute, telling her that he was delayed with a small matter of work. He had sent a car to collect her and had promised to join her by seven.

She was shown to a private table upstairs. Carved screens kept the curious from knowing who sat there, while allowing her a perfect view of the stage. A cluster of musicians sat on one side of the room playing for the diners. Candlelight twinkled from every table.

The waiter lingered for several minutes, talking and staring until Phoebe realized he thought she was attractive. She'd never captured a man's attention before, and while the appreciative gleam in the young man's eyes flattered her, there was only one opinion that mattered.

The waiter disappeared for a few minutes, then returned with champagne. He poured her a glass. When he would have lingered longer, she told him she would be fine by herself. Obviously disappointed by the dismissal, he left.

Phoebe sipped the bubbly liquid. To think that after nearly three short weeks on the island a young man had actually noticed her. Much of it was the dress and the makeover, she thought, knowing she had never looked better. But she suspected there was some other reason. She was a different person than she had been when she arrived on the island.

Being with Mazin had changed her.

She leaned back in her chair. Except for the occasional afternoon when he'd had to return to work or his family, Mazin had spent most of his days with her. They had talked about everything from history to books to movies to her youth to her plans when she returned to Florida. They had shared sunsets, meals, laughter and he had been more than kind the few times she had given in to tears. They had been to every place on Ayanna's list. Every place but one. Lucia's Point.

Phoebe took a deep breath to calm her suddenly frantic nerves. She had little time left on the island, and then she would return to her small, solitary world. She knew that being with Mazin was a once-in-a-lifetime experience, but when she was home things would go on as before. She would attend college and get her degree in nursing. Perhaps she would do better at making friends, perhaps she might even meet a young man. But there, no one would ever be as much a part of her as Mazin. Wherever she went and whatever she did, he would be with her.

She knew that their time together hadn't meant the same thing to him as it did to her, and she could accept that. But she liked to think that she mattered a little. He had indicated that he found her attractive, that he enjoyed kissing her. So she had to ask.

Maybe he would laugh. Maybe he would be embarrassed and try to refuse her gently. Perhaps she had completely misunderstood his interest. But regardless of the many possibilities for rejection, she would not have regrets.

Voices in the hallway distracted her. She turned and saw Mazin slipping between the screens. He was as tall and handsome as ever. The black tuxedo he wore only emphasized his good looks. She rose to her feet and approached him. His smile turned from pleased to appreciative, and their kiss of greeting seemed as natural as breathing.

"I see you are wearing the dress I sent you. I trust you will not punish me for my boldness."

His teasing made her smile. In that moment her heart tightened in her chest, giving her a little tug. Phoebe had the sudden realization that she was in more danger than she had thought. Had she already fallen in love with Mazin?

Before she could consider the question, the pace of the music increased. Several young women took to the stage and began to dance. Phoebe and Mazin were seated and the waiter appeared with their first course.

Something about the rapid movement of the dancers captured Phoebe's attention. Part of it might have been that it was safer to look at them than gaze at Mazin. Apprehension made it impossible for her to eat.

"Some dances are for entertainment," he said, leaning close to be heard. She could inhale the masculine fragrance of him, and the appealing scent made her tremble. "Some tell a story. This is the journey of the nomads in their search for water. The life-giving force is essential."

He continued talking, but she couldn't listen to anything but the thundering of her heart. Could she do this? Could she not? Would she rather ask and know, or would she rather wonder? Hadn't Ayanna made her promise not to have regrets?

"You have yet to touch your food, and I suspect you are not listening to me."

She turned to him. The beat of the music seemed to thunder in her blood.

She studied his face, the way his dark hair had been brushed back from his forehead, the strong cut of his cheekbones, the faint bow in his top lip.

He touched her face with his knuckles. "Tell me, Phoebe. I can see the questions in your eyes, and something that looks like fear. Yet you need not fear anything from me. Surely we have spent enough hours together for you to know that."

"I *do* know," she whispered, unable to look away from his compelling gaze. "It's just…" She drew in a breath. "You have been more than kind to me. I want you to know that I appreciate all you've done."

He smiled. "Do not thank me too heartily. Kindness was not my motivation. I'm far too selfish a man for that."

"I don't believe that. Nor do I understand what you see in me. I'm young and inexperienced. But you've made everything about my time here really wonderful. So it seems wrong to ask for one more thing."

"Ask me for anything. I suspect I will find it difficult to refuse you."

He brushed his thumb across her lower lip. She shivered. The contact made her want so much, and it also, along with his words, gave her courage.

"Mazin, would you take me to Lucia's Point tomorrow?"

His dark eyes turned unreadable. Not by a flicker of a lash did he give away what he was thinking. She swallowed.

"I know the custom. That I may only go there with a lover. I don't have one. A lover, I mean. I've never…" Why didn't the man say something? She could feel herself blushing. Words began to fail her. "I thought you might like to stay with me tonight. To change that. To—"

Her throat closed and she had to stop talking. Unable to meet his gaze any longer, she stared at her lap and waited for him to start laughing.

Mazin studied the young woman in front of him. He had always thought of her as a quiet beauty, but tonight she was the most beautiful creature he had ever seen. Some of her transformation came from the dress and makeup, but much of it was the result of a subtle confidence. At last Phoebe didn't doubt herself.

Until she had asked him to be her lover. He read the uncertainty in her posture, the questions in the quiver of her mouth. He knew she was unaware of how much he desired her, nor would she understand the iron control it had taken for him to keep his distance. Even as they sat there, his arousal pulsed painfully. If she had any experience, she would not question her appeal. But she did not possess that kind of worldliness.

He supposed a better man would find a way to refuse her gently. He knew he was the wrong person to take the precious gift she offered. For the first time in his life, he did not feel worthy.

Yet he could not find it in his heart to walk away. He had wanted her for too long. The need inside him burned. To be her first, to hold her and touch her and make her his own— no one had ever offered him more.

"My dove," he murmured, leaning close.

She raised her head, her eyes brimming with tears. Doubt clouded her pretty features. He brushed away a few tears that spilled over, then kissed her mouth.

"I have ached for you from the moment I first saw you," he said, speaking the absolute truth. "If I do not have you, a part of me will cease to exist."

Her mouth curved into a smile. "Is that a yes?"

He laughed. "It is."

There would be consequences. To make love with a mature woman of experience was one thing—to take a virgin to his bed was another. Honor was at stake. Perhaps in this modern time there were those who took such things lightly, but not him. Not with Phoebe.

He wondered what she would say if he told her the truth. Would she still want him in her bed? His conscience battled briefly with the notion of telling her. But he needed her too much to risk it.

He shifted so he could speak directly into her ear.

"Tell me of your appetites," he murmured. "Would you like to stay for the rest of the meal and watch the dancers? Lingering will increase the anticipation. Or do you prefer to adjourn now?"

"I don't want to wait."

Her simple words sent a bolt of desire through him. His arousal ached. Tonight would be both endless torture and ultimate pleasure. He was determined to show her all the possibilities and make her first time as perfect as possible. Assuming his need did not kill him first.

Seven

They left the restaurant immediately. Phoebe tried not to be scared as they stood waiting for Mazin's car. But instead of his usual Mercedes, a black limo pulled up.

"I wanted tonight to be special," he said with a smile as he helped her into the back seat. "I thought you would enjoy the change."

She'd never been in a limo before, but saying that would make her sound even more unworldly and innocent than she was. Instead she tried to smile her thanks, even though her mouth didn't seem to want to cooperate.

Her brain was a complete blank. The drive back to the hotel would be about fifteen minutes. Obviously they had to talk about something, but she couldn't come up with a subject. What exactly was one supposed to discuss before making love for the first time?

She glanced frantically around the luxurious interior. The seats were camel color, and the softest leather she had ever touched. To the left was a complicated entertainment center with dozens of dials, levers and switches, along with a small television. To the right was a full bar. A bottle of champagne sat in an ice bucket.

"Had you already planned on us..." Her voice trailed off.

Mazin followed her gaze and touched the bottle of champagne. "I had thought we might take a walk along the beach and enjoy the moonlight," he said. "But I had not hoped to have the honor of doing more than kissing you. If I had, I would have been more prepared."

More prepared? Was that possible? Didn't the limo and the champagne spell seduction? Had her invitation simply made things easier for him?

She wanted to ask Mazin, but he was no longer paying attention to her. Instead he seemed to be searching for something. He ran his hands along the back of the seat and pressed against the wood paneling on the doors.

"What are you looking for?" she asked, bewildered.

"There is a storage compartment somewhere." He shifted to the seat behind the driver and examined the leather.

"My oldest son mentioned it to me," he said, more to himself than to her. "He joked about always keeping the car stocked."

Phoebe had no idea what he was talking about. She assumed he meant the older of his four boys, the one away at college.

"Why would your son be using a limo?"

Mazin didn't answer. He pressed against the wood panel. "At last," he said as it gave way.

The paneling opened to reveal a good-sized compartment. There was a change of clothing, more champagne and a box that she couldn't quite see. Mazin reached for the box. She shrank back into the corner of the seat when she read the labeling.

Condoms.

Phoebe's romantic images of what might happen that evening crashed in around her. Reality was not a fuzzy, slow-motion dance of kissing and touching. If they were going to make love, then there were potential consequences of the act. Protection was required. The sensible part of her brain applauded Mazin's sensible nature. Her romantic heart shriveled inside.

He glanced up and saw her. She was unable to turn away before he had a chance to see the expression on her face. She didn't know what she looked like, but whatever it was, it was enough to make him swear under his breath.

He shoved several packets into his tux pocket, closed the compartment and returned to her side.

"You do not want me to be practical?" he asked, putting an arm around her and pulling her close.

"I know it's important." She stared at the crisp edge of his collar rather than at his face. "I appreciate you taking care of me by, um, you know. Making sure you had, ah, protection."

"But it has destroyed the fantasy, yes?"

She raised her gaze to his face. "How did you know what I was thinking?"

"I know you, my dove. I promise to make this night as fantastical as I know how, but I will not compromise your health or leave you with something you did not want."

A baby. He was talking about her getting pregnant. In that second, Phoebe desperately wanted to have his child. What she would give to have a little girl with his dark, flashing eyes and easy grace. Or a sturdy little boy like Dabir, who fearlessly took on the world.

He touched her chin, forcing her to raise her head, then he bent and kissed her.

The soft pressure of his lips chased away her doubts. He kept the kiss light, but just being close to him was enough to make her body tingle all over. Before she could tempt him to deepen the contact, the car stopped.

She raised her head. "Where are we?"

"A side entrance to the hotel," he said, opening the door and stepping out into the night. "I did not think you would be comfortable walking with me to the elevator. At this time of night the lobby would be crowded."

"Thank you," she said as she followed him down a flower-lined path to a glass door that led in from the garden.

Trust Mazin to be so considerate. She would have been embarrassed to have everyone know what they were going upstairs to do.

Once inside, he led her to a service elevator in the back and they arrived on her floor without being seen by anyone. She fumbled for her key until he took her small evening bag from her and removed it. Then he unlocked the door and drew her inside her room.

The balcony door stood open. A single lamp on the nightstand burned, and housekeeping had already been by to turn down the bed. Phoebe could smell the scent of the sea. She told herself to focus on that and not on her jangling nerves.

Mazin locked the door and set her purse on the table by the mirror. He crossed to stand in front of her.

"I see your tension has returned," he said lightly. "Feel it if you must. But feel this as well." He pressed his mouth to her throat.

The warm, damp kiss made her legs go weak. She had to hold on to him to keep from sliding to the floor. He kissed her neck, and licked the sensitive skin by her ear. One of his hands rested on her shoulder, his fingers rubbing her bare skin.

"Beautiful Phoebe," he breathed before taking her earlobe into his mouth and nibbling.

Goose bumps broke out on her skin as he shifted to stand behind her. Her breasts seemed to swell as her nipples tightened. Between her legs she felt a tension and an ache that made her want to press herself against him.

He moved her hair over her shoulder and kissed his way down the back of her neck, to her shoulder blades. She hadn't thought of her back as a very erotic part of her body, but when he lightly stroked her there, and followed that contact by an openmouthed kiss, she found it difficult to breathe.

As he nibbled on her shoulder, he ran his hands up and down her arms. From there he slid his fingers to her waist. Anticipation filled her as he circled slowly, climbing higher and higher. He stood behind her and kissed her neck, even as he moved his hands up to touch her breasts.

She exhaled in wonder as he cupped her small curves, holding them in his hands as if they were most precious cargo. Even through the material of the dress she felt his warmth and the tender way he moved against her sensitized flesh.

The style of the dress was such that she couldn't wear a bra—at least, not any one that she had. At first she'd been nervous about going out that way, but now, with him stroking her, she was grateful. One less layer between his fingers and her aching body.

She loved how he explored her curves. She wanted to beg him to slip off her dress so she could know what it was like to have him touch her bare skin. She wanted—

She gasped as he lightly touched her nipples. She'd known they were tight with desire, but she hadn't realized how sensitive that puckered skin could be. Fire shot through her, racing along her arms and legs before settling deep in her belly. He brushed against them again and again, making her groan and lean back against him as pleasure filled her.

She wasn't sure how long they stood there, him touching her, her savoring the contact. At last he turned her in his arms and kissed her. A deep, satisfying kiss that made her body melt and her toes curl. She wrapped her arms around him, wanting to be as close as possible. This was what she'd waited for all her life. Nothing could go wrong as long as Mazin continued to touch her.

She felt the slide of the zipper being pulled down in back. Cool evening air tingled against her bare skin. She wore panties, a garter belt and stockings under her dress. Noth-

ing more. The ladies in the boutique had insisted on the
latter when they'd seen her dress, telling her that regular
panty hose would be a crime under such a beautiful gown.
Phoebe hadn't been sure, but as Mazin pushed her dress off
her shoulders and she thought of how she looked underneath,
she was glad she had let them convince her.

The dress fell to the floor. She was close enough to him
that she wasn't yet embarrassed about being practically
naked. His large, warm hands moved up and down her back,
touching her, soothing her, arousing her until she longed for
him to do more. Then he slipped lower—to her hips and the
garter belt there. And lower, to the high-cut panties, the bare
skin of her thigh, then to the tops of the stockings. He froze.

Mazin broke the kiss and stared at her. Fire seemed to
radiate from his dark eyes and tension pulled his mouth
straight.

"I want you," he breathed.

There was nothing he could have said that was more perfect. The last of Phoebe's fears faded. She leaned forward
and kissed him. It was the first time she had initiated any
contact. She licked his lower lip, then nipped at the full flesh.
He grabbed her and pulled her close, deepening the kiss with
an intensity that convinced her he was a man in great need
of a woman.

She felt something hard pressing against her belly. His
arousal, she thought, happy to know that she could affect
him so. She wanted to explore her new and wondrous power
over him when he moved his hands to her waist.

The feel of them on bare skin was very different than the
feel of them through her dress. She moved back so he could
move higher. He didn't disappoint her. He slipped up to cup
her breasts, then touched her nipples with his thumbs.

She hadn't known there was that much pleasure in the
world. Her mind faded to blackness and she could only experience what he was doing to her. She wasn't even aware of

pulling away from the kiss until her head sagged back and she exhaled his name.

Instead of being angry, Mazin laughed softly. He bent forward, took one of her nipples in his mouth and sucked. More fire filled her. She cupped his head, running her fingers through his hair and begging him to never stop. He moved from breast to breast, back and forth, licking, blowing, caressing. Between her legs her panties grew damp. Then without warning her legs gave way.

He caught her as she fell. With an ease that surprised her, he picked her up in his arms and carried her to the bed. Her shoes got lost along the way. After standing her next to the bed, he quickly peeled off her panties, leaving her stockings in place, then eased her onto the bed.

Phoebe had a brief flash of panic, but before it could take hold, he was next to her, holding her, kissing her. He rested his hand on her breast, which made her forget everything bad and think only of how he made her feel.

When he moved his hand lower, he kissed her so deeply, she barely noticed. But at the first brush of his fingers against her damp curls, she found herself very aware of what he was doing.

Questions filled her mind. What was she supposed to do? What would it feel like? Before she could ask, he stroked the inside of her thigh. Without her being aware of doing anything, her legs fell open. He touched her lightly, exploring her, finding wonderful places that made her breathing quicken. He found that most secret place and slipped inside. At the same time he shifted his attention from her mouth to her breasts.

He circled her nipple, licking her sensitive skin. She didn't know what to think about—his mouth or his fingers. He withdrew from her and rubbed between her curls. Without warning, his mouth closed on her nipple and his fingers found some amazingly sensitive spot.

The combination made her forget to breathe. Not that it

mattered, because whatever he was doing was too good for her to live through. She was going to die. No one could survive such pleasure. It terrified her. She never wanted it to stop.

He rubbed her gently, moving faster and faster. Suddenly she was breathing again, or rather gasping. She rolled her head back and forth as pressure built.

"Mazin?"

"Hush, my dove. I am here."

And then he was kissing her and touching her and the world began to spin. There was a final push within her, a pinnacle of pressure, and then the most glorious release. She clung to him, shaking, trembling, hungry and satisfied, all at the same time.

When it was over, he drew her close, kissing her face and making her feel as if she were the most precious creature on earth.

"I didn't know," she whispered. "That's pretty amazing."

He stared into her eyes. "There is so much more I long to show you."

"I'd like that."

He sat up and pulled off his coat and shirt. Shoes and socks followed, then trousers. When he was naked, she raised herself up on one elbow to study him. The sight of his body pleased her. She watched as he slipped on the condom, then parted her legs for him.

He waited to enter her, first kissing her and touching her everywhere until that unbelievable pleasure built up to the point of nearly exploding. Just when she was about to go over the edge, he pushed inside her.

Her body stretched to take him. The pressure was uncomfortable at first, then eased. He reached between them and touched that one perfect spot. The feel of him inside her while he stroked her sent her higher and higher. She could barely hold on.

He shifted so that he could wrap his arms around her and

kiss her. The change in their positions forced his arousal in deeper. She clung to him. Everything was so unfamiliar, yet so right, and she lost herself on the next thrust. She called out his name even as he shuddered and clung to her.

She opened her eyes. Mazin stared at her. Even as her climax washed over her and his ripped through him, they gazed at each other. It was a moment of intimate connection, far beyond anything she'd ever experienced. In that moment, she knew the truth. That no matter how far she traveled from this magical paradise, no matter who she met or what she experienced, she would only ever love one man.

Mazin.

Eight

Phoebe awoke just before dawn. An unfamiliar weight draped around her waist and it took her a second to realize it was Mazin's arm. She smiled and snuggled closer to him.

"Good morning," he whispered in her ear. He lay behind her, his body warm and welcoming against her own. "How are you feeling?"

"Pretty darned perfect," she said happily.

Something hard poked into the back of her leg. She giggled. "I didn't realize that people could make love so often," she said.

"I assure you that four times in a night is not usual. You inspire me." He withdrew a little. "However, this is new to you, so I will restrain myself."

She thought about how one of the times he hadn't entered her at all. He'd kissed her intimately until she'd been unable to keep from losing herself in the glory of his attentions. He'd then taught her how to pleasure him that way. As he had promised, there was much to explore.

He glanced at the clock and groaned. "I must return home for a short time, my dove. I have breakfast with Dabir each morning and I would not want to explain my absence. But I will return in a few hours and we can make our way to Lucia's Point." He leaned over and kissed her. "There in the shadow of the waterfall I will make love with you."

She melted at the thought.

He rose and quickly dressed, then kissed her again before leaving. "Miss me," he said. "As I will miss you."

"Always," she promised, and knew it was the truth.

The sound of the waterfall made it nearly impossible to speak. Phoebe stood, transfixed by the sight of so much water tumbling from nearly a hundred feet in the air. A fine mist cooled her bare arms and face. She leaned back in Mazin's arms.

This was, she thought contentedly, a perfect moment. Last night she had learned what it meant to be loved by a man. Over and over Mazin had touched her, kissed her and taken her to paradise. With practice, she would learn to seduce *him*. She wanted that. She wanted to make him ache with longing. She wanted to make him tremble and hunger so that he couldn't hold back any longer.

She wanted to make him love her.

Phoebe sighed quietly. Love. Could a man like Mazin ever care about her? She was young and didn't share his life experiences. He was worldly and wealthy. She hadn't even been to college. They had very little in common. And yet… in her heart, being with him felt so very right. Now, in his embrace, she knew that she had come home. How could her feelings be so strong without him having the same reaction? Was it possible for her to love so deeply and have him completely unaffected?

"What are you thinking?" he asked, speaking the question directly in her ear.

"That the falls are very beautiful. Are we really going to make love here?"

He turned her in his arms and kissed her. She recognized the passion flaring in his eyes. "Do not doubt my desire for you, my dove," he said, taking her hand and placing it on his arousal.

He was already hard. She wrapped her arms around him. "Oh, Mazin."

"Yes. Speak my name," he murmured against her mouth. "Know only me."

He undressed her slowly, peeling away layers of clothing until she was naked on the blanket he'd brought with them. Sunlight shone through the leaves overhead, creating changing patterns of shadows on her legs and torso. Mazin undressed himself, then joined her on the ground. As he kissed her deeply and touched her breasts, she felt herself melting inside.

Heat filled her. Dampness signaled her readiness. When he stroked her intimately, she shuddered in preparation of her release.

He took her to the edge and when she would have slipped off into paradise, he drew back enough to ease her on top of him. The unfamiliar position felt awkward at first, but she soon saw the advantages of controlling his rhythm inside her. While she moved up and down on his maleness, he cupped the apex of her thighs and rubbed his thumb against her tiny place of pleasure. Tension made her shudder. Need made her cry out.

She lost control there in the warm sunlight, with the thunder of the falls in the background. The soft call of birds provided romantic music for their lovemaking. He shuddered beneath her, losing himself as well, calling out her name, making her feel as if she'd finally found her place to belong.

"We must talk," he said later, when they were dressed and walking back to his car. "There is something I haven't told you."

Phoebe didn't like the sound of that. She shivered, as if the sun had disappeared behind a cloud. Was he going to tell her that their time together was over?

"I don't want to talk," she said quickly. "I'm leaving in a few days. Can't we keep these happy memories alive until then?"

He sighed. "Phoebe, I do not mean to frighten you. I am not trying to end our relationship—I simply seek to change it. But before I do that, I must tell you the truth about myself."

She climbed into the car. Where before her flesh had tingled with anticipation, now her skin simply felt cold. She wanted to wrap herself in the blanket Mazin had brought. Except it carried the sweet fragrance of their lovemaking, and if she inhaled that, she would cry. She was determined that regardless of what Mazin said, she would not cry. She would be strong and mature and brave. She owed that to herself, if not to him.

She waited until he slid behind the wheel, then stared straight out the front windshield.

"You're married."

He turned to stare at her. "I told you, my wife died six years ago. I have not remarried. For a time I had thought I would take another wife, but finding someone seemed an impossible task. I gave up the idea."

He started the engine. "I am doing this badly. Perhaps rather than telling you, I should show you. I want—" He hesitated. "Most women would be pleased, but I am not sure of your reaction."

If he was trying to make her feel better, he was doing a lousy job. Phoebe bit her bottom lip as he drove them toward the coast road, and then headed north. Part of her wanted to hear what he had to say, because if he told her to her face that their relationship was over, then eventually she would be able to stop loving him. At least, that would be her plan. But if she ran away, she might never get over him. Although the thought of disappearing back into her hotel and not coming out until it was time for her flight had a certain appeal.

She was lost in her thoughts and didn't notice they'd begun to drive up to the top of the island until she recognized the road to the palace. Her throat tightened, making it impossible to swallow.

"Mazin, why are we here?"

He didn't say anything. Her mind began to race, and not in a good way. Various possibilities occurred to her and she wasn't sure she liked any one of them.

Instead of stopping in front of the palace, he kept driving down a road that led to a large building. One he'd pointed out to her before. The private residence of the prince.

Her entire world shifted slightly. Her brain froze, her heart stopped beating for a second, then began again but this time at a thunderous pace. And before either of them could speak, a small child broke through a grove and ran toward the car.

Mazin slowed, then pulled to the edge of the road. When he parked, Dabir ran to her side of the car and pulled open her door.

"Did you ask her? Did she say yes?"

"Dabir, we have discussed nothing," Mazin growled, although his son didn't seem the least bit impressed by his temper. "We need more time."

"But you've had all morning," the boy complained. "Did you tell her that I think she's pretty? Did you tell her about being a princess?"

"Dabir!"

Mazin's voice echoed through the trees. Dabir squeaked, then grinned. "Say yes, Miss Carson. Please?" he pleaded, then took one look at his father and headed back the way he'd come. The sound of his laughter drifted to them.

Phoebe didn't know what to say or what to think. She felt as if she'd fallen into an alternative universe.

"M-Mazin?"

He sighed. "This is not what I had planned. We are sitting in a car. It is not romantic." He released his seat belt and angled toward her. "Phoebe, what I have not told you is that I am more than a minister in the Lucia-Serrat government. I am Crown Prince Nasri Mazin. I rule this island. The house before us is my home. My sons are princes."

She blinked several times. C-crown p-prince Nasri Mazin? Even her thoughts stuttered. "No," she whispered. "You can't be."

He shrugged. "Yet I am."

She stared at his familiar face, at the dark eyes and firm mouth. The mouth she'd kissed and that had kissed her back in many very intimate places. Heat flared on her cheeks. "But I've seen you naked!"

He grinned. "Yes. As I have seen you."

She didn't want to think about that. "I don't understand. If you're really a prince, why didn't you tell me? And why did you want to be with me?"

He brushed a strand of hair from her face. "When I met you at the airport, I had recently returned from an extended journey. In the back of my mind had been the thought that I should find a wife. I did not expect to marry for love, but I thought I would find a woman with whom I could enjoy life. But that was not to be. The women I met bored me. I grew tired of them wanting me for my position or my money. I came home weary and discouraged."

He shrugged. "Then I saw a pretty young woman walk into the duty-free shop. She looked fresh and charming and very unlike the other women I'd been seeing. I followed her on an impulse. That same impulse caused me to speak with her. She had no idea who I was. At first I thought her innocence was a game, but in time I discovered it was as genuine as the young woman herself. I was intrigued."

She still wasn't thinking straight. In fact, she wasn't thinking at all. "But, Mazin..." She swallowed. "I mean, Prince Nasri—" She squeezed her eyes shut. This couldn't be happening to her.

A prince? She'd fallen in love with a prince? Which meant any teeny, tiny hopes she'd had about a happily ever after had just disappeared like so much smoke.

"Phoebe, do not look so sad."

She opened her eyes and stared at him. "I'm not. I feel foolish, which is different. I should have guessed."

"I went to great pains to see that you did not. I arranged our travels in advance, making sure there wouldn't be anyone around."

And here she'd just thought it was the slow season. She'd been a fool. "I guess no one is going to believe me if I try to tell them this when I get back home."

"Ayanna would have believed," he said softly.

She nodded. Ayanna would have understood everything, she thought with a sigh. Because the same sort of thing had happened to her aunt. And Ayanna had spent the rest of her life loving the one man she could never have.

Pain tightened her chest, making it difficult to breathe. "You should, ah, probably take me back to the hotel now," she murmured.

"But I have not answered your second question."

She wasn't sure how much longer she could sit there without crying. "W-what question is that?"

"You asked to know why I wanted to be with you."

Oh. She didn't think she wanted to hear that answer. It couldn't be good. Or at least not good enough.

He put his hands on her shoulders. "You enchanted me. I do not get the opportunity to meet many people without them knowing I am Prince Nasri of Lucia-Serrat. With you, I could be myself. When you told me about your aunt's list of places to go, I decided to show them to you. I wanted to spend time with you. To get to know you."

That wasn't so bad. She forced herself to smile. "I appreciate all you've done. You were very kind."

He shook her gently. "Do you think kindness was my sole purpose?"

Why was he asking such hard questions? "I thought, maybe, after a while, you might want to seduce me."

Mazin groaned, then leaned forward and kissed her on the mouth. "Yes, I wanted you in my bed, but it was more than that," he said between kisses. "I wanted to be with you. I could not forget you. You became very important to me. I did not plan for you to meet my son, but that turned out to be most fortuitous. Dabir thinks you are very lovely and that you would make an excellent mother."

If the world had tilted before, it positively spun now, swooping and zooming around her until she found it impossible to keep her balance. Her fingers shook as she unfastened her seat belt, then stumbled out of the car. She was going to faint. Worse, she thought she might be sick.

Mazin…make that Prince Nasri…hurried around the car to stand next to her. "Phoebe? What's wrong?"

"You want me to take Nana's place?"

No. That wasn't possible. She couldn't stay here and take care of Mazin's child, all the while watching him with other women. She would be destroyed. Even if her heart weren't a consideration, she had her own dreams and they didn't involve her staying on Lucia-Serrat as a nanny.

Suddenly he was in front of her, grabbing her by her upper arms and shaking her gently. "Is that what you believe?" He stared at her face, then shook his head and pulled her close. "Don't you know I love you, you little fool? What did you think? That I wanted to hire you as a caretaker to my child? I have that for Dabir already. What I do not have is a mother for him and a wife for myself. I do not have a woman to love—someone to love me in return."

She stepped back and looked at him. His words filled her brain, but she couldn't grasp them. "I don't understand."

"Obviously."

And then he kissed her.

His warm, tender mouth settled on hers. As he wrapped

his arms around her, she allowed herself to believe that he might have been telling the truth.

"You love me?" she asked, breathless, but with a little less heart pain.

"Yes, my dove. I suspect nearly from the first." He stroked her hair, then her cheek. "For many years now I have been disenchanted with my life. Everything felt wrong. I loved my sons, but they could not completely fill my heart. I have traveled everywhere and never felt at home, until I met you. When I saw my island through your eyes, it was as if I had seen it for the first time. Your gentle strength, your honest heart, your giving spirit touched me and healed me. I have searched the world only to find my heart's desire standing right in front of me."

He kissed her again. "Marry me, Phoebe. Marry me and stay here. Be mother to my sons, be princess to my people. But most of all, love me always, as I will love you."

"A p-princess?"

He smiled. "It's a very small island. Your duties would not be taxing."

"I wouldn't mind the work. I just never imagined anything like this."

"Will you say yes?"

She gazed into his dark eyes. She didn't care that he was a prince. What mattered to her was that he was the man she loved. This wasn't *her* dream…it was something much bigger and better. It was her heart's desire.

"Yes."

He drew her close and hugged her as if he would never let her go. "For always," he promised. "We will live life to the fullest, with no regrets. Just as your Ayanna would have wanted."

* * * * *

PASSION

Harlequin *Desire*

COMING NEXT MONTH
AVAILABLE APRIL 10, 2012

#2149 FEELING THE HEAT
The Westmorelands
Brenda Jackson
Dr. Micah Westmoreland knows Kalina Daniels hasn't forgiven him. But he can't ignore the heat that still burns between them....

#2150 ON THE VERGE OF I DO
Dynasties: The Kincaids
Heidi Betts

#2151 HONORABLE INTENTIONS
Billionaires and Babies
Catherine Mann

#2152 WHAT LIES BENEATH
Andrea Laurence

#2153 UNFINISHED BUSINESS
Cat Schield

#2154 A BREATHLESS BRIDE
The Pearl House
Fiona Brand